A CALCULATED WHISK

A CALCULATED WHISK

VICTORIA HAMILTON

WHEELER PUBLISHING
A part of Gale, a Cengage Company

LIBRARY OF CONGRESS CIP DATA ON FILE.
CATALOGUING IN PUBLICATION FOR THIS BOOK
IS AVAILABLE FROM THE LIBRARY OF CONGRESS.

ISBN-13: 978-1-4328-9669-0 (softcover alk. paper)

Published in 2022 by arrangement with Beyond the Page Publishing, LLC

Printed in the United States of America
1 2 3 4 5   26 25 24 23 22

For my readers

Some days are extraordinary: weddings, vacations, graduations. Some ordinary days turn out to be extraordinary because you meet the love of your life or make a lifelong friend. My wish for you is more ordinary days that turn out to be extraordinary because of the people you meet.

CAST OF CHARACTERS

Lilibet: Jocie's tabby

IN *A CALCULATED WHISK:*

Alicia Vance: local widow, mom, and co-ordinator at QCB (Queensville Clean 'n Bright)

Mia Vance: Jocie's school friend and Alicia's daughter

Jace Vance (deceased): late husband of Alicia Vance; died in a tragic auto repair accident

Lew (Lewis) Vance: brother of Jace Vance, brother-in-law to Alicia and local tow truck operator

Franklin 'Frank' Vance: father of Jace and Lew Vance, local tow truck company owner

Debbie Vance: ex-wife of Lew Vance, owner of QCB

Kim Hansen: mother of Alicia Vance and Erin Hansen

Erin Hansen: Alicia Vance's younger sister

Wenda Puchala: receptionist at QCB

Charles "Clutch" Roth: local biker

Gus Majewski: co-owner of the Junk Stops Here

Nicki Majewski: wife of Gus Majewski

Skylah "Sky" Majewski: Nicki and Gus's daughter

Lise and Arend Brouwer: owners of the

8

farm and woods across from Jakob and Jaymie's cabin

Brianna Sheridan: journalist and Jaymie's friend

ONE

"I love the smell of old junk," Jaymie
Leighton said to no one in particular. She
stood at one of the sorting tables in the back
room of the Junk Stops Here, her husband
Jakob's junk store, looking through a newly
received box of kitchen tools. "Old junk
smells of dust, and the past, and women's
lives and hope for their children."

Jocie, her nine-year-old stepdaughter,
raced around in circles on a scooter that
had come in with some boxes of kids' toys
left over from a garage sale. Every time she
circled Jaymie she hooted, "Toot toot . . .
Jocie train coming through!" Hoppy, Jaymie's three-legged Yorkie-Poo, raced around
after Jocie barking merrily, his yips echoing
in the big sorting room.

It was a joyful noise, and Jaymie smiled.
The sorting room was a cavernous ware-
house behind the store, with an enormous
garage door that opened to allow trucks to

unload. She stood in front of a box-type table, waist height and about five inches deep, into which she had dumped two boxes of assorted vintage and antique kitchen utensils purchased sight unseen as a box lot at an estate sale auction. Jakob had bid on the lot, and though the topmost stuff had appeared to be dollar store junk, underneath was a treasure trove of fifties and sixties utensils, including red-paint-handled whisks, mashers, spatulas and a knife sharpener, some even older wire utensils and an assortment of spoons, ladles and serving forks. She inhaled deeply. Wood, rust and a soupçon of mold: how many would think that the fragrance of happiness? For her it was better than a bottle of Chanel.

Good thing she married a junkman/ Christmas tree farmer.

She wiped dust and grime from the items with a damp cloth, then piled all that she wanted in a box; some would be for her own collection, and the rest would be for the vintage kitchen display at the Queensville Historic Manor. She priced the rest and dumped them back into a box, hefted it to her hip, and called out to Jocie, "Come on, kiddo, leave the scooter behind. We're going to put this stuff out for sale. Come on, Hoppy!"

The sorting room was separated from the store by swinging double doors. Jaymie put her hip to one and pushed through, carrying the box to the kitchen department. The Junk Stops Here was located in a former factory that had gone bankrupt during the recession. Jakob and his partner, Gus Majewski, initially intended to stock only renovation items like doors, doorknobs, windows, shutters, and vintage gingerbread from old houses torn down as well as other used construction materials, but they now sold everything from jewelry and china to a vast array of furniture, books, clothes, luggage, plumbing supplies, antique wrought iron fencing . . . in short, anything a lover of vintage and antiques could ever want.

Jaymie stopped in front of the wall of kitchen utensils and set down the box, sorting her goods and placing them in the appropriate bin. Hoppy sat patiently at her feet, and Jocie, by her side, stood in silence staring across the sales floor.

Jaymie followed her sight line and saw a woman looking through the boxes of cupboard door handles. A girl about Jocie's age stood beside her reading a book. She was taller than Jocie, who was, in her own words, a *little* little person, but she leaned slightly to one side. Her left leg was a pink prosthetic. "You shouldn't stare, Jocie," Jaymie admonished in a murmur. "You know better than that."

Jocie looked up, a frown on her face. "That's Mia Vance. She's in my class at school. I was waiting for her to look up so I could wave and say hi."

How could she have thought otherwise? Jocie had spent her life being stared at, and if she stared it was not because of a person's differences, but for some other reason — in this case, friendship. "Why don't you go over and say hello?"

"You always tell me not to bother the customers."

"This is different. She's a friend. Go say hi."

Jaymie finished her work and stood back. The kitchen section was her pride and joy, neatly organized shelves and racks with everything to stock a cook's kitchen. She tidied the rest, returning order to the bins, then looked up to find Jocie. She was still with her friend and Hoppy had joined them, staring up intently at the two girls. Together they were perusing the kids' books, arranged in a spinner rack. Joining them, Jaymie said, "Jocie, will you introduce me to your friend?" It was something they had practiced.

Jocie's brown eyes lit up and she stood as tall as she could, plump hands clasped in front of her. "Mama, this is Mia Vance, my friend from school. Mia, this is my mama, Jaymie."

The little girl, sandy hair pulled back with a pink ribbon, freckles sprinkled over her cheeks, smiled shyly. Jaymie gave Jocie's shoulder a squeeze and, as the two girls went back to the books, she looked up at the woman nearby, who glanced over and smiled. "Hi, I'm Jocie's mom, Jaymie Leighton Müller," she said with a little wave. "You're Mia's mom?"

"Alicia Vance," she said. She had light brown hair pulled back in a ponytail, medium brown eyes and some of the same freckles her daughter had but lighter. She was slim and fit, wearing yoga pants, running shoes and a zipped jacket. "I take it the girls are in the same class."

"They are. Mia is probably the kid who is closest to Jocie in height in their class," Jaymie commented.

Alicia smiled, gazing at Jocie and her daughter. "They're so cute together!"

"I've seen you at pickup and drop-off."

The two girls had taken a stack of books over to a chair and were reading together. Hoppy begged to come up, and Jocie lifted him carefully to sit between them, where he was one happy little dog.

"Yeah, I usually do that myself," Alicia said, tearing her gaze away from the two girls. "My mom or sister steps in sometimes. My husband passed away a few years ago, so they pick up the slack when necessary, when I can't get away from work."

"I'm sorry for your loss," Jaymie said. "Do your in-laws live close by? Can they help? My husband's parents are awesome at taking Jocie when necessary."

"It's just my father-in-law, Franklin, and Jace's older brother, Lew. Lew tries to help when he can, but he works long hours. As for Franklin . . ." She rolled her eyes. "Not too reliable. You know?"

"What do you do?"

"I'm service coordinator at Queensville Clean 'n Bright. The job is somewhat flexible."

"Jakob and I work different jobs, so we alternate taking Jocie to school and picking her up."

"I've seen him. I think he owns this store?"

"Co-owns, with Gus Majewski. They have a young couple who run the place much of the time, though," she said of the ex-military couple Jakob hired a year ago.

Her expression sobered and she looked

away, frowning. "I suppose we'd better get going. I need cupboard handles. I hate the cheap ones that are on our cupboard doors."

"Old ones are better made," Jaymie said. "Like most things. I was here sorting a new bunch of kitchen utensils and snagging some for the Queensville Historic Manor. I'm a historical reenactor there and take care of the kitchen collection. We're doing a whole display of vintage whisks called Whisk Me Away to the Past. I'm going to guide Jocie and Mia's class on a tour next month. I hope you'll join us?"

"I'll try. Can't promise." She met Jaymie's gaze and a smile lit up her face. "Hey, I have a whole box of my grandmother's kitchen stuff. I think there are a few old whisks in there. I'll have a look."

"Sure," Jaymie said with muted enthusiasm. Many times she had been offered vintage finds, only to get a box of broken junk. *But you never know,* she thought. "I'd love to take a look at them," she added, with more warmth.

Alicia stared at her for a moment, biting her lip, then glanced over at the girls, still chattering over the books. She then looked back to Jaymie and muttered, leaning forward, "You're the one who solves murders, right? There was one out on Heartbreak

17

Island a few weeks ago and you figured it out when the cops were clueless."

"That's not exactly . . . I mean . . ." Jaymie glanced over at the two girls, then back to Alicia. "I don't usually talk about this kind of thing in front of Jocie."

"I have a couple of questions for you." Her expression had a fervor that was unmistakable.

"I can't talk about the murder. It's police business and an ongoing investigation."

"It's not about that, it's something else. I'd like your . . . your expert opinion."

The hesitation was interesting. What could she need the opinion of a stranger for? "I'm no expert," Jaymie warned. "If I can help with anything, I'm going to be at the historic manor on Monday. Bring me the vintage whisks and we can talk then if you like?"

Alicia nodded. "I've got Monday off. I'd better get going . . . it's my mom's boyfriend's birthday, and we're expected to celebrate." Her eye roll said she'd rather be anywhere else.

"At least there will be cake," Jaymie joked. "Everything is better with cake."

"I wouldn't count on it, not with Russ Krauss as the birthday boy. He could ruin even cake. Come on, Mia," she said, raising her voice to be heard. "We have to go to

Grandma's," she said, gathering up the vintage drawer pulls and cupboard door knobs she had chosen.

Mia trotted to her mother with an armload of books. "Jocie said I could take these," she said, eyes gleaming with excitement. "She said I could read them and then give them back, because her daddy owns the store."

"Mia," Alicia said, with a warning tone and a glance at Jaymie. "You can't ask people to give you things!"

"I didn't ask, Mom, promise!" She hugged the books to her chest with a teary gaze. "I'm just borrowing them."

Jaymie glanced over at Jocie with the intent to admonish her, but her daughter's pleading expression changed her mind. How well she remembered navigating the tricky waters of childhood friendship. "What's the harm?" Jaymie said breezily, looking to Alicia and Mia. "Jocie's right, she does it all the time, *and* she loans books to special friends." She smiled at the little girl. "It looks like Mia is a special friend."

All the way home Jocie talked nonstop about Mia, how her new friend liked horses and animals too, and that her friend loved books, like she did, and how Mia liked unicorns and glitter. She babbled on, even touching on Mia's tragic accident that took her leg, and how she sadly lost her father — someone, Mia said, helped her daddy put a truck up on a jack and did it wrong, and he died — and how she lived on a farm, and how she liked watching the farmer drive the tractor, and how her Uncle Lew always remembered her favorite ice cream.

Jaymie smiled as she glanced in the mirror and looked back at her daughter, who was talking to Hoppy as much as anyone, and how the little dog paid such close attention to everything she said. She sighed, remembering childhood and the joy of making a new friend.

The next day, Sunday, was gloriously sunny and bright, still warm in late September. Jaymie was at the Leighton yellow brick Queen Anne home in Queensville with Jakob, who had brought his chain saw. In his expert control it chugged and whined its way through a heavy limb that had fallen in a windstorm from the tree of their back lane neighbor. Trip Finley had offered them the wood if Jakob would take it away for him, and though they did not need the wood — they had more than they could use — Jakob never denied a request for help.

Jocie was at her friend Peyton's house a

few doors down. Jaymie was on her knees planting spring bulbs along the lawn perimeter, a task her older sister Becca would never do — she didn't like getting her hands dirty. Jaymie sat back on her haunches enjoying the sunshine and watching her hubby. Who would have expected her to fall in love and marry a fellow who had the same loves as she did: old stuff, old homes, old friends.

A sedan pulled down the lane and a thin woman emerged, glanced around, spotted Jaymie, and came through the gate and up the flagstone walk.

Uh-oh. Jaymie rose, dusted off her hands and knees and watched, shading her eyes and waiting. When the woman got close enough, she said, "Detective Vestry. I'm surprised to see you today." Maybe there was something more about the Labor Day Weekend murder she needed to follow up on.

"I come in peace, Jaymie," the detective said with the slightest of smiles. "Look . . . I'm off duty." She gestured to the jeans she wore.

Jaymie nodded, uncertain. Detective Vestry and she had called a truce to hostilities. Jaymie had been certain the woman didn't like her, but Vestry swore that was not true, that she simply had a frosty nature. *And* Jaymie annoyed her on occasion by holding back, the detective felt, withholding information she should share. They had agreed to disagree on that point because Jaymie felt she shared what was necessary. "Pull up a chair. I have to finish getting the bulbs in today. If you don't mind, I'll keep working."

The detective pulled an Adirondack chair closer and sat down, leaning forward, elbows on knees. Jaymie felt tension thread through her. Whatever the detective said, this was not a social call. What did she want?

"What are those?"

"Tulip bulbs."

"Oh. I guess I never thought people planted those. I thought they popped up wherever."

Jaymie, eyes wide, glanced over at her.

"I don't garden," Vestry said in her own defense. "I don't see the point."

"If you buy it at a florist, someone planted it."

"I guess that's true."

Jaymie concentrated on what she was doing as Hoppy, who had been snoozing in the sun, bounced over to the detective to sniff her shoes avidly. Vestry leaned over and scruffed the Yorkie-Poo behind the ears and the little dog, satisfied, wobbled (he only had three legs, so his trot was off-kilter) to the back fence to bark at Trip as he and Jakob tossed the wood into the back of the pickup.

Five bulbs in a cluster, that was Jaymie's method. No tulips marching in a straight line like floral soldiers for her. She glanced over at Vestry, who was staring off in the distance. Finally, Jaymie dusted off her hands, heeled in the last of the bulbs and sat on the ground, cross-legged. "Detective Vestry, if you have something to say, please say it."

Vestry sighed and nodded. "I appreciate that, Jaymie. No beating around the bush. The chief asked me to ask you for a favor."

"Okay." Jaymie had her supporters and her detractors among the local police force. Some, like former chief Horace Ledbetter, appreciated her unique viewpoint, but others, like Vestry, felt she inserted herself in the middle of cases too often. The current police chief, Deborah Connolly, had never expressed an opinion one way or the other.

Vestry looked down at the grass, picked up a twig, twirled it between her fingers, then said, "We received an anonymous tip concerning a death that occurred over five years ago."

"Oh."

"At the time it was thought to be an accident. With this tip, we now believe it was murder."

"Who —"

"Jace Vance, husband of Alicia Vance."

Two

"Alicia Vance? I was talking to her yesterday. She was at the Junk Stops Here. Her daughter Mia is Jocie's friend." Vestry was silent. Jaymie watched her, uneasiness growing in her gut. "You already knew that, didn't you?"

Vestry nodded.

"You're following her?"

Vestry's expression shuttered. It was like a cloud coming across the sun . . . shadows where once there had been light. "I can confirm that we know you spoke with her yesterday."

Jaymie shivered. "Is she a suspect in her husband's death?" She searched her memory for something Jocie had said and a vague memory from the newspaper stories five years before. "It had something to do with a car up on a jack, wasn't it?"

"Jace Vance was a mechanic with a home garage. He had a pickup on a jack and was working under it, the vehicle slipped, and he was crushed."

"Oh, that's awful!" Jaymie gasped in horror, hand over her mouth. "Poor Mia, losing her dad like that." Hoppy, alarmed by her outcry, wobbled over to her and she put a comforting hand on his head. He snuffled, sneezed, settled at her feet and sighed.

"That's the story that was told, anyway," the detective said, rubbing a white scar on her hand. "It was reported as an accident and there wasn't much evidence otherwise except that he was an experienced and exceptionally careful mechanic. No one knew why he was using a flimsy jack except that he had another car up on jack stands at the time." Vestry squinted into the distance and clasped her hands. "There were apparently no other jack stands available for use."

Was that unusual? Jaymie wondered. Did a home garage generally have more than one set of jack stands? "Where were Alicia and Mia?"

"Alicia was supposedly heading to Port Huron that morning to shop for clothes and school supplies for Mia, who was entering kindergarten that fall."

Jaymie noted the use of *supposedly.*

"When she returned home it was mid afternoon," Vestry continued. "She later told police that as she and her husband had a disagreement that morning, she was not speaking to him and didn't tell him she was home. Her exact words were, *He could stay out there in the garage all night as far as I cared.* His body wasn't discovered until the next day when his brother Lew, puzzled that his brother had not texted him back concerning a planned outing, came by to talk to him."

"That's awful," Jaymie said, shaken. "Did he die immediately?"

"We don't think he did."

"Oh, how terrible to lie there for hours . . ." Jaymie's words caught in her throat and she buried her face in her hands. It was too horrible to contemplate, dying like that, alone and in pain. Hoppy rose, whining and licking her hands. "It's okay, sweetie," Jaymie said, letting him climb into her lap and hugging him. "I'm . . . okay." She took a deep shaking breath. "That is horrifying."

Vestry nodded. "A terrible way to die. I was a patrol officer, one of the first on the scene." Her expression was blank, but her voice was guttural with horror.

"When did it happen? Do you know?"

"The morning or early afternoon of that first day. The medical examiner said he probably lived an hour after the vehicle crushed him and he undoubtedly suffered, given the internal trauma. He likely blacked out after a half hour before drowning in his own blood."

Jaymie shivered. She could have done without that imagery, but Vestry had delivered it in a matter-of-fact tone. "Was Chief Ledbetter in charge at the time?" she asked about the previous Wolverhampton police chief, a friend of hers.

"No, this occurred before he came. Remember, he had been a retired police chief and came to us as an interim chief after his predecessor was . . . retired."

Jaymie frowned. There was an old scandal there but after almost six years the details of the incident eluded her. So much had happened in her own life since. "I can't say I paid a lot of attention to the story at the time. What does any of this have to do with me?"

"Are you friends with Alicia Vance?"

"We hadn't met until yesterday. I have seen her before at school drop-off, but not to talk to."

"Oh. Okay." Vestry was disappointed.

Jaymie fidgeted. Hoppy looked up at her, then jumped down and curled up in the grass at her feet. Needing to tell the *whole* story, Jaymie finally said, "However, Alicia *is* coming out to the historic house tomorrow. I'm working on an exhibit there. She said . . . she said she had something to ask me. She mentioned the murder on Heartbreak Island and I told her I couldn't talk about it. She said it was something else. She wanted . . ." Jaymie frowned and tried to recall. "How did she put it? She said she wanted my opinion on something."

Vestry's gray eyes brightened. "Perfect! Let us know what she says."

"That's all?"

"That's it."

"What if she wants my opinion on a school matter?"

"She'd have asked you right there, not made an appointment to see you. We've been . . . putting pressure on her lately. Maybe she'll confide in you or tell you something that will help us."

Jaymie thought of adorable Mia, her pretty eyes sparkling with joy at the thought of new books to read. "Detective, do you think Alicia killed her husband?"

"We believe she knows more than what she has told us, and we'd be interested in anything she has to say."

It was a long day of physical work in the

freshening autumnal air. Back at the Müller cabin there was an early dinner, lunches to prepare, and homework to check. Jocie, after a bath, was happy to get her jammies on and climb into bed with Lilibet, her cat. Jaymie and Jakob cuddled on the sofa together in front of the fire with Hoppy curled up in his basket by the hearth. Jaymie relaxed into her husband; cradled in his arms, she could feel the thump of his strong heart against her back and sighed.

"What did Detective Vestry want that upset you this afternoon?" he murmured against her hair.

"Mmmm. I'd hoped no one noticed I was upset."

"I can always tell. You smile more, but it's not a real smile."

"I suppose that's true. I try to will it away with a smile." She told him what Vestry had told her, and how she felt. "Do you remember that case?"

"I do. I remember in particular because Jocie and Mia are the same age and I was trying to imagine how that poor kid felt, losing her dad, and right before her first day at school. It had to be traumatic. I was getting Jocie ready for kindergarten at the same time."

"I was . . . gee, I guess I was dating Joel at

the time. I thought it was serious." She shook her head in wonder at how much her life had changed since then.

"She knew that you were talking to Alicia Vance? That's troubling."

"I guess they're following Alicia. Vestry wanted to know what Alicia and I were talking about. I told her the truth. But then I made the mistake of telling her that Alicia is bringing me her grandmother's vintage whisks and says she wants my *opinion* on something."

He shrugged. "Maybe Alicia wants to know if she can work at the historic house, or have a sleepover with Jocie or —"

"Vestry thinks it has to do with her husband's death."

"Why?"

"Because she mentioned the murder on Heartbreak Island."

"Everybody has been asking you about that!" he protested.

"She wants me to report back to her whatever Alicia says."

"How do you feel about that?"

"I'm not sure," Jaymie admitted. "The detective implied . . . no, actually, she came right out and *said* that she thinks Alicia knows more about her husband's death than she has told them."

"Sweetie, you do what you want to do," he said, squeezing her tightly. "Don't let Detective Vestry bully you into doing anything you're not comfortable with."

"I'll try not to."

"Now, let's go up and forget about the world for a little while," Jakob said with a smile, pulling her up off the couch and into his arms.

She locked her arms around his neck. "Sounds like a plan."

Fall had officially arrived, coyly tiptoeing into Michigan with frosty mornings and foggy evenings, the chill in the air painting the edges of leaves, darkening the sky, bringing thunder and clouds edged in purple and navy. A sense of impending trouble hovered, the threat of a storm that may or may not arrive. The air was warm and close, the humidity high. There wasn't a soul at the Queensville Historic Manor when Jaymie arrived. She worked in the kitchen uninterrupted for an hour before she heard a voice calling out, *"Jaymie?"*

"Back here!" she hollered.

Alicia came to the door of the kitchen and glanced around. "Wow, it's cool. Not that I would ever want to live like this. Too . . . antiquey."

"I like the look of it, but I need my modern conveniences," Jaymie agreed. She looked expectantly at the woman's hands. Alicia carried nothing but her cell phone and car keys.

"Oh, right . . . the whisks," she said with a distracted half smile. "I lost track of time and then couldn't find the box of Grandma's stuff. Can I bring it out another time?"

"Sure. Want a tour?" she said, waving her hand to indicate the house.

Alicia agreed, and Jaymie took her all over, chattering the whole time, ending back in the green-and-cream-painted kitchen. They sat down at the drop leaf table by the window, and Jaymie pulled back the cherry-adorned curtain so they could look out over the drive. "I love this view, especially that big tree there, the one by the driveway," she said, pointing. "It's beginning to turn. Fall is here."

"It is." Alicia fell silent.

"You said you wanted to ask my opinion," Jaymie prompted, folding her hands in front of her.

Alicia's expression was troubled as she fiddled with her phone and moved her keys on the table surface. "You know the police, don't you?"

Hesitantly, Jaymie said, "I know some officers, but not well. Except Bernice Jenkins, she's a good friend."

"Could you . . . I mean, is it possible . . ." Alicia dropped the keys with a clatter and picked at her nails, tugging at a piece of skin, pulling it back until it bled. She shook her head, unable to continue.

"What is it, Alicia?" Jaymie said. "Is it to do with your husband's death? I remember hearing about it at the time it happened."

The woman quivered and nodded. "I don't know how to ask."

Silent, Jaymie observed her. She was pale and nervous, her shoulder-length mousy brown hair tucked behind her ears, the fragile skin by one of her eyes jumping from a nervous tic. "Tell me about it. Say whatever you want."

After a moment's silence, Alicia said, "I used to tell Mia these stories at bedtime. They would always start with *once upon a time* and would always end with *and they lived happily ever after.*" She sighed. "I loved Jace from the moment we met. Do you know what that's like?"

Jaymie, thinking of Jakob, nodded.

"I guess I was used to louses. Jace was good to me. He was rough around the edges but that didn't matter. He'd buy me funny gifts, you know: a teddy bear, a little box of chocolates, a single rose." She stopped and stared vacantly into space.

Jaymie waited.

Alicia shook herself after a minute, like a shiver had passed through her. "Fairytales don't last, ya know?" she said with a rueful laugh. "After I had Mia things were okay, but Jace didn't get how hard it is to have a kid. I was sick for a while. He started spending more time with his family. He'd take off and not come back until the next day, meanwhile I'm left with a kid, dirty diapers, a filthy home and . . ." She shook her head, pursing her mouth. "If it wasn't for my mom and sister, I don't know how I would have survived."

Jaymie waited. What any of this had to do with what Alicia wanted to ask her, she did not know. After a few moments of silence, she prompted, "You wanted to ask me something?"

Alicia nodded. "Are local cops on the level?"

"About what?"

"Can you trust them? I watch true crime stories and they show the cops talking about how they have these methods . . . ways of getting people to tell the truth. But *is* it the truth? Aren't they tricking people? I've heard they'll even frame people to solve a case."

"I'm not sure what you're asking, Alicia. Are you asking if the local police are honest?"

She blinked and rattled her keys again. "It's just . . . there were some questions when my husband died."

"Questions?"

"About how he died. It was an accident, but it's like they don't believe it. Five years later and they're still sniffing around. I've had two phone calls in the last month, just 'following up,' as they call it," she said, sketching air quotes around the words.

Jaymie's senses went on high alert. She was still confused about Alicia's intent in coming to see her. "But it was an accident?"

Alicia took in a shaky breath. "I . . . I *think* so. I mean . . ." She fell silent.

Jaymie was torn, should she probe for information? Try to get Alicia to confide in her? Was she sitting opposite a killer? "Alicia, did someone hurt him?"

"I don't . . . I mean . . ." She shook her head and broke off, agitated and restless. "I don't know what I think. Or . . . maybe I do." Her phone chimed and she looked at the screen. With a puzzled frown she said, "I'd better take this," then answered.

"Hello? . . . who? Oh . . . *oh.* What do you want?" She leaned back, folding her arms over her chest as she listened, her body language richly expressing sudden fear, anger and uncertainty. "Okay . . . Do I have to? . . . Okay. Tell me what —" Long pause. "I've *told* you," she sobbed, hunching over and half turning away. "I don't know any-thing else, or . . . no, I'm not *saying* I won't come in." Another pause. "No, I . . . I don't have a lawyer now. I can't afford one. Why do you say . . . ? Okay, *okay,* I'll . . . I'll come in . . . I'll be there . . . maybe day after tomorrow . . . I'll let you know."

She clicked off her phone. Wild-eyed, she rose, sobbing and shuddering. She paced to the counter, supported herself for a mo-ment, and then turned, tears streaming down her face. "I . . . I gotta go, I . . ." She covered her eyes, swaying on her feet.

Jaymie, frightened, rose. "Alicia, who was that? Are you okay? You don't look well. What's wrong?"

Alicia put her hands on her knees and bent over at the waist, swaying. "I gotta go. I . . . I have to leave now."

She was in no shape to drive anywhere. "I'm going to drive you home," Jaymie said, ". . . and when we get there we're calling your mom or sister."

THREE

Jaymie picked up the woman's cellphone and her own purse and took Alicia's arm, firmly guiding her out to her own SUV in the parking area. She put her in the passenger seat, buckled her belt for her — Alicia was shaking too much to do it — got into the driver's side and started the SUV. Alicia and her daughter, Jaymie learned when she asked for directions, lived one road over from Jakob and Jaymie, on a patch of land carved out of the Brouwer farm. Lise and Arend Brouwer owned a couple of hundred acres of land across from the Müller farm encompassing the woods opposite Jakob and Jaymie's log cabin and stretching all the way to the next road.

Jaymie drove past the Brouwer farmhouse and bare fields — the soybeans had been harvested — and in moments arrived at Alicia's driveway. She turned in and drove up the rutted dirt lane. "This is your house?" Alicia nodded. It was a run-down sixties-style red brick and yellow-vinyl-sided side-split ranch, with a low cement porch crumbling at the corners. The property was three acres or so, one of three houses that took bites out of the Brouwer farmland. The house was surrounded by trees and over-grown shrubs. Behind the house Jaymie could see an enclosure fenced with chain link protecting a garage big enough to fit several vehicles. Much of the enclosed section of the property was graveled. Jaymie pulled up near the house, stopped, got out, and helped Alicia from the SUV. Looking around, she oriented herself and realized that from Alicia's home across the fields and through the sometimes swampy woods it was a straight shot, as the crow flies, to her and Jakob's log cabin. They were a mere half mile apart.

The woman finally shook herself, took a deep shuddering breath, and led the way into the house through the front door, toss-ing her keys into a ceramic dish, then stalk-ing through the living room to a small square kitchen that overlooked the big back property.

Jaymie followed. "Do you drink tea?"

Alicia nodded as she plunked down at the small table and buried her face in her hands with a groan. Figuring she'd let the other woman be, Jaymie bustled about, finding the teakettle, container of teabags, mugs, teapot, sugar, milk. She stared out the elevated back window, looking down over the big garage where Alicia's husband died. It should look menacing, she thought, but it was just a vinyl-sided garage on a chunk of country property, with fields beyond.

As the kettle started to heat with a rolling grumble of bubbling water, Jaymie turned and leaned back against the kitchen sink. "How are you doing, Alicia?"

"I'm . . . better."

"I hope so." Jaymie poured boiling water in the teapot, used a spoon to squeeze the teabags and speed the steeping, then poured two mugs of tea, handed the other woman hers and sat in the other chair. "What happened back there at the historic house? Who was the phone call from?" She could guess, but wanted to hear it from Alicia.

Alicia shook her head. "Can we not do that right now? I don't . . . I'm tired."

Jaymie let it go for the moment. She glanced around. On the fridge was a drawing of a horse with a girl riding; the rider had a pink leg. "Did Mia do that?" she asked, pointing.

Alicia took a gulp of the hot tea and nod-

ded. "She loves horses and she loves drawing and painting."

"Jocie loves drawing and painting too. But
Mia is so good! She shows real talent. And
she's such a nice kid!" Jaymie hesitated, but
then, watching Alicia, said, "She must miss
her father."

Alicia shrugged. "It was five years ago.
Kids' memories are short. To her he's just a
photo on my phone and a vague memory of
playing horsey in the rec room."

"*You* must miss him."

"It's been hard. You don't realize how
much another person does until you have to
live without them. That first year . . . my
car broke down and I didn't know what to
do. Jace always took care of it. And that
winter the snow was awful, he used to plow
the lane. I didn't know how to work the
plow or snowblower. The bills piled up . . ."
She shook her head. "It was rough."

"And you loved him," Jaymie said.

"Sure."

It felt like the love was an afterthought,
but Jaymie would not judge her. "I have a
friend going through something similar,"
Jaymie lied, trying to dig deeper, as Vestry
had requested. "What would your advice
be?"

"Don't let your husband die without life

41

insurance," Alicia said, draining her cup and slamming it down on the table.

Jaymie wasn't sure what to say. She stumbled back into speech: "It . . . it must have been hard on you keeping up this big property and house after your husband died."

"Jace's family has been helpful. I don't know what I would have done without Franklin and Lew. That's Jace's dad and brother."

"What about Jace's mom?"

"I never met her. She died years ago in an accident. Jace said she was a sweet woman, older than his dad. He missed her, a lot. So did Lew."

"So you lost a husband and Franklin and Lew lost a son and brother," Jaymie murmured. She took a deep breath; this was the hard part, asking someone to relive the worst day of their lives. "How did it happen, your husband's accident?"

Alicia whirled her empty mug on the table until it almost fell over, stopping it just in time. "It was horrible. Mia and I were gone all day . . . shopping. If I'd known . . . but I didn't. Poor Lew found him the next day. It was awful."

Jaymie glanced at the picture on the fridge again and smiled. "Mia seems adjusted to

42

her prosthetic leg. She's been using it a long time, I gather."

Alicia's expression softened as she looked at the drawing on the fridge. Then her face set in a grim glower and her hand fisted. "*Too* long, poor baby. It was Jace's fault. I was so *angry* at him," she said, slamming her fist on the table. "He had her in the car not properly belted in to her toddler seat. He was speeding and he rolled it. Her poor little leg . . . it was crushed and they had to amputate." Her voice was choked, more emotion in it than she had shown about losing her husband. "It was awful, all Jace's fault. And the bills! We almost went bankrupt."

Her phone rang again. She looked at the call display and color returned to her pale cheeks. She took the call, saying, "Hold on." She held the phone to her chest and said to Jaymie, "Thanks for bringing me home. Can you let yourself out? I have to take this call." Her manner was cool, dismissive.

"Would you like me to retrieve your car for you?"

"Thanks, but Lew will take care of it."

"Call me if you need anything, Alicia."

The woman's expression changed, uncertainty in her eyes as she blinked, and looked down at the phone in her hand. "Sure.

I'll . . . I'll find those kitchen tools and maybe bring them out to you?"

Jaymie stood for a moment, gazing at the woman. Something in her eyes tugged at her heart. She looked guarded, like there was something she'd like to say, but not now, not with someone on the line waiting for her. "Okay. Why don't you call or text me about it?"

"Sure."

"Maybe then we can plan a playdate for Mia and Jocie."

Jaymie let herself out as Alicia murmured to her caller. Jaymie backed down the drive and pulled onto the road. A car roared past her as she pulled out, kicking up a plume of dust and spraying gravel. "Rotten driver," Jaymie muttered. Some people did not know to slow down on gravel. Her phone pinged as she headed down the road. She ignored it but it pinged again. She pulled over onto the shoulder and answered.

"Jaymie, it's Detective Vestry. How are you?"

"I'm good. What's up?"

"How did your conversation with Alicia go? Anything new?"

Her heart thumped and Jaymie looked around, spooked. "How did you . . ." Of course. The police knew she was going to meet up with Alicia at the historic house and were following her and . . . "You called Alicia while we were at the historic house."

There was silence for a moment, then Vestry replied, "I did call her."

"You purposely spooked her while I was talking to her." Jaymie felt a spurt of unaccustomed anger. "Why would you do that?"

"I don't report to you, Jaymie," Vestry replied. After a pause, she said, "I will tell you what I said: all we asked is that she come in, that we had details about her husband's death we were following up on."

That sounded innocuous enough, but they had already done it a couple of times. Troubled and conflicted, Jaymie shared her new friend's reaction. "She was rattled enough that I felt she wasn't safe to drive so I took her home, made her a cup of tea and got her calmed down."

"And you talked?"

"A bit."

"What about?"

Silent for a long moment, Jaymie considered all Alicia had said. "Detective, do you suspect she was involved in her husband's death?"

"We haven't ruled her out."

"You know, she was talking to me when we were at the historic house, opening up about it all. I feel like she was on the point of telling me all about it and then your call rattled her and put an end to it."

The detective was quiet.

Jaymie sighed. Who knows how the conversation would have gone without Vestry's interference? "We didn't talk about much once I got her home. I *do* know she is still, all these years later, angry about the accident that caused the loss of Mia's leg. She said it was Jace's fault. That doesn't mean she killed him." She stared out the windshield, tapping her thumbs on the steering wheel. She hadn't driven far so she swiveled to look across the Brouwers' barren rutted fields toward the woods across from which was her and Jakob's home. Five years ago Jace's death hadn't registered on her radar beyond a terribly sad news item, but now it seemed so close. Was it a tragic accident or murder? "You think Alicia was involved or knows something about her husband's death. Why do you think that?"

"I can't share that with you, Jaymie."

"How did Alicia benefit from Jace's death? She had a rough time after he died, looking after the house and property by herself, struggling with the bills. It doesn't make sense."

Vestry was silent.

46

"Wait . . . *did* Jace have life insurance? She implied he didn't. Did she get a big payout?" That would be one big motive.

"She did not."

"That explains her remark, then," Jaymie said, and relayed what Alicia had said about not letting your husband die without insurance. "I'm surprised that they didn't. Jakob and I both have life insurance. If you have a child it's the only responsible thing to do."

"Life insurance can be pricey."

"True. And they almost went bankrupt after the car accident with Jace and Mia. I suppose there were many bills that insurance didn't cover. Maybe they had life insurance but couldn't keep up the premiums."

Vestry was again silent.

"I don't think she killed Jace."

"I'm following the evidence, Jaymie. Things she said at the time didn't add up — I can't tell you what — but there was nothing to go on. I've got go. I'll be in touch."

The episode left her uneasy. She drove into Queensville as rain spotted her windows. There was one person she needed to speak to, one woman who would recall in perfect detail what happened five years ago.

She parked on the street near the Queensville Emporium. The rain held off, though the lowering skies still threatened and there was a faint rumble of distant thunder. Valetta Nibley, Jaymie's best friend and the town's pharmacist, was ready for her break and brought out a thermal carafe of tea and plate of cookies to the Emporium porch to share. They chatted for a moment about Denver's latest trick, unfolding laundry. He liked to burrow in the laundry basket of folded clothes and towels, probably because they were fresh out of the dryer and still warm. The cat was once Jaymie's feline companion but was now living in luxury with Valetta. Val and Jaymie were going to build him the outdoor kitty condo of his dreams, when and if they could get their schedules together.

After tea, Jaymie was silent, staring off down the village street lined with shops: her sister Becca's antique shop, then across the road the Cottage Shoppe, Jewel's Junk, and the Knit Knack Shack. She didn't actually see a thing; she was replaying her conversation with Alicia Vance, trying to pick out anything that would help her decide if the woman had a hand in killing her husband.

"C'mon, kiddo," Val said. "What's bugging you?"

Jaymie confessed to her friend her reluctant cooperation with Detective Vestry and the outcome. Some thought Val Nibley was the town's worst gossip. They didn't realize that as a pharmacist, she knew far more than she ever revealed. Her gossip was filled with harmless stories and fun tidbits, designed to spread information, not titillation.

"Do you know the Vances?" Jaymie asked when she was done.

"Of course I do. So does your sister. We went to school with Franklin Vance."

"Alicia's father-in-law."

"Alicia's mother was in our class too, Kim Hansen . . . once Kim Ellsworthy. She was my biology class buddy. We would team up to do experiments and projects together."

Small-town life: there were always connections.

"Do you know her husband?"

"Her ex, you mean? I know she married some guy named John Hansen years ago, but he took off, leaving her with the two girls. You actually know Alicia's younger sister, Erin," Val remarked.

"Erin Hansen, of course! She's the receptionist at the *Wolverhampton Weekly Howler,*" Jaymie said of the newspaper where she had a weekly food column, "Vintage Eats." "How about that?" Shaking her head, she added, "Val, someday they are

49

going to erect a monument to your memory . . . not *in* your memory, *to* your memory! Your brain synapses must look like a vast spiderweb of connectivity."

Val snickered and gulped down the last of her tea and recapped the thermos. "That's not actually how the brain works, Jaymie, but I get your drift."

"Do you remember the accident that took poor Mia's leg?"

"I do," she said, sobering. "It was horrific. Poor kid was only about three."

"And you remember Jace Vance's death?"

"Sure, another blow to that family. Fate seems to have it in for them. Even since his death they've been put through the ringer. Poor Alicia had a car accident and there was a fire that almost destroyed the garage on her property."

"I guess I knew all that . . . I mean, I'd heard about it, but didn't connect it all together. That's a lot. The garage was damaged?"

She nodded. "The structure was still sound, though. It was repaired with new siding and a few support beams were replaced."

"Val, did you think there was anything odd about it at the time? Jace Vance's death, I mean. Anything suspicious?"

Val frowned and twisted her lips, staring out through her thick glasses at the street in front of them. "Jace was a super mechanic and exceptionally careful. Brock said at the time that it was an odd accident for the guy to have," she said. Brock was Val's older brother. "Still, people get hurried and careless. One moment can be the difference between life and death. As a pharmacist, I stay mindful and never *ever* let my mind stray. I hold people's lives in my hands. Accidents happen to even the best of people." She paused, then looked directly at Jaymie. "If I'm being honest, and I'll always be honest with you, I did think it was suspicious at the time, how Jace died, but I kept it to myself. When no arrests were made, I assumed my suspicions were uncalled for. Not the first time, probably not the last."

"And now, with Vestry following up on it all these years later?"

"It gives me pause."

Jaymie sighed and fidgeted. "I didn't like reporting on what Alicia said to me. The detective thinks Alicia is hiding something."

"And what do *you* think?"

Flexing her shoulders, Jaymie tried to shrug off her thread of unease and tension but it remained, gathered in her muscles, settling in her backbone. "There's some-

51

thing there. She was upset by Vestry's call. Why would she be if she isn't hiding something?" Jaymie shook her head. "It's maddening. She was on the verge of confiding in me, I could *feel* it. I wish the detective hadn't called. If she had trusted me . . . but Vestry always has to go that extra mile, push harder."

"To be fair, she didn't know that Alicia might confide in you."

"I don't want to be fair, I want to be grumpy. What did she enlist my help for if she didn't think I'd get somewhere?" Jaymie flashed a look over at her friend and grimaced as a rumble of thunder rolled across the village. "I know I'm being unreasonable, but my sense that Alicia was going to confide in me doesn't mean she was going to tell me she killed her husband. It doesn't even mean that she *conspired* to kill her husband. I don't think she did anything of the kind."

"Okay. I trust your read on people, Jaymie, you know I do."

Jaymie rose and dusted off her bottom, then cast a look at the threatening sky. "I'd better get home. I have a column due day after tomorrow and it won't write itself."

"Me too. Lots to do today."

"I suppose that's likely the end of it, anyway."

"What will you do if the detective calls you again?"

Jaymie hunched one shoulder. "I don't know. Alicia is supposed to bring me kitchen tools from her grandmother, but I'm not holding my breath. Talk to you later, Val!"

FOUR

It rained overnight, but Tuesday dawned
clear and cooler, the smell of fallen leaves
wafting on the breeze through the windows
Jaymie opened to enjoy the last lingering
warmth of early fall. It was a busy day.
Jaymie got her column done, the recipe
photographed, cropped and edited the
photos, and sent it all by email to Nan, her
editor at the *Wolverhampton Weekly Howler*.
She had an upcoming appearance for Sid
Farrell's radio show on antiques and needed
to plan for it. In her regular timeslot she
talked to his audience about vintage kitchen
utensils and dishes; since she was working
on the display of vintage whisks for the
historic house, she'd talk about the history
of whisks. She believed in being prepared,
so she wrote bits of dialogue and a list of
fun facts to fall back on in case she got
tongue-tied.

The word "whisk" is Scandinavian in origin,

she wrote. The kitchen utensil and the verb *to whisk* came from similar roots. The first kitchen cooking whisk was simply a bundle of slim sticks tied together, but by the nineteenth century Victorians had invented the wire whisk, virtually unchanged for years, though different shapes and sizes all had their day. Julia Child, who popularized the use of the wire whisk in American cooking via her TV show, was an avid kitchen utensil collector and had hundreds, as she liked trying different types.

Jaymie then researched types and shapes of whisks to share on her blog, as she would point Farrell's listeners there for more information. Her passion for vintage kitchen utensils and dishes made her a favorite on the radio host's show, and it had in return increased her blog readership.

Alicia did not call or text about the box of utensils. Jaymie gave a mental shrug. It was not as if she had expected the woman to follow through.

It was Jaymie's turn to pick up Jocie from school. Her daughter had begun ballet lessons, so after-school pickup was delayed by three-quarters of an hour. Jaymie pulled up to the mostly deserted pickup zone in time to see Alicia park and get out of her car. Jaymie followed, parked next to her and got out. They reached the pickup zone together and Jaymie smiled over at her. Alicia, wearing a cable-knit cardigan sweater in a gorgeous cobalt blue over a T-shirt and jeans, nodded. After a moment she sidled over to Jaymie.

"Hey, thanks for taking me home yesterday." She glanced toward Jaymie, then away, squinting into a slanting beam of afternoon sunlight that had broken through the clouds. "That call I got, it kind of . . . alarmed me. Nothing important, but it threw me for a loop."

Jaymie, knowing the caller was Vestry, was interested in Alicia framing it as "nothing important." She waited a moment. Alicia didn't mention the later call at her home, when she had asked her guest to leave. "I'm glad you got your car back. Is Mia here for dance class?"

"She's taking ballet. She saw a ballet-dancing teenager online — a girl who also has a prosthetic — and she wanted to try it. Her doctor said that it could help her with balance."

Jaymie smiled. "Jocie's in the same class. She takes dance because she loves it, but it's good for her flexibility, too. That's important for her."

There was silence for a long minute, then

Alicia turned to her. "Look, I didn't get to ask what I wanted to ask. I know you've helped the police with murder cases. I wondered, do you ever just help *people*?"

Taken aback, Jaymie stared at her. "I'm not sure what you mean?"

Reddening, Alicia shook her head. "I don't know what I mean. I don't *know*." She fidgeted, shifting from foot to foot and clutching her phone tightly in one hand. "I still have something I want to ask you."

Jaymie hadn't intended to involve herself further, but this sounded serious and she could not deny her. She watched her new friend's face, the furrowed brow, the bit lip, turning red, the dark shadows under her eyes that spoke of a sleepless night. "Ask me now."

"I have to think about it first. I can't . . . oh, look, there are the girls!" Alicia said, her tone brightening, waving as Jocie and Mia came out together arm in arm. "Aren't they sweethearts? I love your Jocie. She's so smart and kind and cute as a button!"

Jaymie smiled at that description. "Mia, too. Such a talented girl, and a reader, like Jocie. I think they'll be good friends."

"I hope so." She sounded hesitant.

"I'm sure they will, Alicia. We'll make sure they get that chance," Jaymie said warmly, glancing over at the other woman.

"I hope . . ." Alicia broke off and shook her head, mumbling under her breath something that sounded like "life is unpredictable."

"What was that?" Jaymie asked, wondering if she'd heard her correctly. "I didn't hear what you said?"

"Nothing," she muttered. "Mia is shy. It took someone outgoing like your Jocie to bring her out of her shell. I love my little girl so much," she said fervently, watching the children. "Every decision I make is for her benefit. I just wish she was as good at making friends as your Jocie." She turned back to Jaymie and hurriedly muttered, "Can I come out to your place in an hour? I have to drop Mia off with my mom, first. I'll call before I come. Or I'll text. Okay?"

Jaymie nodded as Jocie threw herself at her, chattering nonstop. She waved to Mia, and Jaymie waved to Alicia and they got in their respective vehicles and drove away.

They had an early dinner. Jaymie kept checking her phone, but Alicia never did call or text. She had probably changed her mind. Maybe it was better that way, Jaymie reflected, staring out the kitchen window. She didn't like feeling that she had to report whatever Alicia told her to Vestry. She dried the last of the dinner dishes, plopping a wire whisk into the vintage tin on the windowsill she used to store cooking utensils, as Jakob got ready to go out. He was taking the store's accounting books to Gus so he could ask him about a couple of expenditures that had not been correctly entered. "I'll be back in half an hour, okay?"

Jaymie held her cheek toward him for a kiss — his lips were warm, and his beard tickled — and said, "If we're not here, we'll be in the woods across the road. Jocie has to collect acorns for a school project, and I'm collecting dried weeds for a fall wreath."

Five minutes later, as the light was waning, Jaymie hung the damp tea towel on a hook to dry and called out, "Jocie, it'll be dark in an hour. If we're going to do this, let's do it!"

Jocie bounced into the kitchen followed by Hoppy, who wobbily bounded after her, barking. Jaymie laughed. "Okay, Hoppy, you too. We'll combine a walk with treasure hunting."

She leashed Hoppy while Jocie got her cloth bag to carry her acorns. "Get a sweater, kiddo, it'll be darker and chilly by the time we get back." She grabbed a bottle of water, her cellphone, and a flashlight. Her phone had a flashlight app, but it wasn't strong enough for them to see their way.

At nine Jocie was too old for a lot of the parental things, but Jaymie still took her hand when they crossed the gravel road. They climbed down the dusty ditch on the other side, and then back up and went over (Jaymie) and under (Jocie) the wire fence and through the stand of sumacs that were turning a brilliant scarlet. The Brouwers were friends of the Müller family going back forty years, both immigrants, though from different countries, both with sons who were friends and former schoolmates. The woods were open to Jakob, Jaymie, Jocie and any other Müller who wished to wander them. There was no hunting allowed — signs stating it were on every fence post — so it was safe.

After the rain from the night before the ground was marshy in places. While searching for acorns and gathering them, and as Jaymie looked for dried branches and weeds for a wreath, Jocie chattered ceaselessly about ballet class. "Did you know that Mia said there was a ballet dancer she saw online who had a prosthetic, just like her? She said she'd never seen a little person ballet dancer, though, so I said maybe I'll be the first little person ballet dancer."

"That would be awesome. Maybe we can

film your class? I'd love your grandparents to see you dance." Jaymie's parents had fully embraced Jocie as their grandchild and were thrilled. They made special efforts to visit. They were coming north to Canada for Canadian Thanksgiving in October — Jocie and Jakob would join them across the border for that — and then would stay at the Queensville house through American Thanksgiving in November, before returning to their home in Boca Raton. "They could watch you online!"

Hoppy was getting impatient. He yapped and tugged on the leash. "Hoppy, I swear, you are an obedience school dropout!" Jaymie scolded as a blue jay swooped and screeched at the yappy Yorkie-Poo. A buckle on his harness broke, he squirmed free and was off, bouncing through the forest, yapping and chasing something.

"Hoppy, come back!" Jaymie screamed into the darkening depths. Coyotes roamed the fields and countryside; her little fellow would be a tasty morsel. "Jocie, stay here. I need to get him." She set aside her gathered weeds and followed the little dog through the woods, finding his path by listening to his echoing barks, stumbling over tree roots and branches as she went. *Darn that little tripod pup!* He was much more nimble with three legs than she was with two. She still heard him yapping, but it sounded like he had come to a stop. The light was failing. It was dusky and shadowy in the forest, and she hated that she had left Jocie alone. She had to get back to her daughter!

"Hoppy! Where *are* you?" she shouted angrily.

He yipped and she followed. There he was, standing guard over . . . something? She slowed, catching her breath, not wanting to spook her dog. Though he was often obedient, other times he liked to play *chase me!* She caught her breath and kept her gaze on him, stepping over tree limbs, crunching through leaves, until she was close.

What was that? In the dusk she noticed an unnatural shade of blue. A tarp? No . . . it was . . .

"No, no!" she gasped, choking back a sob and staggering back a step. Lying on the forest floor in a crumpled heap, kitchen tools tumbled about her from a torn paper bag, was Alicia Vance, wearing the same blue sweater she had worn when she picked up her daughter two and a half hours before. Fighting back an urge to scream, aware that Jocie was yards away, tamping down tears and horror, she stilled, deliberately calling upon her inner strength to slow her thudding heart. She closed her eyes, drew in a deep breath, and opened them.

Jaymie approached and dropped to her knees in the mat of dead leaves. Hoppy whined and nosed at the body. "Alicia? Alicia, speak to me!" The woman was dead. By the waning light Jaymie could see that her eyes were wide open and staring, filmed over with a hazy, cloudy appearance. A large vintage kitchen whisk was on her chest, with a small spot of blood turning the blue wool to purple. Looking closer, Jaymie could see that the whisk was twisted violently, one of the long wires that made up the whisking head wrenched from its place and pushed deep into her chest, on the left side of her breast. She gasped — the kitchen tool had been turned into a stiletto, a wire dagger to the heart.

There was rustling behind her. Jaymie straightened.

"Mama? Mama, it's getting dark!" Jocie was trying to find her. "Did you find Hoppy? Can we go home?"

Jocie! She could not let her little girl see this. "Honey, don't come any closer. I've found . . . we have to . . ." Jaymie shook herself, trying to come to terms with what she'd found, trying to figure out her next step. Cell phone. "Jocie, honey, stay right where you are! I'm okay. Hoppy's okay. But we have a little problem and I need to get your daddy to meet us. You won't move, right? You're a brave girl. You're not afraid of the woods." There was silence. "Honey, can you call Hoppy? Get him to come to you?"

Jocie's voice, a little thin and wobbly, called, "Hoppy, come here, Hoppy!"

The little dog looked at the body, looked up at Jaymie, then looked back to where Jocie's voice was coming from.

"Hoppy, Jocie *needs* you," Jaymie whispered. "Go to her. Go on . . . please, my brave little guy."

The dog quivered, then bounced away as Jocie kept calling.

"Do you have him?" Jaymie called, as, with trembling frigid hands, she pulled up Jakob's contact info.

"He's here," Jocie called.

"Okay, hold on, I'll be with you in a minute." She sighed in relief when Jakob picked up and said hello. "Where are you? Are you home?" she whispered.

"I'm here. Are you okay? Honey, is Jocie all right? What's wrong?"

"I'm fine, Jocie is fine," she muttered, trying to keep her voice down. "Jakob, we're in the woods across the road and . . . and I've found a body. I've found Alicia Vance!" Tears welled and streamed and a sob caught in her throat. She knuckled the tears out of her eyes. "I need you to come out to the edge of the woods to retrieve Jocie and Hoppy and get them out of here while I call the police."

"Honey, let me come get you and —"

"No, no, I'm okay. I'm worried about Jocie. I don't want her to see this. It's her friend's mommy!" She choked and sobbed. "I'm okay, really, I am. I know it sounds like I'm falling apart, but I'm not. *Please*, Jakob, come out, cross the road and wait. I'm going to come to the roadside and wait for the police." He agreed and hung up.

She used a GPS app to mark her place, then joined Jocie and Hoppy, picking up the little dog and leading her daughter to the road where, in the dwindling twilight, Jakob was waiting. Along the way Jocie kept asking questions, but Jaymie didn't know what to say. Finally, she said, "Honey, please. I'll explain later but I need to get help, okay? Right now. No more questions. Go with your daddy."

They had reached the road. Jocie looked up, examined her gaze and nodded. Jaymie handed Hoppy over to Jakob, who hugged her and murmured in her ear, "Tell me what you need."

"I need you to take Hoppy and Jocie and make them safe," she said, squeezing his shoulder. "Don't worry, I'm not going back into the woods. I'll wait right here until the police come."

As the two loves of her life crossed the road to the warmth of the glow from the cabin kitchen window, Jaymie called Detective Vestry and, in halting words, explained what she had found.

"Good Lord, how do you do it?" was the woman's reply. "How do you manage to stumble over so many bodies?"

Jaymie gritted her teeth; that flippant response was not helpful. This would never have happened if the detective hadn't asked her to befriend Alicia to the extent that Alicia decided to confide in her. "Detective, just come! With police cars and an ambulance . . . or . . . or the medical examiner. No sirens. Come out to my home. I'm by the woods across the road."

Vestry, more intent and serious, said, "Are you safe? Is the assailant nearby? Did you hear or see anything?"

"I'm safe. I don't think the assailant is nearby. Alicia's been dead a while, judging by her eyes. I'm out at the road, and I can

66

see Jakob at the kitchen window." She waved to her husband, who waved back. "It's getting dark but I can guide you back to poor Alicia. *Hurry!*"

"I'll be there in five minutes, a squad car will be there in three."

Jayme guided them. Detective Vestry followed, with two uniformed officers. More had been left at the roadside. They could have used her phone's location finder to locate the body, but she couldn't stand by and do nothing. Several beams of flashlights danced in the forest. She explained, as she went, what had happened, that she had met Alicia at the school, that the woman had said she'd call as she had something she wanted to talk to Jaymie about, how she didn't call, so Jaymie had gone into the woods with her daughter to look for acorns, leaves and dried weeds.

Jaymie knew she was over explaining, and that it came from a need to calm her own nerves as they got deeper into the woods. "Detective, you may not know this, but Alicia's property is on the other side of these woods. She must have been coming on the path through here to bring me the kitchen tools. It's a shortcut." Why wouldn't she drive? Was she trying to avoid someone? Was she trying not to be seen? Haltingly, she expressed those thoughts to Vestry as they approached the position and Jaymie pointed out the body. "There she is," she said, directing her flashlight beam to the spot of brilliant blue. "Poor Alicia." Jaymie shivered with mingled cold and horror.

Alicia did not kill her husband, Jaymie was sure of it now. But what did she know? There was something on her mind. What was it?

FIVE

Jaymie stood at the kitchen window watching across the road as police crime tape was run along the fence. Lise and Arend Brouwer had driven over and stood holding vigil on the roadside. Arend, a vigorous balding man in his late seventies, had one arm around his wife's shoulders. She slumped against him, her gray hair tight in a bun, her head on his shoulder, one hand on her cane. This would make those good people heartsick, Jaymie thought, her eyes brimming with tears, a young woman losing her life on their land. She turned away from the window. She couldn't stop thinking of Mia, now an orphan. Whatever else Alicia was or was not, she was a good and loving mom.

Jakob had kept Jocie busy with homework, making sure she had her bath, and bed. He finally came to Jaymie and hugged her, confessing that he had not told Jocie all that

69

happened. He didn't yet have the words. She laid her head on his shoulder and slumped against him. Tears streamed and she sobbed. "Who would do that to her? Oh, Jakob, it's so awful. And the first thing Vestry said on the phone was, how do I keep finding bodies, l-like I want to!" She buried her face in his shoulder.

Jakob hugged her to his sturdy body, murmuring soothing words into her ear.

If only she had pushed Alicia a little harder, probed a little deeper, maybe she'd still be alive. "Why didn't she tell me what she wanted when I asked? Why did she say 'later'? Why did she come through the woods rather than get in her car and drive?"

"Shhhh." He rocked her. "We don't know if any of those things would have saved her, honey. Even if she had told you whatever it was she was going to, this still may have happened."

"You're right," Jaymie said wearily. She pulled away from her husband and filled the kettle.

"I can do that for you."

"No, it's okay. I need to . . . to fidget." Jaymie smiled at Jakob, who looked at her with worry in his beautiful brown eyes. She cradled his cheek and scruffed his beard. "I'm okay. Or at least I'll *be* okay. But poor little Mia! The ache that sweet child is in for." She took in a long shaky breath, trying to calm herself.

He nodded. "Poor kid."

An hour and three cups of tea later, Vestry, hands shoved in her jacket pockets, strode across the road, head down. Jaymie was waiting at the door and ushered her in. Vestry looked around. "Wow, this is quite the place you have here."

"My husband built it with his brother," Jaymie said. "Come in. Tea?"

"Nope. Not a tea drinker."

"Coffee?"

"Sure."

They settled in the living area near the fire. Jakob hovered, watching Jaymie anxiously. She smiled and he finally sat in one of the chairs by the hearth. Jaymie sat on the sofa and Hoppy climbed up in her lap as she faced the detective, who took out her cellphone and set it on the coffee table, tapping the screen to a recording app. "Detective Angela Vestry with Jaymie Leighton Müller," then she stated the date and time and circumstances. "Witness testimony. Can you tell me how you happened to find the body of Ms. Alicia Vance in the woods across from your home?"

Haltingly, Jaymie described meeting Alicia

at the school, what the woman said, and how she waited for her call . . . the call that never came. "I had promised Jocie that we would collect acorns for a school project, and the Brouwers — they own the land across the road — told us it's okay to go in there whenever we want. I knew there were oak trees in a certain spot, so we went." She hugged her Yorkie-Poo to her. "Hoppy — this little guy — got off the leash and ran ahead. I followed him, telling Jocie to stay where she was. I saw the blue ahead of me . . ." She stopped and stared at nothing, her heartbeat accelerating. "Such an un-natural color in the forest," she said, her voice sounding ghostly.

"And then?"

"I found Alicia and knew she was dead immediately. Her eyes . . . they were wide open and staring and filmed over." The sprung whisk, one beater wire pulled out and straightened into a deadly weapon . . . that was not a spur-of-the-moment crime, Jaymie thought.

"Did you hear or see anyone while you were in the woods?"

"Not at all."

"Are you sure you don't know what Alicia wanted to talk to you about?"

Jaymie frowned and petted Hoppy, who

72

looked up at her and whined softly. She picked at a bundle of weed seeds stuck to his fur and tugged them out, putting them carefully on the coffee table. "I'm trying to recall her exact words. First, she said she knew I helped the police sometimes, but did I ever help people? And then I think she said, *I have something I want to ask you.* I asked her what it was. She said she had to think about it first. And that's it." *Do you ever just help people?* What did Alicia mean by that? "I think it had to do with her husband's death, but I'm not sure of that. She complained about the police, how they had been hounding her."

Vestry waited a moment, then nodded and said, "End of interview," leaned over and tapped the cellphone. She drained the rest of her coffee, pocketed her phone and stood. "If you think of anything else, call me."

"Where is Mia?" Jaymie asked, looking up at the detective.

"She's with her grandmother. I'm heading over there now to speak with Alicia's mother."

"To tell her what happened to her daughter," Jaymie said, setting Hoppy aside and standing, tugging at her T-shirt to straighten it.

Vestry nodded. Her expression was carefully neutral, not a flicker of emotion.

Jakob joined Jaymie and pulled her to him. "We'll be thinking of them. Poor little girl. I hope she's going to be okay."

Vestry nodded. "I'd better get going."

Wednesday morning, phone calls came in one after another, along with text messages. Jaymie refused to comment. Traffic past their home increased once word got out. The *Wolverhampton Weekly Howler* online edition was headlined "Local Mother Found Murdered in Woods," and Jaymie was named as the one who found Alicia. Nan, her editor, begged her for a comment. Jaymie, increasingly distraught, said *no comment* and hung up on her. She tried to stay busy, but didn't feel she could leave the cabin other than taking Hoppy for a walk in the Christmas tree field.

When Jakob brought Jocie home that afternoon, the little girl was in tears. Mia was not at school, of course, but the news of her mother's death had spread like a small blaze fanned into an inferno. Jaymie had thought adults would shield their kids from it, but information flowed through social media. With most kids having phones . . . it was a disaster. Kids had plied

74

Jocie with questions since it was her mom who found Mia's mom, and it happened in the woods opposite their house.

Solemn and withdrawn, Jocie retreated upstairs with Lilibet and Hoppy. Jaymie wrung her hands and paced, working herself into an agitated mess. They had considered keeping Jocie home from school, but their cabin was no refuge for the moment. Sending her to her grandparents would only be a stopgap. In general, Jakob believed it was better to keep things normal for a child, but in this case he had demurred. They had a minor argument about it that morning, with Jakob fearful that she would hear the news the wrong way and Jaymie sure it would not have gotten around yet. "I was wrong," she said to Jakob, turning her back on the kitchen window and fretting about Jocie. "I should have known better. This is awful."

"Honey, honey, it's okay," her husband said, grabbing her to stop her from pacing. He hugged her, a good long squeeze. "I wasn't sure either way. We can't always err on the side of caution. Maybe we should have told her, but what's done is done. She'll be okay. We need to talk to her about it."

Hand in hand, they climbed the stairs and tapped on the door to Jocie's room. Slant-roofed and beamed, it was crowded with stuffed toys, books, games, puzzles and a plastic tote of craft supplies, one drawer open. She sat on her bed stringing beads.

"Whatcha doing?" Jaymie said, sitting on the end of the bed. Jakob circled and sat down next to her on the other side.

"I'm making Mia a bracelet."

"That's a nice thing to do," Jakob said. "She may not be back to school for a while."

Jocie looked up, her round cheeks tearstained. "Can we go see her?"

Jaymie met Jakob's gaze.

"We'll look into it, but it may not be possible," Jakob said gently.

She nodded, sniffing back tears that trailed over her chubby cheeks. "Her mom was going to take us for ice cream next time after ballet. Mia was going to see if you'd let us. Where is Mia?"

"She's with her grandmother."

Jocie nodded. "She went there a lot. She has her own room and her Aunt Erin lives there too."

"What did you hear at school?" Jakob asked.

Jocie's tears had stopped for the moment, but her expression was shadowy and pained. She kept her gaze down on the beads as she strung them one at a time. "One of the kids, his dad is a police officer and he said that some lady found Mia's mom dead in the woods." She looked up. "And then he looked at me and said it was my mom. Why didn't you tell me last night? Why didn't you *tell* me?"

Jakob opened his mouth but Jaymie looked at him and shook her head. He nodded, got up, came around the bed, kissed his daughter on the top of her blonde head, and said, "I'll make dinner."

Jaymie took Jocie's small pudgy hand in hers and met her gaze. "You know what? I should have. You're a big girl. It was wrong of me to keep it from you. I was worried you'd have nightmares and that it would scare you."

Jocie nodded.

"I'm sorry I let you be blindsided —"

"What does 'blindsided' mean?"

"It means that learning about Mia's mom . . . you didn't see it coming. I should have told you the truth. Then it wouldn't have come out of nowhere."

Jocie nodded again and returned to stringing the beads. "Why was Mia's mom in the woods so close to our place?"

"We — Detective Vestry and I — think she was coming to see me. When we picked you and Mia up from ballet, Alicia told me she wanted to talk. She asked if she could come by in an hour, and I said yes. She didn't call like she said she would, so I didn't think she was coming."

"Who killed her?"

"We don't know."

"What's going to happen now?"

"I don't know exactly. But Mia is being taken care of. She's got her grandmother and her aunt, and I think her grandfather and uncle, right?"

Jocie nodded. "Her grandpa lets her ride in the back of his truck."

Taken aback, Jaymie said, "A pickup? That's dangerous, Jocie. *Really* dangerous. I hope you'd never do that?"

She rolled her eyes. "Dad would never let me do that." She was silent for a few moments, then said, "You won't go back into the woods, will you?"

"No, of course not. You saw the police there. I'm letting them look after it."

"I mean ever."

"Jocie, I can't promise never to go into the woods again," Jaymie said.

She sighed and looked up into Jaymie's eyes. "But . . . Mama, sometimes you investigate." She said the word carefully. "Why do you do that?"

That was a tough one. "Jocie, I never do

anything I think will be dangerous."

"That's not what I asked."

"I know, honey, it's a tough question. It's different every time."

"Will you promise?"

"Promise what?"

"Not to do anything dangerous ever again." Her lip was in a pout, her expression verging on sullen.

Jaymie watched her for a moment. What to say? She couldn't promise. Danger occasionally came at one; she would deal with it when it did. And yet she saw — and understood — Jocie's fear. Carefully, she said, "We all manage ourselves as best we can. We're careful and we take care of each other. I promise I will not take unnecessary risks." She smiled. "Like, we let you climb up into the tree house even though we get scared you could fall, but we don't let you . . . oh, drive the car, or swing from branches thirty feet in the air."

Jocie watched her eyes, then nodded. "Okay."

For now, her expression hinted. Those answers had sufficed for now.

"Let's go downstairs and help your dad make dinner. Will you set the table?"

The police had finished with the site the

following day. Jaymie hadn't heard anything. It was unnerving. Now whenever she looked across the road at the woods she had a foreboding feeling. On the other side of those woods and across the fields beyond it, Alicia had walked to bring her the kitchen tools and whatever problem she had in her heart that she needed to share with Jaymie.

The problem she hadn't felt free to tell Jaymie at the school parking lot.

What could it have been? Something about Mia? Something about Jace and his death? She shook her head . . . all these years later? It didn't seem likely. And yet what else could have been weighing so heavy on her that she felt compelled to reference Jaymie's experience with the police and involvement in murder cases?

She knew the police suspected her of involvement in her husband's death. It worried her gravely, judging from how she broke down when Vestry called her in for more questioning. She was scared. If she did it, she would have been scared, but would she have had anything to ask Jaymie? It was more likely that she knew or suspected who did it and was trying to figure out how much to tell the police, if anything. That jibed with her questions about fearing police entrapment. She may have felt Jaymie

80

could help her decide what to do.

It was another lowering day, with dark clouds churning under a high ceiling of lighter clouds, and no hint of blue. Jaymie exited the cabin and stood staring across the road at the woods, shivering, rubbing her arms. There was still police tape fluttering in the breeze, yellow and sinuous like a draped snake, from fence post to fence post. She imagined Alicia's home, a half mile away on the other side of that wooded grove.

Perhaps Alicia had set out alone. She carried the bag of kitchen tools thinking ahead to what she would ask or tell Jaymie, not aware that someone was following her, perhaps stealing, in the twilight, from clump of bushes to small grove of trees until Alicia entered the woods, offering the killer safety from prying eye. Then he (or she?) accosted her and argued? But that didn't make sense. If they had intended to kill her, surely they would have brought a weapon, not had to improvise one, ripping a metal wire out of the whisk and plunging it into Alicia's heart.

Maybe it was spur of the moment. Someone caught up with her . . . *Alicia, we need to talk. I didn't* (do whatever Alicia thought they did), *I didn't, really!* An argument, a struggle, and the improvised weapon, a harmless whisk made over into a stiletto to

81

the heart.

No, neither of those made sense. The conviction she had, that Alicia's assailant was someone she knew, had grown stronger. Jaymie pictured anew the scene on the other side of the woods: Alicia walked across the rutted field, holding the paper bag of kitchen tools in her blue-sweater-clad arms and talking, as the sun set, with someone she trusted. Someone she felt comfortable enough to head toward the path through the woods with, to enter them with, to not suspect. Did that person turn around and wrench the kitchen tool out of her hand, rip it apart and stab her, once they were in the depths of the woods? Or perhaps the person offered to carry the bag and thus had easy access to the tool, growing more sure each minute they spoke that Alicia had to die and fashioning the lethal weapon.

Jaymie shuddered and took a deep breath. Imagining the scene was fine, but this time she would let the police figure it out. The police were good at investigating alibis, timelines, fingerprints, DNA, blood spatter.

However . . . Jaymie was good at talking, commiserating with, comforting people. And even murderers feel pain. If she had learned anything over the past three years it was that people who killed were often frightened, or angry, jealous, hurt, reeling from their tragic criminal deed. There were undoubtedly cold-blooded killers out there, but most were first-time murderers who were unprepared for the guilt and fear they experienced in the days after. She had seen how the knowledge of what they did took a toll on the perpetrator. People are not stone, and even the most deliberate and hard-hearted hurt.

Jaymie was good at getting people to confide in her. This was too close to home. It was time to find out who was hurting. And why. Her first question was . . . why did Alicia have to die right then? What was she going to tell Jaymie?

Six

She returned inside and called Valetta, who knew everyone's last name, where they lived, and who with. Armed with the full name and address, Jaymie popped a casserole in the oven to bake while she showered and changed, dressing carefully in soft autumn patterned leggings and a long sweater. She grabbed her purse and the still-warm casserole dish of homemade macaroni and cheese, then headed out to the SUV, with one troubled look across the road at the forest. She hoped soon she could look at the beautiful woods without shuddering.

Kim Hansen lived in Wolverhampton in a part of town that was lined with ranch and Colonial-style homes built in the sixties and seventies. Her house was a Colonial, red brick on the bottom and white siding on top, with an attached side garage. There were three cars in the wide drive. Jaymie parked on the street, grabbed her purse and the casserole and headed up the sloping pavement. She shifted the dish to her left arm and rang the doorbell.

A harried-looking woman answered the door, her gaze unfocused, her gray-rooted blonde hair mussed and her eyes red. "Yes?"

"Hi. Are you Kim Hansen?"

The woman nodded, her gaze focusing on Jaymie.

Taking a deep breath, Jaymie introduced herself, then said, unnecessarily, she was sure, "Your daughter, Alicia, was on her way to my place when she was . . . when it happened. May I come in?"

Kim stared for a long moment, then stood back, holding the door open. Jaymie passed through and waited as the woman closed the door behind her.

"I wanted to . . . to bring you this." She handed her the foil-covered casserole. "It's homemade macaroni and cheese. You must be devastated right now, but people need to eat, and I know you'll have people dropping in. Kids love macaroni and cheese. Is . . . is Mia here?"

"She's up in her room," Kim said, hefting the casserole. "You didn't have to do this."

"I know but . . . Mia and my Jocie are friends," Jaymie said, her voice cracking. "They're in ballet together and are becoming good friends. Jocie is fond of her. And worried for her."

Kim's expression cleared and her eyes watered. She nodded. "Come to the kitchen. Have a cup of coffee. Or tea."

"Tea if you have it."

The woman led the way through the entry and past a formal living room into which fall light filtered through sheer curtains. They entered what had likely started as a small kitchen, but now the wall between it and a dining room had been torn down, the wallboard raw and freshly plastered but not yet sanded and painted. "We're renovating, making a more open floor plan," Kim said.

Two women sat at the plain blond-wood kitchen table, places indicated with fringed woven striped placemats in a sunny color combination of red, orange and yellow. Jaymie recognized both. "Erin," she said. "I'm sorry for your loss . . . your poor sister." Tears welled in her eyes as she thought of how she'd feel losing Becca.

"Thanks." Erin was a pretty woman, reddish hair, freckles sprinkled over her nose, blue eyes. She was cool at all times, even in the sometimes hectic office of the *Wolverhampton Weekly Howler,* where she was the receptionist.

Jaymie turned to the other. "Nicki, how

are you? I didn't know you knew the Hansens?" Nicki Majewski was Gus's young wife.

"I've known them for years," she said. "Tami used to babysit Mia before . . ." She paused, then said, "Before."

Jaymie nodded; "before" was sometime prior to Tami's incarceration for a crime she committed back in the eighties. Jaymie had helped solve it before her wedding to Jakob, leading to Tami's arrest, confession and plea deal.

"And I lived at Tami's. That's how I met Gus."

Jaymie nodded again. She knew that, of course.

Kim put the kettle on the stove and turned to lean back against the counter. Her glance flicked upward and she stilled for a moment. Music drifted down from upstairs. "Poor sweetie. Mia has been listening to her mom's favorite music all day. Carrie Underwood's "Jesus Take the Wheel" on repeat." She smiled, a wobbly expression that quivered with suppressed tears. "I'm letting her do what she needs to do."

"I think that's wise, at least at first," Jaymie said. "I hope I'm not interrupting?"

"We were . . . reminiscing, I guess you'd call it," Kim said with a weary sigh. "Erin is going in to work this afternoon." She pushed a sturdy chair toward Jaymie.

"I'm sure Nan would give you time off?"

Erin nodded, swiping bangs out of her eyes. "She would, but I need to do *something.* I can't just sit here crying. This way I can talk to Nan about how they're handling this in the paper."

"What do you mean?"

A glanced flicked between mother and daughter. "You saw the headline online this morning?" Kim asked.

Jaymie nodded. "And I read the article."

"It was okay, for now, but we don't want them dragging all that other nonsense up." Kim's expression hardened. "All that stuff about Jace. All the doubts. Suspicions. Gossip."

"Nan will be fair," Jaymie said uneasily. Nan Goodenough was, above all things, a news editor. She hoped what she was saying about her was true.

"Fair?" Erin said with a skeptical look at Jaymie. "In what universe is the press ever fair?"

Jaymie stayed quiet. What they had experienced in the aftermath of Jace's death had scarred them. No one came through a police investigation and the resulting press coverage unscathed.

Nicki snorted and rolled her eyes. "As if. The way they covered Tami was horrible."

Jaymie still remained silent. Nan had gone out of her way to be factual and refrain from innuendo in that case, but that was the past, now. Tami had made a plea deal and was serving her time.

Erin looked at her cell phone. "Speaking of . . . time for me to get gone." She gave a brief smile to Jaymie. "See you at the *Howler.*"

"I've got to see Nan for a planning meeting."

"I know. I'm the one who keeps her schedule up to date." The young woman hefted her leather bag over her shoulder and stalked out, no farewell even to her mother. The front door banged behind her.

Kim seemed to relax once she was gone. She made a pot of tea, put the casserole in the fridge, brought the teapot and clean mugs to the table and took her daughter's vacated chair. She carefully straightened the placemat, lining it up with the table edge, then buried her face in her hands and sighed.

"I'm sorry," Jaymie said softly.

"I keep thinking, *what if,* you know?" she said, her voice muffled. "What if I had picked up Mia that day instead of Alicia? I was supposed to — Mia was coming to our place to stay the night — but I lost track of time and had to call Alicia at work, tell her I couldn't get there. She left work early to pick her up. If I had just done what I was supposed to do Alicia would have still been at work and would never have met you, never have headed toward your place." Kim looked into Jaymie's eyes and appeared to rethink her words. "Not that I blame you. Of course. How did she seem? Was she worried about anything, or anyone? I can't figure out what happened. Was someone lurking in the woods, do you think? Maybe she startled someone who was doing something illegal?"

"I think the police would have told the Brouwers if there was evidence of camping in the woods. We live right across from there and I'm in those woods often. I've never seen any indication of that."

"But it could be, right? Some tramp or bum? A drug addict or homeless person?"

Jaymie watched her, unable to find a way to say the truth without hurting her: Alicia was killed by someone she trusted enough to walk through the woods with her.

"Why was she coming to see you anyway? I don't understand."

"I'm not sure myself. She said she needed

to talk to me, but she had to think about it first." Jaymie watched Kim, but she had calmed. "Did she tell you how we met? We ran into each other at the junk store. Jocie went over to talk to Mia, and I followed and introduced myself. She said she had kitchen tools from her grandmother. She wanted to give them to me, so she came out to the historic house, where I volunteer. A phone call upset her so much I drove her home."

Kim nodded, fiddling with the placemat fringe. Her expression hardened. "That was that witch cop, Vestry, who called her. She's the latest, all of them convinced Alicia had something to do with, or knew about . . ." She stopped and shook her head.

"About . . . ?"

"The cops were bugging her about that old stuff with Jace," Nicki blurted out.

Kim gave her a look, but nodded. "Like I said, Vestry had decided Alicia was involved or had information she wasn't sharing. Alicia was convinced that the woman was trying to build a case against her."

"What do *you* think?"

"I think that detective is a woman-hating witch. That's what *I* think." Kim then went over what Jaymie already knew about Jace Vance's death, then added, "The cops are convinced she knows more than she said."

She paused. "Knew. *Knew* more," she said, her face twisting as she put her daughter firmly in the past tense.

"Did she know more? Innocently, I mean. You can know something but be too afraid to tell. Or you can belatedly realize you have pertinent information." Jaymie watched her eyes carefully.

"There's nothing to know," Kim said, her tone flat. "Jace was killed in a tragic accident. It happens every day."

Not *died,* but *was killed.* It was an interesting but possibly innocent way to put it. "Would Erin know what her sister was thinking?"

There was a flicker in Kim's eyes, and then it was gone. She was alert to movement upstairs that made her half stand. Her gaze returned to Jaymie. "I'll have to let you go," she said, standing fully. "I don't like leaving Mia alone right now, and this is the last thing I want her to hear about."

Jaymie nodded and rose. She put her hand on the woman's shoulder. "I hope Mia is okay." She shook her head with a sigh. "That's such an empty platitude, but . . . I do. I'm thinking of you all, but mostly, Mia. At least she has you and Erin." She paused a beat, squeezed and released the older woman's shoulder, then said, "My daughter made her a bracelet. Can she bring it over?"

Kim's expression softened and she smiled through tears. "Mia likes Jocie. She was so excited that another kid that was different was in the ballet class. I think they'll be good friends." Her voice clogged and she cleared her throat.

"I hope so."

"Kim, I got to go too. The babysitter is expecting me," Nicki said, rising.

The two women hugged, Kim thanked Jaymie for the casserole, and Nicki followed Jaymie out. Once the door was closed, she muttered, looking back at the door, "Can I follow you out to your cabin? I need to talk about this with someone who isn't already a basket case."

"Sure," Jaymie said.

"I'll pick the baby up and be right out."

As Jaymie got in her SUV and clicked her seatbelt she saw Nicki talking to a man who had just arrived. In his fifties, balding, wearing slacks and a golf shirt and jacket, he was nondescript. In a crowd he would go unnoticed. He appeared angry, or at least irritated as he spoke to Nicki. He shook his head and firmed his lips, then watched as she got into her car. As she pulled away, Jaymie felt an uneasy tug in her stomach. It occurred to her that she had been assuming that Alicia's murder was tied in with her husband's death, but it had been five years. There had been a lot of life lived in the meantime, plenty enough for there to be other reasons someone would want her dead.

Skylah, or Sky as she was most often called, was a sweet little toddler with the usual manic energy of one her age, and a fascination with animals. Jaymie and Nicki sat together in the living room of the cabin. Sky, Hoppy and Lilibet played a spirited game of keep-away — that's what the animals would have called it, Jaymie was sure — around and around and around the living room area. Jaymie watched intently to be sure the little girl didn't accidently hurt one of the pets.

As she poured tea, Jaymie asked, "Who was that who pulled up and talked to you as you were leaving Kim's home?"

"Ugh." She grimaced. "That was Russ Krauss."

"Kim Hansen's boyfriend."

"Yeah. Do you know him?"

"No, but Alicia spoke of him. I got the impression she didn't like him at all."

"I swear, Kim is the only one who does. Erin keeps her opinion to herself but I know she has no use for him."

"And you don't like him either."

"Not even one little bit. In fact, he's my least favorite person in the world."

"Why is that?" Jaymie asked, feeling the quiver of curiosity. Someone so universally disliked piqued her interest.

Nicki frowned. "I don't like to gossip."

"But?"

"I hate how he treats Kim. I know Alicia didn't like it either."

"In what way?"

"He's controlling. Everything has to be his way. He wants Erin and Alicia to call him Dad. He wants Mia to call him Grandpa."

"He doesn't have kids?"

"Nope. But it's more than that. He wants final say in everything, even, like, family vacations and stuff."

"And Kim doesn't object?"

She rolled her eyes. "When he acts like that she ignores him, or tells him to shove off."

Jaymie frowned. It sounded like Kim had found a way to deal with Russ and it certainly didn't seem like she was under his thumb. "How long have they been together?"

"Years and years. As long as I've known them."

"Before Jace's death?"

"Sure."

"Did Jace like him?"

Nicki stared at Jaymie, frowning. "You're not thinking . . . gawd, Jaymie, I'm not saying Russ is a *murderer.*"

"Okay. All right. I'm not saying that either. I'm getting to know the family."

Nicki still stared at her. "Did Alicia ask you to find out who killed Jace?"

"No."

"Oh. Okay." She looked deflated and her gaze returned to her little girl, who was now dancing around the room as the animals watched intently.

"Why do you ask?"

"I talked to Alicia after you ran into her at the store. She told me about it, and then she said stuff. Asked questions."

"Like . . . ?"

"We went back over the stuff about Tami and all that happened. I told her how you had figured it out before anyone else, even the cops. She asked, were you trustworthy? Like, should she talk to you? And I asked her about what, but she didn't answer. Or at least, not directly. Then she started . . ."

Nicki sighed, fidgeted, then smiled as she

96

kept her eye on her daughter. Skylah was now sitting on the floor with a book "reading" to Hoppy and Lilibet, who looked relieved that the chase portion of the afternoon was over. Nicki leaned toward Jaymie and said, "Alicia was convinced the police were going to arrest her. They followed her and tapped her phone."

"Tapped her phone?"

"That's what she told me. She thought they were going to arrest her for Jace's murder."

She was pretty close to right, Jaymie thought. "Do you think she did it?"

"Of course not!"

"I know that Alicia was furious with Jace over Mia's accident. If you're right, and the police considered her a suspect, there's your motive, her anger at her husband."

Nicki looked over at Skylah, her expression soft with love. "He was careless and Mia paid the price. I don't know what I'd do to Gus if that ever happened." She met Jaymie's gaze directly. "I might divorce him, but I wouldn't kill him. I mean, what would be the point? Jaymie, doesn't Jace's death — if it even *was* murder, which I don't think it was — seem more like a man's crime to you?"

"A man's crime? I don't remember all the

particulars. How exactly did it happen?"

The young woman nodded. "Okay, well . . . Mia was about to go into kindergarten. Alicia told Jace she was going to Port Huron to shop for Mia for school."

There was significance in the way Nicki said it, an emphasis on *told.* "That isn't what she was doing that day?"

Nicki shook her head vehemently. "Alicia was having an affair. She was meeting her lover that morning."

"Who was it? How do you know?"

"I don't know *who.* I only know about it because Alicia dropped Mia off at Tami's for her to babysit that morning. I was boarding there and going out with Gus. That afternoon when Alicia came back to pick up Mia she was steamed! I guess, from what I heard" — meaning she was eavesdropping — "Alicia's boyfriend didn't show up. She complained to Tami for a bit, then took Mia and went home."

"I remember part of the story," Jaymie said, thinking of Alicia's house, the enclosure behind it, and the big garage. "Alicia claimed that she didn't check on Jace in the garage because she was still angry after a fight they'd had."

Nicki nodded and said, "Once upon a time they were so in love . . . you should have seen them! Alicia adored Jace. But he wasn't great when she was sick after having Mia, and then he was the reason Mia was so badly injured . . . that poor little darling could have died! It killed Alicia's love, I figure. She felt betrayed, worse than if he'd cheated on her. I think I'd feel the same, you know?"

Jaymie remembered what Alicia had said, that every decision she made was for Mia's benefit. Cheating on Jace didn't benefit their daughter, but maybe Alicia had regretted that choice and had tried since to make up for it. This was all conjecture, but the deep love in her voice when she spoke of her child was unmistakable.

Nicki leaned forward. "They weren't even sleeping in the same room at that point, when Jace died," she whispered, with a glance toward Sky, who was still reading aloud to the snoozing animals. "Since Mia was starting kindergarten, Alicia was going to work full-time. She had started at the Queensville Clean 'n Bright as a part-time cleaner, but the woman who scheduled the cleaners was retiring for medical reasons, and Alicia was offered the job. It had more regular hours and more money and was an office job, straight days. She was going to start her new job the Monday after Mia started school."

"Did she have any friends there?"

"At QCB? Sure . . . Wenda . . . what's her last name? Starts with a P. Poochie. Pooch. Ah! Puchala!"

Jaymie filed that in her memory. A talk with Ms. Puchala might help if she was going to figure out who killed Alicia. If. Or when? The crime had left her angry, furious, in truth. Such a despicable premeditated murder leaving a little girl an orphan must be punished. "You say Alicia wasn't speaking to Jace?"

"Only to fight. I guess they *did* have a fight that morning — she said as much to Tami — but that had been happening regularly. I'll never believe that Alicia . . ." She paused and set down her cup. "That is . . . I can't believe . . ."

Jaymie watched her face, the shifting gaze, the faltering speech. "You say you can't believe it, but you have wondered whether Alicia killed Jace."

Admitting it with a shrug and grimace, Nicki said, "Her death proves that's not true, right? I'll admit I considered it, but the way Jace died . . . if it was murder that was more of a man's crime, right?"

"You said that before, but . . . how?"

"You know, in the garage."

100

"As I understand it a jack failed and the car —"

"Truck."

"Okay, the truck fell on Jace. If it was murder, arranging it may not have been that difficult. A woman could have done it." She frowned and thought about it. "Whose truck was it, anyway?"

"I . . . don't know."

Jaymie frowned. "Nicki, do you know anything about what happened that day that you're not saying?"

"What do you mean?" Her tone was defensive, edgy.

"Do you know who put the truck up on the jack?"

"No, of *course* not. I wasn't there. As far as I know it was Jace. I mean . . . who else?" She took in a deep breath and glanced over at Sky, who was getting sleepy. "I think it was an accident," she said, with finality in her tone. "The police are making something out of nothing, harassing poor Alicia to death."

"That's not fair, Nicki. Someone hated or feared Alicia enough that she was murdered and that's not the fault of the police."

"It could have been a homeless person living in the woods, or . . . I don't know. It's not necessarily all about Jace's death, you know."

"I know it's possible it had nothing to do with Jace's death," Jaymie replied. "But it may. I don't know a lot about jacks. Could someone push the truck off of it?"

Nicki shrugged. "You say you don't know a lot about jacks? I don't know *anything*."

Hoppy wobbled over to sniff Jaymie's pant hem and she put her hand down to her little dog and helped him up on the sofa, cuddling him on her lap. While it was possible that Alicia's murder had nothing to do with Jace's death, she couldn't overlook that the woman had been killed just as she had decided to ask or tell Jaymie something. Worry gnawed at her brain; were she and her family in danger from Alicia's assailant? Killers are generally anxious and paranoid, Jaymie thought, a combination that can lead a perpetrator to more attacks.

"Did Alicia ever say what happened after she got home the day Jace died?" As Nicki nodded, Jaymie continued, "Can you tell me whatever you remember from that?"

Nicki's gaze turned inside. She thought for moment, then told Jaymie everything she could remember. It was a blazing hot August day, Nicki said. Alicia and Jace had argued about Alicia's plan to work full-time at QCB once Mia was in kindergarten. She told Nicki that Jace knew he'd have to do more around the house and pick their daughter up from school sometimes. They were constantly fighting and this was another of those morning battles. Alicia was fed up with Jace and ready to call it quits.

"Alicia was having an affair. That may have contributed to them not getting along," Jaymie said.

"I always thought it was the other way around, like, she had the affair because she was mad at Jace after what happened to Mia. You know? It turned her against him and made her want to hurt him."

"Like he had hurt their little girl," Jaymie mused.

"Right. She turned to some other guy for comfort, you know?" Nicki continued her story. Alicia's lover stood her up. She had been going to meet him at a motel along the highway, but she waited and waited and he never showed. She ended up shopping in Wolverhampton, picking Mia up and heading home.

"And she never checked on Jace."

"Why would she? He was in the garage. He was *always* in the garage. He had a sofa bed, a radio, a TV, a fan . . . he even had a fridge stocked with beer. He slept out there sometimes in nice weather."

"What did Alicia do when she got home? Do you know?"

Nicki nodded. "She got a couple of calls. Lew —"

"That's Jace's brother?"

Nicki nodded. "Lew called and said Jace wasn't answering his cell, where was he? Alicia told him Jace was out in the garage working. She said he probably had the music on too loud, or the generator, and that's why he hadn't heard his phone, or maybe he didn't have it on. Lew asked that when Alicia saw him, could she remind him that they were meeting up at another car auction the next day? She said sure." Nicki bit her lip and eyed Jaymie. "I'm pretty sure Alicia got a call from her lover apologizing. He got caught up in something."

"How do you know?"

"Tami called to check in on her because she seemed upset when she picked up Mia. I was there when Tami called, and I heard them talking. Or at least I heard Tami's side." She frowned and grimaced. "It's, like, five years ago now. I'm trying to remember why I got that impression. Tami knew she had a boyfriend. They talked a lot. Tami babysitting Mia and all, they got close. Anyway, Tami was on the phone with her that afternoon, asking if she was okay, and I heard Tami say *He got caught up in something? That's no reason to stand you up.* I asked about it later and Tami told me to keep it to myself, but that Alicia had a lover."

"Did she know who?"

"I . . . don't know. Tami may."

"Who else did Alicia talk to that day?"

"I think Kim had called Alicia. I do know Erin called her and they had an argument. It had been Kim's birthday the week before and Alicia was supposed to go in with Erin on the gift, but Alicia hadn't paid up. She told me her sister always bought gifts that were too extravagant. She had a house and kid, while Erin lived with their mom. Then Erin would expect Alicia to pony up her half. Erin is pretty sticky about money owed to her. I always got caught in the middle, with both Erin and Alicia complaining to me about the other one. I think she was complaining about all of that to Tami . . . at least that's what I got from Tami's side of the conversation."

"You're pretty good friends with the family."

Nicki nodded and sniffed a tear back. "After what happened with Tami, Gus was . . . distracted. Troubled, you know?

Alicia was nice to me. She helped me through it."

"Nicki, you must have some idea of who Alicia was having the affair with?"

"I don't know for sure."

"But you have a guess?"

Nicki nodded, her gaze clouded. "I'm pretty sure it was Russ."

"Russ Krauss? Kim's boyfriend? Nicki, you said that Alicia didn't like Russ, and now you're saying they were lovers?"

"I know it sounds crazy, but why else would she hide who she was seeing from her mom? And maybe she acted like she didn't like him because they broke up."

Rapidly, Jaymie considered Nicki's assertion: pretty and vivacious twenty-something Alicia with Russ Krauss, her mom's forty-five-year-old boyfriend? "I don't believe it. I can think of plenty of reasons why she wouldn't want her mom to know she was cheating on her husband."

"You don't understand, Kim didn't like Jace. She was against them from the beginning. Kim wouldn't have cared if Alicia was going out with some other guy. There had to be a reason Alicia was hiding her affair, and it fits if the guy she was seeing was Russ."

Frowning down at the rug, Jaymie laced

her fingers together. She didn't buy Nicki's argument. "I can't picture Alicia with Russ. Would she do that to her mom?"

The young woman's expression faltered. "Alicia and Kim's relationship was . . . complicated."

"What about lately? Did Alicia say anything to you about what was going on in her life right now?"

"I didn't see her much. We were close at first, after what happened with Tami, but lately we kind of drifted apart." She stood and picked up her purse. "I'd better get going. I'm taking lunch to Gus at the store, and then I have to shop for dinner. Sky!" she called. But the little girl was asleep, curled up on the rug in front of the fireplace with Lilibet.

"I'll help you get her out to your car," Jaymie said, and, setting Hoppy aside on the sofa, stood and crossed the room. She gently picked up the child and followed Nicki out to the car, helped her buckle her into her seat, and waved goodbye. She stood for a long moment staring at the woods across the road, the remnants of yellow crime scene tape flapping in the breeze. "And now to make a difficult call," Jaymie muttered, returning inside, where she called Detective Vestry.

Seven

Jaymie expressed her concern to Vestry that whoever had targeted Alicia had known that she was about to confide in her new friend. "Detective, don't you think it could put me and my family in danger?"

"You're looking at this the wrong way. Unless Alicia spelled out to her murderer that she was about to take you into her confidence there's little reason to worry. Even if Alicia literally said *I'm going to tell Jaymie Müller this or that,* then killing her took care of it; they got to Alicia before she spilled the story. You and your family are no danger to the perp. If anything, they'll stay far away from you. Harming you or yours would put them in more peril, exposing them to detection."

"I guess," Jaymie said. She saw the detective's point. But on a visceral level she didn't feel that they were safe.

"What else do you have?"

She filled the detective in on what Nicki had said. "Don't tell her I told you, please!"

A gusty sigh from the other end told her what the detective thought. "Jaymie, how often have I revealed confidential matters to you?"

Jaymie admitted, "Never. Okay, I get it . . . you're not about to blab to anyone else, either. I feel awkward, I guess, getting people to spill their guts and then tattling to you."

"You mean you're not accustomed to working closely with the police."

"I get your point," Jaymie said stiffly. "I will continue to tell you anything I find out."

"I'd rather you didn't."

"You'd rather . . . what?"

"This is out of your hands now, Jaymie. I know I asked you to get Alicia to confide in you, but it is not your responsibility to discover who killed her. It's *our* job. Please let us do it."

"I won't get in your way."

"That's not what I asked. I said you were safe a moment ago, but all bets are off if you keep poking your nose into it. I *asked* that you stay out of it."

"I know what you asked, Detective. I promise I won't interfere in your investigation."

Vestry was silent for a long moment. "I guess I'll have to be satisfied with that, won't I?"

Jaymie was perturbed and antsy. Vestry had used her to get information, but now that Alicia was dead her services were no longer required. That was not good enough. She was in this now and despite what the detective said, despite how reasonable she made it sound, Jaymie still felt she and her family were at risk until whoever killed Alicia Vance was behind bars. Jakob, who had come home early, sat at the desk along the far wall working on a plan for the Christmas tree season as Jaymie searched online for every article she could find on the tragic death of Jace Vance five years before. She found a few video clips from the Detroit TV station news; a younger Alicia, with tears streaming down her face, spoke of her husband's death as a tragic accident.

Jaymie then searched the *Wolverhampton Weekly Howler* archives and came across an in-depth story about Mia's injury. It related a story similar to what Nicki told her, but it added a few interesting facts. Jace Vance had been drinking when he crashed the car with his daughter in it. His blood alcohol was under the legal limit and it was a first offense, but there were additional charges of child endangerment because she was not properly buckled into the toddler safety seat. He pled guilty and was penalized with a short stint in jail, probation and fines. Jaymie could understand how furious Alicia must have been, and how corrosive it would be to their marriage. How do you recover from a betrayal so enormous that it could kill every vestige of love in your heart? Was her affair retaliation, like Nicki suggested? Who would ever know, now that Alicia was gone?

Jaymie's heart hurt thinking of poor Mia, who lost her leg and then barely two years later her father and now . . . her mother. Such a sweet and sensitive little girl! Tears rolled down Jaymie's cheeks, but she wiped them away impatiently and carried on. If she could figure out what happened to Alicia it would do more for Mia than her tears ever could.

Having spent a few years writing a column for Nan, she had learned a bit about the newspaper business. She had observed that there were code words, careful write-arounds, for crime stories. Jace's death was deemed to have "suspicious circumstances," though it could simply be an accident, the reporter wrote. Eventually news items on the tragic incident dwindled and then stopped as the police admitted they had no new information. Still, it was clear that they were investigating it as a murder.

She recognized the name on the byline. Interesting. She picked up her phone and made a call. "Brianna, hi!" she said to Brianna Sheridan, who she remembered from high school. They had lost touch, then became reacquainted. She was a reporter for the *Howler* for a few years but left the newspaper on maternity leave and never went back, moving on to work in sales at a radio station. Jaymie had married since they last talked. Brianna was now working free-lance for a news aggregator.

"What is that?" Jaymie asked, sitting cross-legged on the sofa.

"It's kind of technical, kind of not. I get to use my tech training as well as my journalism experience. Basically an aggregator uses computer technology to collect news items and categorize them. An algorithm or a bot can do it, but still, it takes a human to fine-tune the technology. I've been working on refining local news feeds, teaching the algorithm what to collect, but . . ." She sighed. "My mind is crap lately."

Jaymie got down to the meat and potatoes

of her call. "There's something I wanted to ask you about. You reported on the death of Jace Vance in late August five years ago."

"I did. What's up?"

Jaymie told her about Alicia Vance's death and her own part in talking to Alicia and then discovering her body.

"That's terrible!" Brianna said, her voice warm. Years as a news reporter had not dulled her natural sympathy. "I missed that. I've been out of the news biz lately. Since I had my second baby I'm so deep in diapers and midnight feedings and toddlers and preschool I can't even think most days. Probably why I'm having so much trouble with this freelance gig. I mean, it's good in one way, it's work I can fit in around all of that, but I have been so focused I haven't seen the news, I guess. Gosh, *murder*?"

"I know. It's a terrible thing." Jaymie tried to keep her voice level. She was still shaken by finding the body, and it had stayed with her. She tried to brighten her voice as she congratulated Brianna on the new baby.

Their conversation turned to that for a moment. Then Brianna said, "Are the two deaths, Jace's and Alicia's, connected?"

Jaymie relayed the info she had read in the day's stories on Alicia's murder. The reporter had delved into the family's past tragedies. The police offered the reporter no concrete statement that the two family deaths could be connected, nor did they say they definitely were not. The reporter was left with bare bones. He created a timeline of the family's bad fortune, from Mia's tragic accident to Jace's death, finishing with Alicia's murder. "So much has happened to that family that I have to wonder . . . *is* there a connection? Or am I seeing links where none exist? I don't want to jump to conclusions."

"Hmm. Now I'm curious."

"Was there anything back then about Jace's death that you didn't say in the article because you didn't have verification? Anything the police asked you to leave out? Any rumor you heard?"

There was silence for a long moment. Jaymie thought Brianna may have drifted off, but then she said, "Don't mind me, I'm thinking back. There are things I found odd at the time, but we couldn't get any comment from the police. First: no one would say who the pickup belonged to, the vehicle that fell on Vance. I'm sure the police knew, but maybe it wasn't germane to the investigation, or perhaps they were holding back. They do that all the time during an investigation, hold back info for a multitude of reasons. They did say, though, that the garage had proper jack stands but that a vehicle was already up on those, so a jack was used on this occasion to 'take a quick look,' if I remember the quote from his dad."

"I don't know anything about jacks and online information is confusing. I have changed a tire before, don't get me wrong, but other than that —"

"Gotcha. I did a lot of research when it happened and spoke to three different mechanics." Brianna explained what she remembered of jacks and jack stands and the different types. "I don't remember exactly what kind he was using, but the official theory was that the jack failed. It sometimes happens if you don't engage secondary and even tertiary safety mechanisms. Even though each professional I spoke to said adamantly that no one should crawl under a vehicle that was only up on a jack, I know that there are lots of injuries from similar accidents every year. People still crawl under vehicles that are up on jacks."

Jaymie was silent for a moment, and then said, "I can kind of understand why a random home mechanic might do it. He wouldn't know the risks. But a professional should know better. Why would Jace have gone under a vehicle propped up on a jack?"

"I don't know. Maybe he was in a hurry."

"Did the truck fall off the jack, or did the jack fail?"

"Good question. If I recall correctly, the jack was said to have collapsed — to me that means it failed — but the medical examiner stated he didn't die immediately. I assume that means if he had been found right away he may have lived."

"How could it be murder? Could someone make a jack fail?"

"If the jack was released prematurely or the safety mechanism was altered, causing it to fail, it would be murder. If that's what happened it would take a cold-blooded killer to walk away from their victim. I heard stories from those who had vehicles drop on them and lived, it's horrific. Lifelong injuries."

"Did you do any background on the family dynamics at the time?"

"Sure. I interviewed Vance's father and brother, his mother-in-law, sister-in-law. I felt for Mia Vance, let me tell you, poor little girl. I was trying to start a family, and I ached at what that little girl had gone through and was going through. I feel even worse now, knowing she's lost her mom." She paused. "My impression of Alicia

116

Vance's mother, though . . . I have to tell you, that woman gave me the chills."

"Kim Hansen? Really?"

"She had almost no emotion about Vance's death. I got the impression she couldn't have cared less."

Kim had no use for Jace, Nicki had said, and hadn't from the beginning of her daughter's relationship. Could her anger over what Jace had done to her beloved granddaughter motivate her to kill her son-in-law? "What about Erin, Alicia's sister?"

"She was pretty young at the time, a teenager. She seemed flighty, but nice enough."

"What about Jace's father and brother?"

"Shady, both of them, but especially Franklin. He's into bikes and belongs to a biker club. He is most definitely rough around the edges."

"How did he react to his son's death?"

"He seemed distraught."

"Seemed?"

"What can I say? He's stoic, you know? A man's man. Shed no tears, be brave, all that garbage. Lewis Vance — Lew, the brother — was crushed. His life was crashing, if I recall correctly. He was breaking up with his wife at the time and seemed like he was in a tailspin."

"Breaking up with his wife; breakups are devastating. Was he on edge to the point of being dangerous?"

"To his younger brother? I can't think why. No motive that I can imagine."

"Thanks, Brianna," Jaymie said absently. "You've been a real help."

"Hold on, *hold on* . . . you can't hang up without me asking questions. Like, are you talking to the police? I know you've helped them in the past. Are you helping right now?"

"Uh . . . I'm not . . . uh, equipped to tell you." Brianna may not be a reporter anymore but she still had those instincts and connections.

"Okay, I get it, you don't want to say. But if you are, I may be able to help. I still have my old notes. How about I look through them?"

"That would be great, but I still won't be able to tell you anything."

"Doesn't matter at this point. I'm a little stir crazy here, and talking to an intelligent adult is manna to a starving ex-journalist. I'm happy to provide you with as much info as I have in return for your promise to tell me what you can when you can."

"You've got a deal.

EIGHT

The next day, Friday, was an increasingly rare full day of working at the Queensville Emporium for Jaymie. Since the Klausner granddaughter Gracey had started working regular hours, and other grandchildren worked part-time after school and other jobs, Jaymie was redundant. Today was a special day, though, the Klausners' seventieth wedding anniversary, and they were having a big party at the Queensville Inn. Jaymie was working all day. Valetta was attending the anniversary party after she closed her pharmacy for the day.

The morning was busy for both her and Val, so when the store finally emptied at about noon they combined their morning tea break with lunch, sitting out on the front step of the Emporium with tomato sandwiches, made with the last of the season's ripe red beauties from Valetta's garden, tea and oatmeal chocolate chip cookies. The weather had changed once again. It was a brilliant sunny day, warm, but with that hint of autumn in the breeze and the color tingeing the edges of the maple tree in the triangular village green opposite the store. They chatted about the tragedy of Alicia's murder.

"I'm still trying to get over it," Jaymie confessed. "I feel . . . I feel . . ." What *did* she feel? Sad, certainly, for all of them, but most especially Mia. Angry that someone had stalked and slain Alicia. And scared. She was still processing it, trying to get over finding the body, the fear of it happening right across the road from their home, the guilt that the poor woman was on her way to see her when it happened. "There are no words to even describe how awful it is. I can't get past it. Why didn't she tell me what was on her mind at the school?"

"She wasn't ready. There is nothing you could have done to prevent this from happening," Val said, touching Jaymie's bare arm and squeezing lightly, a comforting gesture.

"My mind knows that but my heart doesn't. I keep thinking of Mia, that poor sweet girl. She has suffered so much in her life and it breaks my heart to think of her losing her mother. It's tragic. It's brutal.

Life is so *unfair.*" She choked back a sob.

Val put her arm around Jaymie's shoulders and let her mourn. That was the wonderful thing about her; she knew when to speak and when to stay silent. Taking a deep breath and dashing the tears from her cheeks, Jaymie sat up straight and gulped down hot tea. Turning her mind to the puzzle of who did it might help.

She told Val about calling Brianna. "She said that she found Kim Hansen *chilling,* that the woman's reaction to her son-in-law dying was muted. No, not muted . . . what did she say?" Jaymie cast her memory back to the previous day's call. "She said she got the impression that Kim couldn't have cared less about Jace's death."

"We all react differently. Because she didn't choke up to a reporter doesn't mean she didn't care."

"True."

"Besides, she had a right to be angry at Jace after what he did to Mia. It was understandable if he wasn't her favorite person."

"He was her daughter's husband, and father to her granddaughter —"

"Who caused them both incomprehensible pain and suffering."

Jaymie nodded. "I was trying to imagine how Kim felt after Mia's accident . . .

toward Jace, I mean. Would she be angry enough to hurt him?"

"That's a little far-fetched," her friend said, blinking behind her thick glasses. She pushed them up on her nose.

"Val, you seem a bit . . . heated in Kim's defense."

"Do I?" Val shrugged. "You know we went to school together."

"You said you were lab buddies."

She nodded. "I see her sometimes. I know that she's had a rough . . ." She paused, frowned, and looked off across the road.

Jaymie examined her expression, recognizing internal turmoil. She wondered how much Val knew about locals because of meds they were on for depression and other problems, things she could not, would not reveal. Pondering that was like peeking behind a curtain in Val's mind, a hidden compartment that held knowledge she would never share with anyone. This was exactly why she trusted Val and why her insight was valuable. "You can say whatever you think, Val, you know that. When you do, I'll know it comes from a place of knowledge you may not be able to share with me."

"Kim Hansen has had a rough time," Val said simply, finishing the thought she had started. "She loves her daughters and her granddaughter fiercely. I know she was furious with Jace and disliked him. *But . . .* I don't think she would ever hurt Mia by harming Jace, if that's what you're thinking."

That made sense, but would Kim see killing Jace as hurting Mia, or freeing her from a lifetime with a careless father? She didn't share that thought but did wonder, how much of what we believe about other people is influenced by our own internal personhood? Val, for all her good sense, would never conceive of someone she knew and liked killing anyone. Jaymie wondered, was she the more cynical or realistic of the two of them, that she assumed there were depths she would never plumb in those she knew even on the most intimate level?

She poured herself more tea from the carafe into a vintage melamine cup and cradled it in her hands, resting it on her hunched knees. One of Jaymie's favorite things about Val's friendship was how she bridged the gap between Jaymie and her older sister in ways that Becca never could, or would. Where Becca was pragmatic and had left behind their youth in profound ways, Val was a continuous link — young Val and middle-aged Valetta — a bridge that included Jaymie on a walk from the past to the present. She could see Becca and their other friends through Val's lens. "Tell me about Kim."

"Kim was the popular girl in school. She was a cheerleader and on the yearbook committee and she was even voted by the boys as Best Kisser." Val smiled. "When she asked to be my lab partner I was thrilled, to put it mildly. The popular girl chose *me*! I think I was envisioning instant popularity: party invitations, sleepovers, shopping trips. Those never materialized."

Jaymie didn't say it, but Kim would have chosen young Valetta Nibley as a lab partner because Val was brilliant in science, showing early the promise that would bring her a scholarship to pharmaceutical college. Kim would have known that she had a shot at better marks with a lab partner who would do more than her share and be able to explain things along the way. "Was she nice?"

"To me? Sure. We worked together okay. But I always had the feeling she had other things on her mind. She would blow me off when I suggested working on our project on the weekend."

"You ended up doing more of the work, I'd bet."

"I did." Val sighed. "She was nice to me though . . . nicer than she had to be. She even tried to set me up with a guy."

"Who?"

Val rolled her eyes. "Russ Krauss."

"She set you up with *Russ Krauss*?"

Val nodded, with a chagrined smile. "We went to a movie together but he wasn't into me. I knew even then that Kim was the only girl for him. It's all he talked about even on our 'date,' " she said, sketching air quotes around the word.

"He got his wish, didn't he? They're together now and have been for a long time."

"Funny how things turn out."

They returned to work. Jaymie considered what she had learned; it wasn't much. But maybe someone else knew more.

Unexpectedly, she was relieved of working the full day when another non-Klausner came in ready to take over. Young Gracey Klausner had mistakenly penciled them both in on the schedule. Jaymie, with her mind on the mystery, was happy to let the other girl, who attended Wolverhampton College, have the hours. It was two in the afternoon . . . time to sleuth. She said goodbye to Val and headed out on foot across the village to the Queensville Inn.

125

She sought out the room at the inn she wanted as she walked along the road. Mrs. Stubbs was in her usual place, on the terrace in her mobility chair bathing in the warm sun, book open on her lap and teapot on a small table beside her.

Jaymie smiled and hiked up the grassy slope. The trees along the road had started shedding leaves and she swished through a pile of them with pleasure, wishing she had Hoppy with her; he loved to visit the town's grande dame. Mrs. Martha Stubbs, Queensville's third oldest resident, lived in a special suite in the Queensville Inn, which her oldest son owned. She didn't notice Jaymie until her young friend topped the slope. She then put one arthritic finger in the book to hold her place, smiling. One swift look at the cover told Jaymie it was a large-print version of a modern mystery, one of a slew from a few years before with *Girl* in the title.

"Jaymie, how nice to see you!" She raised her free hand in greeting.

It must be a good day. On a bad day, when the arthritis was painful and the weather gloomy, Mrs. Stubbs could be pessimistic and sharp-tongued. Jaymie sat carefully in a chair pulled up to the small table. Normally she would have plopped down on the grass, but she was wearing good slacks and a pretty blouse, so, prim and proper it was . . . though she did slip off her shoes. They exchanged greetings.

"Say, I had a phone call from your writer friend the other day," she said, about Melody Heath, an author of romance novels and lately suspenseful detective books. "She's sending me author copies of her whole . . . what did she call it?" She frowned, thought, then put up one finger. "Ah, yes, her *backlist* of books. She needed my address. I must say I am pleasantly surprised. I never thought she'd follow through."

"When Mel says she's going to do something, she does it. She has an amazing memory when it comes to her career. Other stuff, not so much." Jaymie launched into the purpose of her visit, catching Mrs. Stubbs up to date with what had gone on in her life recently. The woman nodded along; she had heard much of it from Dee, her daughter-in-law and Becca's best friend, as well as the garrulous Edith, her son Lyle's girlfriend.

Mrs. Stubbs was an avid reader of mystery fiction and true crime and watched true crime TV shows. She was, as she put it, a student of human nature, and crime was human nature at its most extreme.

"I feel . . . uneasy. It happened in the woods right across from the cabin, and yet Detective Vestry says I don't need to fret. Am I crazy for worrying that it was too close to home?" Jaymie said.

"I know you have your squabbles with the detective, Jaymie, and I'm sympathetic, but in this case I think she may be right. It would cause more trouble to the perp than it would be worth to give you grief." She had begun sprinkling police talk, like *the perp,* in her conversation.

"A part of me can't be easy about it."

She folded her hands in her lap. "Make your case."

Jaymie looked down at the grass and toed a late dandelion trying to bud. "Whoever killed Alicia knew where she was headed. The only reason she'd be going through the woods would be to get to our cabin."

"Go on."

"If they knew she was on her way to me, they also knew she may have confided her worries to me. We'd met a couple of times; who's to say she didn't tell me everything? Whatever 'everything' is. Vestry is assuming that whoever it was knew Alicia so well they'd know that she hadn't told me what was on her mind. Even if that was true, they could be watching me, waiting for me to talk to the police. Murderers aren't an especially reasonable bunch, in my experience, and I do have experience. If he or she gets antsy or suspicious of something I do, even unwittingly, it could trigger the kind of paranoia that leads to murder."

She took in a deep breath and let it out, trying to calm her stomach. "We both know killers in real life aren't as logical as they seem to be in murder mysteries. I mean, I've tried to read a few murder mysteries but end up throwing them against the wall because everything is so logical and tied up in a neat bow at the end. Killers are so *rational* in books, but in real life they're human, which means they are irrational and do stupid things out of fear, or anger, or spite. They sometimes do things so outrageously idiotic it takes your breath away and when they do, it's because they thought someone was on to them, even when they weren't. They're paranoid and panic.

"That's how they get caught, they act out of fear. Melody complains that readers expect book characters to be more reasonable in fiction than people are in real life, and I understand what she means." She paused, and felt the fear trembling in her gut. "I don't want to be the killer's second victim. Or the third, if we count Jace."

Mrs. Stubbs had a worried look on her face. "I hate to say this, Jaymie, but you've made a compelling case."

"I'll only feel secure when Alicia's killer is in jail. I don't care what Vestry says, I'm going to figure it out with or without her help. If the police get there before me, and I believe they have the perpetrator, all the better, but I'm not going to rest easy. I'll be looking over my shoulder forever. I'm already too spooked to go back into the woods again." She sighed and shivered, feeling a quiver of fear down her back. "I'd be interested in your take on it. How do you think I should proceed?"

Mrs. Stubbs looked down at her gnarled fingers, flexing the arthritic joints. "I agree that this all likely does go back to five years ago, to Jace Vance's death. You should start from there. Find out, if you can, who Alicia's lover was."

"You think that's important?"

"I do."

"Why? I'm not saying I disagree, but . . . why?"

Mrs. Stubbs frowned and put a prescription receipt in her book as a bookmark and shoved it down beside her on the seat of her mobility chair. "It feels like there's an emotional component to this crime."

"Isn't there always?"

"Not always. There are crimes of profit. No emotion there. Some are the result of an emotionally disturbed person — your serial killers and the like — but it's true that from what I've seen most *are* emotional crimes that come from jealousy, or anger, or feeling slighted, no matter how misguided the feeling is. Or there's a combination of motives, crimes of passion that also profit the killer. We already know there's an emotional tangle in that family, the detritus left from the little girl's accident. I don't doubt that it's the reason for Alicia Vance's faithlessness. Find out who she was cheating with; it will get you somewhere, I'd bet."

"Maybe. How do I even start to find that out?"

Mrs. Stubbs stared at her. "You know the answer, Jaymie. Do what you naturally do."

"Maybe I'm being stupid, but I can't think how to proceed."

"That's because your horror at what happened across the road from you is interfering with your instincts," the woman said sympathetically. "As Melody would say, get out of your head and let your instincts take over."

"Since when did you start quoting our

mutual writer friend?" Jaymie said with a smile.

Mrs. Stubbs smiled too, but ignored her question. "Worm your way into her life. Find out who her friends are or were. Who she worked with. Any clubs she belonged to, or places she habituated."

"Her coworkers at Queensville Clean 'n Bright, maybe," Jaymie mused.

"Good place to start. Lyle hires cleaners from there. They have an office manager . . . what's her name? Not Wendy but . . . ah, yes! Wenda."

"Wenda Puchala. Her name was mentioned to me. It's a good start."

"I'm sure more will occur to you once the investigative juices start flowing."

Edith came through the room's sliding doors. "Ah, Mother Stubbs! Thought I'd find you here. Hello, Jaymie. How are you today? No Hoppy?" She loved animals, and the little Yorkie-Poo was a favorite.

"I was working at the Emporium and stopped by to say hi."

"Mother Stubbs," she said, turning to her partner's mother. "You have friends who have dropped by for tea in the dining room. Mrs. Bellwood and Ms. Frump."

"Ah, the Snoop sisters!" Mrs. Stubbs said with a cackle, using Jaymie's nickname for the fearsome duo. "Some new scheme hatched for searching out the Sultan's Eye, no doubt," she said about a fabled local treasure, a painted pendant of an eye seen in a portrait of one of the town founders' wives. It had disappeared long ago. "They've been trying to get me to use my leverage with the historic society to let them take up the floorboards."

"You're not going to do that, are you?" Jaymie asked, alarmed.

"Of course not," she said with a wink. "But it's fun to let them try to convince me. Mrs. Bellwood makes the most delicious scones. And Ms. Frump is an excellent hairdresser," she said, patting her white newly coiffed curls.

They said their farewells and Edith accompanied Mrs. Stubbs back into her room to get ready for company. Jaymie started to walk away but stopped and looked back up to the inn. She hadn't even thought to mention Kim Hansen and the high school connection. Did Mrs. Stubbs, who was a constant library and board volunteer at the high school while her younger son attended, at the same time as Val and Becca, know Kim Hansen, or Kim Ellsworthy, as she was then?

She'd have to remember to ask next time. It may not be important, but she left no

133

stones unturned when it came to discerning the truth. It wouldn't be the first time a modern tragedy had its roots in the past.

Which led to her own realization: she must have gone to school at the same time as Lew Vance. Jace and Alicia may have been in the same school in lower grades just as she was graduating, but Lew was close to her age. What did she remember of him? Virtually nothing. She would have been a senior and he would have been a sophomore, plus, they clearly moved in different orbits. Given the family's interest in vehicles, maybe she knew someone who was there for at least part of it: Johnny Stanko. Having failed a few grades, he was older than every other student in the school, but he had a love for cars, engines and anything that moved fast and thus may have been the type to hang out with the Vance boys.

She knew where to find Johnny, most days. She changed direction and headed back toward the main street and Cynthia Turbridge's Cottage Shoppe.

NINE

Shops along the main curved avenue in Queensville had the benefit of deep lots left from a bygone era of gracious wide treed streets. A few of the places had taken advantage of that depth by erecting small outbuildings and in some cases there were old sheds or barns that had been converted to modern usage. The Knit Knack Shack had, a few years before, built a small windowed annex where they held craft workshops. There was a big old barn behind Jewel's Junk that Bill Waterman, the local handyman, and Jewel now shared for woodworking and furniture repair.

Cynthia's Cottage Shoppe was a quaint cottagey bungalow built in the late eighteen hundreds. She had turned it into a sweet shabby chic shop where she sold vintage knickknacks, cottage-style furnishings, but also repurposed and rebuilt treasure from her own skilled and meticulous hands. Cynthia's other passions were yoga and meditation. They had helped her to sobriety, and recovery when that sobriety failed a while back. What she had learned she was passing on to other alcoholics, among them Johnny Stanko. They made an odd couple — petite, lithe, pretty fifty-something Cynthia and lanky, shabby, shambling thirty-something Johnny — but both were goodhearted recovering alcoholics trying to find their way through an often inhospitable world. Whether they were actually a couple or just friends nobody was quite sure.

Over the summer, behind her shop, Johnny had built for her a yoga/mediation suite surrounded by pines. Glass-windowed with a stained wood exterior, it was a serene rustic studio. Since he was doing it only in off hours from his job at the marina he was just now putting the finishing touches on the interior. Jaymie checked in with Petty Welch, who worked for both Cynthia and Jewel; the woman told her that Johnny was indeed back at the yoga studio. She took the pine-needle-covered path and found him taping and mudding the back interior walls of the main studio.

They chatted as he worked, Jaymie perched on a step stool. After a few minutes Jaymie said, "Johnny, do you remember Lew

Vance from high school?"

"Sure do. Still see him."

"How did he take it when his younger brother, Jace, died?"

"Don't know," Johnny said, spreading mud along the taped join of two sheets of wallboard. He reminded her he had come back to Queensville four years ago after time away, trouble with the law, and a long time drunk. It took his sister's death, inheriting her house, and a new commitment to sobriety for him to stay in Queensville, the site of youthful torment. "Sorry I can't help you," he said, looking over his shoulder as, with grace surprising in someone so lumbering, he ran his knife along the tape, taking off excess and leaving a smooth layer of compound concealing the taped line.

"But you're hanging out with Lew now, right? You must have talked about family. Has he ever said anything about what happened to Jace?"

He turned as he scraped the drywall knife on his hawk, a flat aluminum sheet with a handle. "He thinks Jace was murdered. He doesn't think the cops give a . . . care."

"They've never closed the case," Jaymie said.

"News to me. Lew thinks they've written it off as an accident." He turned back to the wall and picked up more mud on his knife, spreading it further along the taped joint.

"They haven't. If Lew thinks Jace was murdered, he must have an opinion as to who did it?"

Johnny stilled, then threw Jaymie a look over his shoulder. He scraped the side of his mudding tool. He was a slow thinker. Wild and impulsive in his youth, time and trouble had taught him circumspection. He set down his tools, covered the pail of compound, and pulled up a lawn chair that sat by a plastic tote on which were a paper cup of cold coffee and the remains of lunch. "He won't say. I've known Lew a long time." He fell silent again, chewing his cheek absently, his long legs stretched out, booted feet crossed at the ankle. "I wasn't here when Jace died, but Lew did tell me about it. Said it didn't sit right. Jace was careful when it came to work."

After another moment of silence, Jaymie softly said, "He was the one who found Jace, right?"

Johnny nodded. "Wouldn't wish that on my worst enemy. Those guys may not have been super close, you know? But still, they had each other's back."

"They weren't close?"

Johnny frowned and grimaced. "Different

as chalk and cheese, as my sis used to say."

"How so? What makes — made — them so different?"

"I know Lew better than I knew Jace, but I'd say Lew and his dad are closer. Jace was more of a straight arrow, you know? Did things right. Got married. Had a kid. Worked hard."

"But he drank and ended up in an accident that cost his little girl her leg."

Johnny nodded. "Also before I got back, but . . . yeah. Heard about it. His missus was real angry."

"Was he . . . I don't know, involved in anything illegal?" she asked, casting around for questions to unlock the mystery of Jace Vance

Johnny's gaze shifted away and he looked faintly troubled. "Like what?"

Something had changed, Jaymie thought, watching him. "Anything that Jace may have been involved in that led to his death, if it is murder. Did anyone have it in for him?"

His expression cleared, and he looked back into her eyes. "I don't know of anything illegal that Jace was involved in, and if I knew of anyone who had wanted to do him harm, I'd tell the cops, much as I hate them."

"Lew thought Jace's death was murder?"

Johnny nodded.

"Yet he never expressed any opinion of who did it?"

"Not in so many words."

There was evasion in that phrase *not in so many words.* "He said something that made you wonder?"

A series of fleeting expressions chased across his face . . . uncertainty, worry, resignation. Johnny trusted Jaymie. He finally nodded. "I know you won't take this for more than it is, Jaymie, just my feeling. Lew once said there were only two people who hated Jace."

"Yes?"

"Alicia and Kim."

"For the accident that took Mia's leg." He nodded. "Enough to kill him? I mean, how would they do it?"

"If the truck was only up on a jack it could be pushed off."

"I don't think I understand."

Johnny moved restlessly. "Pretty simple. Okay, so, if you're safety-minded like Jace was, in the normal course of things you put chocks by the wheels that are gonna stay on the ground so the car doesn't roll back when you put the jack under. Then you hoist the car up with a jack and put jack stands underneath, make sure they're stable, and let the car down to rest on the jack stands."

"So you don't hoist a car up on a jack and crawl under?"

"Not if you have half a brain. Only an idiot doesn't take the time to put the jack stands under. Damned *fool* hoists a car up on a jack and crawls underneath."

"That would be unstable and dangerous."

"*Damned* dangerous."

Jaymie thought of what Brianna had said about jacks and jack stands and the accidents that happen when mechanics got careless. But Jace was, by all reports, *not* careless. She shared what her reporter friend had told her about the number of similar accidents that happen every year. "You don't think it's something Jace would do."

He shrugged. "Look, I wouldn't do it. That's all I know."

"What if . . . Johnny, what if someone he trusted was there, and he put the vehicle up on a jack for a quick look. Could someone . . . oh, this sounds awful, but I have to ask. Would it be difficult to push a vehicle off a jack? Could a woman do that?"

His expression darkened. "You're asking about Kim or Alicia?"

"I guess I am."

"Anything is possible. A jack — 'specially the flimsy ones that come with a vehicle — aren't safe, not for anything more than changing a tire at the side of the road."

"If Jace died under a vehicle collapsing on him, the tires must have been off?"

"At least one of 'em, I'd say." He shrugged. "Only reason it would be up on a jack."

"Why would you take a tire off, though, if you were checking a vehicle over quickly?"

"Maybe to check for brake pad wear? Some cars and trucks you need to take a wheel off for that, others you can see without taking the wheel off."

She sighed. "I don't get it. If Jace was as careful as you say, then how did it happen?"

He folded his arms over his chest. "Maybe someone got him all riled up and he got careless?"

"Then we're back to an accident."

He shook his head. "I'm saying someone took advantage."

"Say Jace and Alicia have a fight," Jaymie said. "She eggs him on, maybe, knowing he's about to go out to work on vehicles. And so he slams out of the house and in a hurry puts a truck up on a jack and . . . what happens then?"

"Someone pushes the truck off the jack to

make it fall on him."

Jaymie shuddered and hugged herself. The vision she had, of a faceless, formless villain creeping into the garage and shoving the pickup truck off its jack to fall on Jace Vance was horrendous. It still didn't make sense. Wouldn't he hear someone coming in? Maybe he did, and maybe he called out to them. If it was Kim or Alicia he'd trust them enough to stay under the vehicle. She didn't want it to be one of the women, but it was possible. Still . . . it was an awful lot of supposition. "Surely Jace had others who didn't like him?"

"Don't we all? It would take awful deep hatred to do what was done to him." Johnnie shook his head. "*Awful* deep hate."

"How did his father take it? Did Lew tell you?" Jaymie said, remembering how Brianna described Franklin, a tough shed-no-tears kind of guy. It didn't mean he was emotionless, but it made her curious. "I've heard he's a shady character."

"Franklin? He's a good guy. Loves his kids. If you want to know more about him — and about the whole mess, he helped those guys through it — you should talk to Clutch."

"Clutch Roth?" Clutch held Jaymie in special reverence for finding his daughter's

143

body and seeing that her killer was convicted. If she approached him he'd tell her anything he could.

"Sure. Him and Franklin used to be good friends. Both rode in the Wolf Pack; that's a bike club."

Interesting. "I don't have Clutch's number anymore."

"I don't got it on me, but I'm seeing him later."

"Can you give him my number and ask him to call me?" She gave Johnnie the cards she had made up with her number and her Vintage Eats blog address on it. "Johnny, my dad taught me how to change a tire, so I know how to jack up a car and I *have* changed my own tire before, once, because I had to. Is it any different for a heavier vehicle, like a pickup truck?"

"You're not gonna test it out, are you, crawling under a jacked-up truck?"

"Good heavens, no. I get professionals to do anything under my SUV. I add oil, change my wiper blades and lightbulbs in my headlights, things like that, but I use a mechanic for everything else."

"What are you thinking?" Johnny asked.

"Nothing. It's . . . nothing." In truth, she was still wondering about Alicia's possible involvement in Jace's death, but there wasn't anything Johnny could answer. Jaymie thanked him and said she'd let him get back to work, then left. She had questions she knew Vestry wouldn't answer. Who to ask? That was a tough one.

She headed home to get supper started. It was Friday, the weekend was ahead. What to make? Another vintage recipe column was due soon, and she had to get in to have a meeting with Nan. Time had gotten away from her again and she didn't have a column idea. Maybe she could combine the two: supper *and* the vintage recipe she needed. She had two large cooked chicken breasts in the fridge and a thawed package of puff pastry, too, so . . . chicken à la king, the most vintage of vintage recipes!

She got out her grandmother's recipe book from the fifties and found the page she wanted. It was a cutout chicken à la king recipe from an old Canadian magazine, yellowed with age but still legible. She photographed the list of ingredients, and then, while she cooked, she video-called her Grandma Leighton. The video call technology was a new link to her grandmother, and she loved seeing her grandma's sweet face while they chatted. They talked about the recipe, and how it was going.

"You know, I always wondered what it

would be like with cooked turkey."

"Grandma, what a great idea! How about I try it on you at Thanksgiving, when we're up in Canada?"

"I'll look forward to it, dearest!"

"And Grandma . . . thank you for this," she said, indicating her vintage tools and bowls and the old handwritten cookbook. "I'm grateful that when I was a kid you shared the kitchen with me and taught me to cook."

"I knew Becca wasn't interested," she said with a chuckle. "*Someone* has to carry on the Leighton family recipes!"

They said their goodbyes and hung up. Time with her grandmother was exactly what she needed to center her. Clutch Roth called. He didn't want to talk over the phone, though, he wanted to see her, and suggested she come out to the farmer's market the next morning. She agreed and hung up as Jocie and Jakob, who had been at his parents after school, came in, hungry and ready to eat.

She served it up, took pictures of her own "beauty" plate for her newspaper column and then sat down at the trestle table, where her hungry family had already demolished half their dinner. "Is it good?" she asked with a smile.

Both nodded.

"What are these little red things?" Jocie asked, pointing with her fork.

"Jarred pimentos."

Jocie looked askance, ready to not like the item she had already been eating because it had a funny name.

"Eat! I'm not sure what they do besides add color, but . . . vintage is what vintage does."

"You just made that up," Jocie accused.

Jakob chuckled, whisking flaky crumbs from his beard. "I think she caught you."

"Trust me, it's something my grandmother would say."

Later, as Jocie got ready for bed and twilight closed in around the cabin, Jaymie and Jakob sat on the bench outside the front door, staring across the road. "I can't get over it," Jaymie said softly, her breath puffing in the chill of the evening air. She pulled her plaid wrap more closely around her as a chill shuddered through her. Malaise had returned, creeping in on her like a soft-pawed cat, preying on her peace of mind. "I can't get past feeling I could have done something to keep Alicia from getting killed. And now poor Mia will have to grow up without her mom."

Jakob put his arm around her and pulled

her close, sharing his solid warmth. "I'm the last one to pretend that what has happened to that poor little girl won't have consequences, especially since she also lost her father. It's not your fault, *liebchen*."

"I guess I know that in my head. It's my heart that hasn't caught up."

He put his hand on her head and pulled it down, kissing the top. "That's because you're a good person." He frowned thoughtfully. "Jocie is suffering too. I didn't realize she was such good friends with Mia. I know they're classmates, but I never heard the girl's name mentioned until they started taking ballet together a couple of weeks ago."

Jaymie was silent for a long minute. "I think I understand. When I was in school I had friends but most of them, like Valetta, were older than me. Then this girl moved to Queensville and we met and . . . I took her under my wing. She was grateful to have a new friend. Like me she loved books, and food, and going for long walks. For a while we were inseparable. From the first day, I was protective of her because I felt how scared she was, in a new school and new town."

"You think that's how Jocie feels?"

"I know it's not quite the same, since Mia

148

isn't new in town. They've gotten closer because of ballet. You know what Jocie's like . . . such a big heart, and always for the underdog. You've raised her with self-confidence and Mia is shy. She's timid. I think it was a budding friendship before this happened but now she feels like poor Mia has been cut adrift, you know? Losing her mother. Having lost her father. And Jocie knows what it's like to lose her mother."

"Let's go talk to her."

"I think we should."

They went inside and climbed the stairs together. A long quiet talk with their little girl left all of them in a better frame of mind. Sleep came easier for Jaymie that night, warmed by the love that surrounded her.

TEN

Saturday morning at the farmer's market, on a sideroad off the highway halfway between Queensville and Wolverhampton, was busy, especially in autumn. As Jaymie drove she reflected on her and Jakob's conversation with Jocie at bedtime the night before. Jocie felt cut off from her friend and was worried for her. They reassured her as best they could, and by the end of the conversation all felt somewhat better, but . . . they knew they'd have to stay aware of Jocie's concerns. Especially troubling was her sudden fretfulness over Jaymie's well-being. Alicia's murder had started her worrying and she wouldn't easily stop.

Jaymie well remembered a bout of child-hood anxiety she suffered through when her grandmother was in the hospital. She became acutely aware that people she loved could die, and for a while she worried about every little thing, following her parents and

Becca around like a shadow, obsessing over every sniffle or ache. Reassurance — and her grandmother's recuperation — had helped her recover. She would use that memory to help Jocie through it.

The farmer's market parking lot, a long graveled fenced area along the highway, was almost full. Jaymie parked at the far end and walked. Clutch had told her how to find his booth, but he hadn't told her what he sold. She followed his directions, strolling past woodworking stalls displaying cute country signs with chickens and hearts and apples, a fragrant stand featuring artisanal soaps and bath bombs, food booths with shelves of homemade jam, salsa, breads and artisanal cheese, and a leather booth with belts and handbags. She happily inhaled the smells. This was what she needed, something completely different to get her mind off her sorrow and fear. Christmas was coming — maybe she'd look for a new hand-tooled belt for Jakob, and a handbag for Valetta.

When she reached Clutch Roth's stall she was surprised, and then baffled. It was filled with shiny metal objects: chain-mail jewelry, coin purses and even gloves to use when wielding a sharp knife. But there were others not easily described, a display of shiny steel gadgets that puzzled her until Clutch, a tall, gaunt man with a long graying pony-tail and sunglasses pushed up on top of his head, greeted her and demonstrated his fidgets, handmade from shiny metal gears and nuts and other metal bits and pieces. They were ingenious toys to keep hands and minds busy. She bought one for Jocie to play with.

"Let's get a coffee and walk around," he said, leaving the booth in the calm control of his "lady," Gabby.

They strolled the aisles as the sun climbed in the sky, got coffee from a local bean roaster, and sampled a baker's pastry. Everyone knew Clutch and gave them special treats because he was a fellow vendor. "You've known the Vances a long time," she said as they walked, then asked him about his background with the family.

"Frankie and me . . . we grew up to-gether," he said, his gravelly voice contemplative.

"Frankie?"

"Short for Franklin. We used to be real close."

"Used to be?" Jaymie shaded her eyes against the brilliant autumn sun and looked up at her tall companion.

"We've drifted apart. Kids and wives and

other stuff over the years. Used to be we were tight, but now . . ."

His gaunt face was shadowed and Jaymie said, "You look worried. Tell me why?"

"I feel for the guy, you know? He lost his wife 'bout the same time I lost mine."

"That was quite a few years ago. How did Franklin's wife die?"

"Car accident. Real tragedy . . . she lost control in an intersection." He shook his head. "Frankie and me, we've both suffered through the years. I tried to talk to him after Jace died, but Frankie was all frozen up, and then . . ." His jaw flexed and tightened and he looked away. "He didn't bother returning the favor when Natalie . . . when we found my daughter." His beloved daughter Natalie had been murdered.

Jaymie put her hand on his arm. He turned back and looked down at her with a smile that died, to be replaced by puzzlement. "Frankie's changed."

"How?"

"Losing your kid the way he lost Jace . . . it changes you. Some families get more than their share of tragedy, mine and his both. You'd think old friends . . ." He shook his head and shifted uneasily, squinting into the sun and flipping his sunglasses down over his eyes. "Truth is, he changed long before he lost Jace. Guess we all have, me too. What did you want to know?"

She watched him for a long moment, feeling that there was more he wasn't saying. "You've heard that Alicia Vance was murdered in the woods across from my husband's and my home."

He nodded.

"I found her." Her voice caught in her throat and the words came out in a whisper.

"I heard that, and I'm sorry. Awful thing."

"She was on her way through the woods between her home and mine with a bag of vintage tools she had promised me. She referenced my past, helping to figure out things in murder cases. Clutch, she was afraid the police were going to arrest her for Jace's death."

He gave an inarticulate sound in his throat.

"As far as I know they don't think she did it but they thought she might have an idea of who did."

"Is that so? An' how do you know that?"

Clutch was antagonistic toward the police. He felt the local PD had been unwilling to help find his daughter. They had dismissed her disappearance as a woman who left town without telling her father where she was going. Jaymie saw both sides. Clutch had known Natalie wouldn't stay away so long without telling her dad where she was, but the police walk a fine line; adults have a right to walk away from their lives without interference.

Jaymie evaded her friend's question and went on. "I believe that Alicia may have been murdered because she knew — or suspected — who killed her husband. I'm scared that they know she was coming to see *me,* that they'll think Alicia confided in me. I'm worried because my little girl is friends with Mia, Jace and Alicia's daughter," she said. "That poor little girl, no father and now no mother! I guess my way of dealing with it all is figuring out who did that to her."

They had stopped in a private corner of the market at an unused tarp-draped stall. He stared down at her. "I s'pose the police are behind you trying to figure it out —" She was about to respond but he put up one hand. "I don't want to know another thing. Maybe they finally figured out that you got your ways and they work better than the cops. I trust you, when I don't always trust the cops. I'll tell you anything I know. We got mutual friends, Frankie and me. We might not be friendly now but we're still in the same circles, and I see Lew all the time.

He runs a tow truck outta Wolverhampton — Frankie and him are partners; they got two, three operators, doing real good for themselves lately — and I throw him business whenever I can. There's been rumors of . . . let's go sit and I'll tell you all about it."

They found a spot in the far reaches of the farmer's market, an unused corner by vendor parking where lawn chairs were set up for vendor breaks. Clutch lit a cigarette and puffed for a moment, then his gaze slid toward her. "Bad habit, I know. Helps me think." He pinched the burning end off and put the butt back in the cigarette pack, and the pack back in his jacket pocket.

"You've known the family for a long time."

"Frankie and I ran together back in the day. I could always count on him. He was a pistol, that's for sure . . . had a way about him. Natural charm, I guess. He could talk himself outta any trouble. Even back in high school he pulled pranks and got other kids in trouble." He chuckled, then sobered. "Didn't always turn out for the other kid. You gotta stand up for yourself, though, 'cause no one else will. Anyways, back in high school me and my girl and him and Kim would —"

"Wait . . . Kim? As in Kim Hansen?"

"Uh . . . yeah. Kim Ellsworthy she was back then. Cute little cheerleader going out with the bad boy. Every teen movie stereotype there was, right? A frickin' John Hughes film."

"So she went out with Franklin in school. I understand that she got pregnant young with Alicia?"

Clutch looked mystified for a minute, then broke out in laughter. "You're not thinking . . . gawdamighty, no. Alicia was not Frankie's daughter. Kim would have said so when Alicia and Jace started going together. No, she had Alicia after high school. By then she was with . . . another dude."

Jaymie's cheeks turned red. "Okay, good. I thought that was going to put a weird twist to the tale. I heard that Kim didn't like Jace, and I thought . . ." She shook her head, feeling stupid.

"Didn't like Jace? Hmph. There's nothing wrong with those two boys, Jace and Lew. Kim was always a stuck-up little . . ." He stopped.

"You didn't like her?"

"She acted like she was better than us, even while she was going out with Frankie. Acted like I didn't exist in the school hall." He scuffed his boot in the gravel. "Aw, I shouldn't of said that. She just lost a daughter, and I know how that hurts. Me and the old lady are gonna send her flowers."

"What were Jace and Lew like as kids? Did you know them?"

"Sure. My kids and Frankie's were friends. Those two boys were a handful. They'd fight about anything."

"Fight? Between themselves, you mean?"

"Sure. Boys do, you know. Me and my brothers about killed each other. Best of friends now. Jace and Lew fought 'bout everything, but if anyone touched one of 'em, they'd band together."

"Lew and Jace got along, then?"

"As much as any two brothers. They got real competitive, always one-upping the other."

"How so?"

"Frankie had a hand in it, always urging them on, you know, comparing them to each other. Jace was younger, but he got married first. Lew got married soon after."

"Coincidence?"

" 'Spose. But it was always one big coincidence after another. Lew got a Bonnie, so Jace had to get a CB750. Classic competition." Jaymie looked puzzled. Clutch explained that those were nicknames for two types of classic motorbikes. "Both boys were motorheads but Jace had the real talent for fixing anything. If it had a motor, he could make it run."

"I kind of remember Lew from high school," Jaymie said. "Franklin was in school at the same time as my sister and her friends, and Becca's just fifteen years older than me. Franklin and his wife must have had Lewis pretty young."

He nodded, with a noncommittal expression. "Sure. Senior year of high school."

That implied that either he got a girl pregnant while going out with Kim, or he and Kim split up. She tried to think of a way to ask Clutch, but she didn't want to get off track. She'd file that for later investigation. "I've heard that both guys — the whole family, in fact — were super careful about safety."

"That's what made the accident so gawdawful odd."

"Johnny explained to me about jacks and jack stands. What do you think happened? I mean, we can't get around the fact that the truck was up on a jack and he was underneath when the jack collapsed and the truck fell on him."

Clutch nodded, his thick salt-and-pepper brows knit. "We all talked about it after it happened. Nine outta ten guys admitted that when they had another vehicle up on

159

their jack stands and someone asked them to take a quick look, they had put a car up on a jack and crawled under." He shrugged. "Not smart, but we all think it won't happen to us." He frowned. "Jace was wrong about that."

"So it may have been an accident after all? Nothing suspicious?"

"May have been? Likely was. Bad luck, bad timing, whatever. Crap happens."

"He had to have a tire off, though, right? Or the vehicle would not have come down on his body."

He nodded. "Wheel was off, from what I understand."

"And it was reported as an accident."

"Like I said, prob'ly was."

But then, why were the police still investigating it, why did they suspect that Alicia knew more than she was saying, why was she afraid, and what was she coming to talk to Jaymie about? The only explanation that made sense was that Jace had been murdered, and Alicia knew more than she was saying. "I heard that someone helped Jace put the car up on the jack and did it wrong."

His head whipped around and he stared at her. "New to me. Who said that?" His tone was sharp.

"Mia said that to my daughter."

160

"She was only what, five at the time?"

"About that."

"How would she know? She wasn't there."

Jaymie shrugged. "Kids pick things up from adults. She may have overheard someone say it."

"I guess. Coulda been someone who didn't know what they were talking about though." He was silent, taking one of his fidgets out of his pocket and spinning a nut around on a wire. "Lemme ask around."

"Clutch, don't —"

"I'll be careful. I know how to do that," he said wryly.

"I know you do." Jaymie took a deep breath.

"Hey, Clutch? Gabby said get your butt back to the booth." A guy with shaggy dark hair held back from his face with mirrored sunglasses, a scruff of beard on his chin and dark eyes approached. "She needs a break."

"Hey, Lew," Clutch said with a glance at Jaymie. "Me and Gabby were gonna come around, but you know your dad. How you and Frankie doing? All this crap with Alicia . . . it's gotta hurt."

The man stood about ten feet away and looked at her, his eyebrows knit, then he looked to Clutch. "We're okay," he said, his voice cracking. "We're mostly worried for

Mia. Hard on her, losing her . . . her mom." He cleared his throat and flipped his mirrored sunglasses down over his eyes.

An older man who looked a lot like Lew Vance came up behind him. He studiously ignored Clutch. "Lew, come on back. We got a guy who wants to look at that seventy-nine Charger. I said you'd take him out to your car lot."

The younger man nodded.

"Hey, Frankie," Clutch called out, his tone carefully neutral. "I was saying to Lew I was real sorry to hear about Alicia."

Franklin Vance, dressed in dark jeans and a leather jacket, was heavyset, with bloodshot eyes and sunglasses holding back long salt-and-pepper hair in exactly the same way as his son. He stared, fleeting emotions flickering over his face like shadows over a wall, there, then gone, too fast for Jaymie to recognize. What was he feeling: regret? Sadness?

He ignored his old friend and whirled about, departing. Lew gave an apologetic expression and turned, following his father.

"What caused the rift between you?"

Clutch's expression was guarded. "Old crap. Nothing important."

"What do you know about Kim's boyfriend, Russ Krauss?"

162

There was a veiled look in the biker's eyes. "Can't say I know much about the dude."

Evasion; Jaymie was sharply attuned to it. "You may not know him well but you've heard something. What?"

Clutch grimaced. "Okay, yeah, I know him," he admitted. "Don't like him."

"Why not?"

"He's a . . ." He paused, then said, ". . . blockhead, to put it politely."

"There's got to be more to it than that."

Clutch moved restlessly. "Guy's got a rap sheet."

She eyed her unlikely friend, surprised that having a rap sheet would matter to Clutch. Given the crowd he was rumored to have been affiliated with in the past, he must know others who had records. "What did he do?"

"I'd rather not get into it."

Jaymie watched Clutch closely. He had always been straight-forward with her, and now he was not. "He's from around here?"

"Sure. You already know that."

"What did he do?" she prodded.

"Coupla breaking and enterings, stole a car. Maybe two. Then he got in real trouble." He frowned and looked away, squinting into the rising sun. "He killed a guy in the nineties."

"*Killed* a guy?" Jaymie cast her mind back to Krauss as he appeared outside of Kim's home. He looked like a peevish accountant, not a killer.

"Manslaughter, not murder. He got jumped by a dude in an alley. They fought and the guy hit his head and died."

"Does Kim know about it?"

"It's not a secret. He did his time. Everyone gets a second chance."

"Of course," Jaymie said absently. She thought it through. Nobody liked Russ, according to Nicki. But then Nicki also posited that Alicia's affair was with Russ. Jaymie thought that was unlikely, pure speculation on the young mom's part and not based in any actual observation. And she still had no motive for Russ to kill Jace or Alicia.

"I gotta go and let Gabby take off," Clutch said, standing and straightening.

"Sure. But Clutch, a couple more questions," she said, standing too and hoisting her purse up on her shoulder. "Where does Russ Krauss work? Do you know?"

"He drives for Queensville Clean 'n Bright, where Alicia worked."

Startled, Jaymie said, "Drives for them? What do you mean?"

"They have a passenger van that they use

for their cleaners. Drop them off at clients . . . you know."

"Okay. Sure. Is that a coincidence, or did Alicia get him the job? Or did Russ get her the job there?"

"That I do not know."

"Clutch, does his job include vehicle maintenance?"

Clutch frowned and scruffed his graying whiskered chin. "Don't know. Maybe."

"How long have him and Kim being going together?"

"Long time. Ten years, maybe?"

"How long have they *known* each other?"

He gazed at her steadily. "She's known him as long as she's known any of us."

"Since high school."

He was getting restless. "I gotta go, kiddo. If I leave Gabby in charge for too long she'll start giving stuff away."

"One more question, I promise," Jaymie said, touching his arm. "Clutch, if Franklin had a child before leaving high school, was he still going out with Kim, or had they broken up by then?"

"You got better sources than me for all that stuff. Ask Valetta Nibley; she can tell you all about it. Or old Mrs. Stubbs . . . she was always there as a volunteer, snoopin' around, tattling on us kids. If I think of anything, I'll give you a call. Sorry I wasn't more help. I don't know much."

As often happened in the early stages of trying to elucidate a mystery, Jaymie came away from her conversation with Clutch with more questions than answers. Back in her SUV, she got out her notepad — she was never without one anymore — and wrote down questions she now had.

What's up between Clutch and Franklin? And why is Clutch not talking about it?

How much does Russ Krauss know about car repairs?

The man's name kept popping up from multiple sources. If she was to add him to the list of suspects, what could be his motivation? she wondered. He had a checkered past. Had that followed him?

Was Nicki right that Alicia's lover was her mom's boyfriend? If so, did that give him a motive to kill Alicia?

Vance family . . . so much tragedy? Mia was hurt in car accident, and Jace died in garage accident. So much trouble in one family. Was there a connecting thread?

What did Alicia know, and what did she want to ask me?

That was the question that nagged constantly. Even if she discovered nothing else, she needed to know that. Maybe Wenda

Puchala would have answers. Jaymie resolved to contact her on Monday. But right now . . . home.

Jaymie wolfed down a quick lunch, changed into work clothes, and then met Jakob, Jocie, and other Müllers out in the tree fields. It was almost time to start tagging them for the year's Christmas tree market and cut-it-yourself season!

Normally this would be the time when they would groom the fields and remove any trees that in Jakob's expert assessment would not be good quality for the customers. This year, Jakob was trying something radical — so radical it was an ancient technique — he had learned from a book on Christmas tree farming. Normally as they cut trees for the Christmas market, they would pull the stumps from the field and infill the hole, planting a seedling to take its place the next spring. This year he would be "coppicing" part of the field, or cutting his pines higher up the trunk than normal and allowing the stump to stay in the field. A new tree would sprout from the stump and grow up to become a Christmas tree in another few years. It was an ecological approach to tree farming, an experiment he was excited about.

Though it was too early to cut trees for the season, he was starting his new approach by identifying those that would not make desirable Christmas trees. In another month those would be cut above the lowest skirt of branches. The evergreen boughs from the top part would be trimmed and used in pine wreathes, while the trunk would dry in time to be burned. He and Helmut, his brother, spent the day grooming the tree field for the cut-it-yourself buyers by removing diseased trees, which would also be burned.

While they did that, Jaymie and Jocie worked on cleaning up the customer area of their property, moving — with some difficulty, more determination and a lot of laughter — a couple of picnic tables so folks who couldn't walk the fields had a place to sit. They strung lights around the tables, as evening fell early that time of year, clapping with joy when the lights worked, sparkling in the autumnal gloom. Though the season was still a month and a half away, it was good to get all this done while the weather held.

It was a long day that ended with a frozen pizza at eight, and a tired little girl who had to be carried to bed by her dad. Jaymie curled up on the sofa with Hoppy, who was in a huff because he hadn't been allowed out during the work for fear he'd get in the way of the tractor and be hurt.

Jakob came back and stretched out with her and Hoppy. He yawned. "How did your talk with Clutch go this morning?"

She told him about it, and then said, "Darn! I have a gift for Jocie from his booth. I'll have to remember to give it to her tomorrow."

"Do you think there *is* something fishy about Jace's death?"

She thought about it for a long minute, fighting sleep, her eyelids heavy. "I do," she whispered. "The police call it a suspicious death, too. It's more than an accident." She turned and gazed up at his face in the dimness of the fireplace glow. "What was Alicia coming to tell or ask me? I'll never know. It's awful. Poor little Mia."

He kissed her gently. "Don't take it all on your shoulders, sweetheart." He held her and rubbed her back.

"I won't. I promise. If I can help the police, I will."

ELEVEN

Sunday was family day. They had breakfast with Jakob's parents and brothers. Jaymie made pancakes and they drenched them in maple syrup tapped from their own grove of sugar maples. Jaymie had brought her tablet and they had a video call with Jaymie's parents in Boca Raton so they could take part, as the Leightons ate their sensible breakfast of egg white omelets and fresh Florida orange juice.

Jocie played with her cousins for a while as Jakob and Helmut — a slimmer version of Jakob — headed out to the fields to finish yesterday's work. Jaymie and Sonya, Helmut's life partner, cleaned the highest cupboards that Jaymie's mother-in-law couldn't reach anymore. With much laughter they discovered forgotten gems: *many* packages of paper plates and napkins, plastic cutlery, old margarine tubs and a whole plastic bag of restaurant salt and pepper packets that their mother-in-law saved for picnics and camping. It all went into the donation box to be taken to a charity.

They parted ways and retreated to their own homes for supper and Sunday night rituals, including homework. Jakob, barbecue apron on over his clothes, was making chili for dinner while Jaymie sat at the kitchen table with Jocie helping her decide on a topic for a presentation she had to give. It had to be a topic of special importance to her, so she decided on Little People Who Made History. She would focus especially on Charles Proteus Steinmetz, the German-born mathematical genius dubbed the Wizard of Schenectady, who happened to be a little person.

Once they were done outlining what research she would need to do, Jocie closed her notebook and looked up at Jaymie. "I want to send Mia the bracelet I made her. Can I make a card to go with it?"

"That would be a nice idea. Your teacher sent an email to the parents to say that any of Mia's classmates could make cards and she'd make sure they were forwarded, but if you make one to go with the bracelet, I'll see if we can take it over to her grandmother's tomorrow afternoon. No promises.

I'll see if it's possible."

Jocie retrieved her craft supplies and set to work while Jaymie brewed a pot of tea, made herself a big cup, grabbed a shawl, and took it out to the bench in front of the cabin. Sitting cross-legged, cradling her mug, she pondered as she stared at the darkening woods across the road, sinister to her now when once they were a welcome retreat. She was fearful and obsessed, the view magnetic to her. She pictured Alicia starting out from her home on the evening of her murder. Walking through her backyard, she would have passed by the garage where her husband died five years before. Then she continued on to the back fence and . . . was there a gate? Did she walk *with* someone, chatting amiably — or arguing — until they attacked her? Or did her killer follow her as she strolled into the dark woods?

And *why*? Why kill her, and why now? Jaymie was virtually certain that Alicia was not involved in her husband's murder, if that's what his death was. She could have known something, though, and maybe she had decided to tell what she knew. There were other possible motives that didn't involve the death of her husband, but the timing led Jaymie to believe her theory was

172

most likely. Jaymie sighed and sipped her rapidly cooling tea, trying to decide how to proceed. Alicia had still been involved with the Vance family; she had said how helpful Lew was when she had car trouble. And there was her own family too. If Jaymie was going to poke around, it would be wise to start with those people: Russ Krauss, Kim Hansen, Erin Hansen, Franklin Vance, and Lew Vance. If she found anything out she'd pass it on to Detective Vestry.

She'd start with the obvious questions: With whom had Alicia been having an affair five years before? Had she since spurned him? Had she plotted with him to kill her husband and dumped him afterward? Someone must know. Tomorrow she'd drop in to Queensville Clean 'n Bright. While she tried to discover more about Alicia's life, she'd investigate Russ Krauss. She drained her cup of cold tea, stood, and with one long brooding look at the shadowy woods, returned inside to the warmth of the cabin and her family.

"Dinner's almost ready," Jakob said.

"I'll set the table." She slipped off her shawl and tossed it aside.

"Mama, what do you think of this?" Jocie held up her handiwork.

She took the card from Jocie and exam-

173

ined it. The front was a picture of a beautiful rainbow, glittering with pearls and gems. Inside, Jocie had hand-lettered, *I'm thinking of you Mia. I hope you feel better soon. We miss you.* Simple and to the point.

Jaymie's vision blurred with tears. "It's beautiful, Jocie. I'll see if we can take it to her with the bracelet. Now . . . let's have dinner."

Some weeks start off organized and perfect, but more start out with breakfast gulped and a mad dash to catch up. This first week of October started with a mad-dash kind of Monday. The weather had changed overnight and rain had swept in, leaving behind a gloomy cloud-strewn sky, gusty wind, and leaves tossing and twirling on the breeze. Jaymie got Jocie to school in time, making sure she took her backpack. She kissed her cheek, then waved goodbye as Jocie trotted up the sidewalk. When Jaymie turned, she noticed Kim Hansen standing on the pavement in the parking lot staring at the school. She approached and touched the woman's shoulder gently. "Kim? Are you okay?"

"What?" She turned, looking lost. "Oh . . . Jaymie." Her eyes were red and swollen and she looked weary, shoulders sagging under the weight of a thousand cares. "I don't know."

"You don't know what?"

"We decided last night that Mia should go back to school today, but is it too soon? Is it the right thing to do? I worried if she sat at home it would make her sadder, but now . . . what if someone says the wrong thing?"

"How did Mia feel about it?"

"I asked and she said okay. I think she's in kind of a numb place of denial. Her mom would go on vacation, leaving Mia with me for two or three weeks. It must feel like that for her right now, like her mom is on vacation and will be back."

Jaymie made up her mind quickly. She took the other woman's arm. "Let's go in and see Sybil."

"Sybil?"

She tugged Kim's arm, leading the other woman, who stumbled after her. "The principal, Sybil Thorndike. You'll like her." Jaymie had spoken to the principal often, first over a year ago concerning an old sad crime from the eighties, but since then regarding Jocie's schooling and the case of a bully her daughter handled a little too forcefully.

A half hour later they came back out and Kim impulsively turned and hugged Jaymie.

175

"Thank you," she said, her voice choked. "I feel better."

Sybil had listened to Kim's fears about Mia's first day back following her mother's death, and had offered solid advice — including that in Mia's case she thought letting her come back to school had been a good thing — and that she'd make sure the little girl was okay, without letting her feel she was being watched. She advised the services of a crisis counselor. The police had one on hand for victims of crime, but there were private counselors who may be better suited to a child suffering the violent loss of a parent.

Kim sighed and wrapped her arms around herself. She glanced back at the school with a calmer expression. "You'll never know how much I appreciate your help, Jaymie. I'm heading back to Wolverhampton. I have to drop off Erin's cell phone; she forgot it this morning. Maybe we could go somewhere and grab a coffee?"

"Sounds good. Meet me at Wellington's Retreat?" Jaymie said and gave her directions.

"Okay."

A half hour later Jaymie secured a table in the window of the tearoom. Kim arrived a few minutes later and they ordered. Jaymie thought that the pale thin woman needed sustenance. She ordered the day's scones, lemon cranberry, with lots of butter and strong black tea. When it came less than two minutes later, she coaxed Kim to eat. "You'll be no good to Mia if you don't keep your strength up."

Kim smiled. "You sound like Erin. She's no-nonsense too. I don't know where she got it from."

They made conversation. The holidays were going to be hard, Kim admitted. Maybe they'd go away over Christmas to Disney World, or a tropical beach.

Jaymie hesitated to give advice, but then said, "I know you'll figure it out . . . what's best for Mia, I mean. This holiday season she may cling to rituals and things she did with her mother, you know . . . going to the same places, doing the same things. It may be confusing for her if things are upset too much. I know it's going to be hard for you all, but maybe let Mia have input in the decisions? I know you're already doing that by letting her decide if school was a good idea."

She frowned, then nodded. "I'll think about it and have a talk with Mia." She scrubbed her eyes. "My life changed over-night when Alicia died. I was a grandmother, now I'm a mom. I feel tired and resentful, and bad for feeling that way."

"You have to let yourself feel what you feel," Jaymie said gently. "Otherwise you'll never process it. There's no guidebook for grief."

Kim gave a trembling smile. "Are you kidding? A couple of friends have already sent me online grief resources and guides. It seems like everyone has an answer, and none of them work for me. I want to forget it all. It's been awful. We haven't decided on a funeral or memorial service . . . it's . . . I can't even think about my Alicia without crying." Her eyes welled. "I'm having nightmares . . . someone stalking my baby, following her." She sighed and shuddered. "I was so young when I had her, and now she's gone. Gone *forever.*"

"How old were you when you had Alicia?"

"I was twenty-two. Old enough, I thought. Now it seems so young."

Jaymie pushed another scone over and encouraged Kim to eat. "Do you think you will have a memorial service for Alicia at some point?"

"We will. I can't even think about it yet. I know I have to decide what and when." She took in a deep breath and nodded. "I'm going to wait for a few weeks. We have some

cousins out of state who will want to come."
She took another bite. "I don't know how
I'm going to handle it all alone."

"But you've got Russ to lean on, right?
You two have been together a long time.
How long have you known him?"

"High school." She smiled faintly and
continued nibbling on the scone.

Jaymie said, "I was at the farmer's market
the other day and I ran into a mutual friend,
Clutch Roth. You and Franklin Vance and
Clutch all knew each other and hung out
back in high school?"

At the mention of Franklin's name, Kim's
head whipped up and she stared. "Oh . . .
Clutch," she said. "I knew him. A lifetime
ago, it seems."

"You all went to school with my sister,
Becca, and my friend Val Nibley. But you
and the two guys were close?"

Kim demurred. "We weren't that close."
She pushed away the plate of scones and
hurriedly said, "I don't suppose Valetta ever
told you, but I tried to fix Russ up with her
once." She laughed self-consciously. "*That*
was a disaster."

"How so?" Jaymie asked, interested in
another view of the story she had heard
from her friend, that Russ was too into Kim
to be open to any other girl.

179

"She was too straitlaced for him. You wouldn't know it to look at him, but he was a bit of a wild child in high school."

"You two dated in high school, you and Russ?"

She looked down at the scone, pulling the plate back toward her. "This is good!" she said, taking another bite. "I'll have to get some for Mia and Erin. Mia said that Jocie talks about tea parties all the time. Maybe we'll get the girls together to have one?"

"Sure. Jocie loves tea parties. Kim, about Franklin Vance . . . you went together in high school, right?"

She met Jaymie's gaze. "We dated."

"His son, Lew, is my age, almost, only a couple years behind me in school. Franklin is about the same age as Val and my sister Becca and you. Who was Lew's mother? Was she Jace's mother too?"

"Why do you care?" Kim asked with a confused look.

"Oh, I don't. I'm just —"

"Snoopy. I've heard that about you." She dusted her hands off and gathered her bag.

"Kim, I didn't mean to snoop."

"Sure you did. Maybe that's why Alicia wanted to talk to you."

"What do you mean?"

"Oh, never mind. Don't worry . . . it's no

big secret, you know," Kim said, staring across the table at Jaymie. "Lew's mom was an older chick who hung around that gang . . . Clutch, Franklin, some other guys. Franklin ran around. He ran around a *lot,*" she said, a bitter tinge in her tone. "While we were going out. While he was with her. Before they married. *After* they married." She shook her head. "But yeah, she was Jace's mother too." She looked pensive. "She loved Franklin and she was a good mom, I'll say that for her. We were actually friends, for a while."

"Clutch told me she died in a car accident."

"No mystery about that, either, in case you're wondering. Some jerk ran a red light and crashed into her."

Jaymie nodded. The conversation had been disjointed, at times hostile and other times emotional. Ruefully, she said, "I'm sorry if I've asked too many questions, Kim, or been insensitive. I guess I *am* snoopy. My fatal flaw."

Disarmed and surprised, Kim laughed. "You're different than your sister, that's for sure. Becca was always . . . she seemed older than she was."

"She had to look after me a lot when she was a teenager. I think it made her seem more mature than she was," Jaymie said.

Her eyes glittered with tears. "I wish I'd had a sister."

"Becca was a good big sister. My mom and dad were going through a rough patch, but Becca was there for me. I'll always be grateful to her for that."

Kim sobbed, then took in a long shaky breath. "God, I miss my Alicia! I don't know how to explain her; she could be wild. Stubborn. We didn't always get along, but that girl was like Becca in that way, I guess . . . rock solid. Determined. Mature despite her wildness. Grew up too fast . . . we grew up together, in a way. I had my own rocky period." She sighed and shook it off. "I guess I thought if I was on a beach in the sun it would be easier," she said, going back to her idea of going away for Christmas.

"You're not going to forget if you're here or on a beach," Jaymie said gently. "A friend of mine once said that grief is like a shadow, it follows you wherever you go." Those were Mrs. Stubbs's words of wisdom she learned after she lost her husband. Jaymie paused a beat, then said, "Is that how Alicia and Jace met, because you and Franklin and his wife were friends?"

Kim shook her head. "Nope. The kids met at school. I wasn't a big fan of them being together, but you can't fight your children, you know?"

"You didn't like Jace?"

Kim looked away. "It's . . . complicated."

"It was a horrible thing, what happened to him," Jaymie mused.

"I feel like this whole family is cursed. First the accident with Mia, then Jace's accident, and since then the garage burned and Alicia was in a crash. It's terrible!"

"Alicia was in an accident? How did that happen?"

Kim shook her head and hugged her purse. "Just one of those things, according to my daughter. She was going through an intersection when she was T-boned. She's lucky it was on the passenger side and she was alone in the car. She wasn't badly hurt."

"What about the other driver?"

"Hit-and-run. The police never found him."

"And how did her garage burn down?"

Kim's expression darkened. "I have a feeling about that. I think it was arson. Some local kid. There was a string of them a couple of years ago, sheds and barns and garages burning in the night, cars torched."

"And again . . . no one arrested?"

"Our local force is a joke. Alicia was sure they suspected her in the arson. Insurance fraud was the accusation."

"She was never arrested."

"Because she wasn't even here when it happened! She was on vacation. The police implied she had paid someone to set the fire while she was out of town so she could establish an alibi. As if! She had stuff stored in that garage. My mother's antique furniture was up in the rafters and it burned to ash."

"If she wasn't there, who reported it?"

"Luckily Arend Brouwer was out checking a fence — one of his goats got out and was killed on the road — and saw the blaze. If he hadn't seen it early the whole building would have been gone. Alicia had *nothing* to do with it." Her tone was fierce, argumentative, and angry.

Who could blame her? If she was the suspicious type she would think that Alicia's string of misfortune was a targeted campaign of terror. "How did Alicia seem lately? I saw her a couple of times and she appeared upset."

Kim nodded. She had relaxed, set her purse back down, and pulled the plate of scones toward her again. She tore one into pieces. "Something was worrying her but she wouldn't tell me what."

"Would she have told her sister?"

"Erin?" Kim laughed in derision. "Those girls can't stand each other. Never could. Like oil and water, so different. Like Russ says, if you didn't know, you'd never suspect they were sisters. Erin is my sensible one, never took a risk in her life. Alicia was my wild child." She paused and frowned, moving her cup around in circles. "Wild, and yet . . ." She shook her head. "I know it's a contradiction, but Alicia was old beyond her years sometimes."

She was repeating herself. Jaymie let her talk.

"She was kind. She was smart. I think she was trying to decide a lot of things. She was talking about moving away."

"How did you feel about that?"

A short bark of laughter and Kim said, "I wasn't crazy about the idea. I think I'd die if I couldn't see my granddaughter every day. I'd have followed them wherever they went. Anything to have my Mia near me."

"But you've got Russ and Erin to consider."

"Mia is my life. I'd do anything for that child. *Anything.*"

Jaymie got a chill down her back as she watched the other woman. *Anything* — there was a guttural ferocious grit in her voice when she said the word. "So you and Alicia

185

didn't always get along?" It was an under-statement, from the sounds of it.

"I loved her, but she was a handful. We argued *all* the time." She sighed. "But Mia . . . she's my soulmate. I'd do anything for that child."

There it was again, that intensity, that vehemence. Did doing *anything* for Mia include killing the man responsible for Mia losing her leg, and even the daughter who was thinking about taking her away perma-nently? Surely not. That was preposterous, dark, disturbing. However . . . now Kim had Mia all to herself, virtually guaranteed to have her granddaughter forever. "Did Alicia have a boyfriend?"

"She was seeing someone but never told me who. She was secretive."

And yet she was thinking of moving away. Maybe *with* this boyfriend? How could she keep his identity from her mother? Did Mia know who it was? "Was she close to the Vance family? I suppose Franklin and Lew want to see Mia often."

"She was too close to them if you ask me," Kim said. There was taut anger in her voice. "Franklin, Lew . . . even Debbie Vance, Lew's ex!"

"Really?"

"Alicia and Debbie were friends while

Lew and her were married, but it's a little much that they stayed close after the divorce."

It didn't seem odd to Jaymie; friends were friends. "I don't think I know Debbie Vance."

"She'd be . . . a year or two younger than you, maybe?" Kim put her cell phone into her purse. "I'd better get going. I have some stuff to do . . . stuff about Alicia."

"Before you go, Kim, my daughter made Mia a bracelet and card. Could we come over after school so she can give it to her?"

The woman paused and looked down at Jaymie. "I guess it's all right."

"We'll see you about four?"

With a tight smile, Kim nodded and left.

Time to head back to Queensville and have a word with Wenda Puchala at Queensville Clean 'n Bright, but first . . .

Jaymie drove toward Queensville via a detour and pulled up the lane at Alicia's home, deserted now, already feeling like it was neglected. Or had it always looked like that? The lane was rutted and sloping, running up alongside the house and past it to the chain-link-fenced yard. The gate was ajar, the padlock hanging open. Jaymie slipped through, walking a hard dirt path toward the garage, a large yellow-sided building with double garage doors on the front and a row of windows along the side, one of them with a broken pane. Cords of wood were stacked by the wall, and the yard was littered with an old plastic playhouse listing to one side, a decrepit rusting swing set, and a sagging clothesline attached at one end to the garage, at the other to a T-post, white paint flaking to show rust and other layers of paint.

She looked beyond the yard toward the woods. There was a gate on the back fence that opened onto the field belonging to the Brouwers. She strolled toward it, staring from the slight elevation of Alicia's land over the downward-sloping field. Striped in the gold stubble left after the harvest and wide bands of muddy earth, evenly spaced ruts collected water from the rain the night before. Through the field was a faintly visible path toward the woods. Jaymie wasn't sure what she expected to see . . . Alicia's ghost, haunting the dark shadows of the wooded grove? A shudder passed over her. Through that gate Alicia had headed and someone had followed or accompanied her.

Who would she trust to walk with her though gloomy woods? Maybe her assailant volunteered to carry the bag of utensils. She could imagine that . . . *Here, let me carry that. I'll walk with you. It'll give us a chance to talk.* Then, falling behind, taking the whisk, pulling one of the beater wires out and straightening it, and then, getting to the right spot in the middle of the shadowed woods . . . attack. How skilled did the person have to be? The wound was a stab piercing the heart, from what Jaymie had observed. Alicia would have bled out in minutes.

The woman had seemed afraid and troubled even to her mother, but there would have been people in her life she trusted. If Jaymie was right about her final stroll in the woods, someone had betrayed that trust.

Jaymie shivered and rubbed her arms. Autumn was pressing in, pushing the last summer warmth away with gloomy skies and cold winds. A sudden noise alarmed her and she heard the garage door opening, as if a spectral hand had pushed a button. She whirled and saw, standing and staring at her, Russ Krauss. A flush passed over her; she was trespassing, she supposed. When in doubt, launch a charm offensive. She pasted on a smile and walked toward him. "Hi. Russ Krauss, right? I'm Jaymie Leighton." Her smile faltered, and she said, "I'm the one who found Alicia."

"I know who you are. You're the snoop

who gets her name in the paper all the time."

Middle-aged and of middle height, he was the kind of guy who gets overlooked all the time, Jaymie thought, and yet he had won the woman with whom he was obsessed — according to Valetta — even in high school. Balding, with a fringe of salt-and-pepper hair rimming his hairless pate, he wore wire-framed glasses on a pudgy oval face stubbled with a three-day growth of beard that was likely purposeful, to give his face character. It didn't. He wore khaki trousers held up by a thin brown leather belt that swooped under a belly over which was stretched a beige golf shirt. He hadn't said another word, simply stared, light glinting on his glasses.

"I guess I'm here trying to grasp what happened," Jaymie said, settling on a small dram of the truth, the best way to defuse a situation most times. She should leave. And yet . . . she had questions. So *many* questions. She turned and waved at the field beyond the fence. "I can't believe that Alicia started across that field and into the woods and someone followed her." She turned back and regarded him closely, then examined the back of the house and the garage. "Her murderer followed her. Is there a

190

surveillance camera on the house? Have the police discovered anything?"

"Wouldn't you be the first to know?" He tossed the garage remote in his hand. He hadn't moved and didn't appear about to.

"Don't let me stop you from doing whatever it is you came here to do," she said, uneasy in his presence.

"Leaving you free to roam around and take whatever you want? I don't think so."

"What would I take? Really . . . what would I take from here?" she asked, irritated more than outraged. "I was just speaking to Kim. We had coffee in Wolverhampton. Do you think I decided to come out here and rob the place, but oh, let me stand and stare at the back field first?" A smirk lifted one corner of his mouth. It was a weird kind of standoff; though she didn't have any reason to be there, she hated to let him win and chase her off. "You've known Alicia a long time," she observed, moving closer. "You must miss her too."

"I feel bad. Kim is suffering so much," he said. He cleared his throat. "She loved her daughter, and I love *her* so . . . yeah, it hurts."

He said the right words, but his tone was impassive and lacking in depth. Maybe he was the kind of guy who didn't go in for

191

emotional displays. "Did she ever confide in you? Alicia, I mean. Did she ever tell you she was worried or alarmed about anything?"

"We didn't exactly have a father-daughter relationship," he said dryly. "No, she did *not* confide in me. You should ask Franklin. Maybe she talked to him."

She cocked her head and regarded him closely. "Why do you say that?"

He raised his brows and shrugged. "Since you're bound and determined to snoop, *they* were close enough . . . closer than her and me."

She frowned. What was there behind his words? "What do you mean by that?"

"Take it as you want to. I've said all I'm saying."

"How did you and Jace get along?" she said.

"Me and Jace? Look, little lady, what are you trying to say? What . . ." He drew back and his mouth hung open for a second before he said, "Are you accusing me?"

Taken aback, she said slowly, drawing out the first word in puzzlement, "Accusing you of what? Why would I do that?"

"It's time you got out of here."

Jaymie watched him, remembering what Clutch had said about his violent past. And yet he looked more like an irritated accountant than a dangerous assailant, a classic case of underestimating someone, maybe. She wasn't about to test him further. "Okay, I'm leaving. Go ahead and do . . . whatever you came here to do."

"I'm picking up some things for Kim, if you must know," he said.

Interesting that he chose to answer just as she was leaving. Anxious to deflect suspicion? But suspicion of what? Lifting one hand in farewell, she turned and headed out the gate and to her SUV.

TWELVE

Jaymie picked up a couple of fresh salads from the Queensville Inn takeout and headed back to the main street in Queensville to her sister's antique store. It was Georgina's day off, so Becca would be in all day. Kevin, Becca's hubby and partner in the store, was at an estate sale in Port Huron. Becca was in the big front room setting an antique dining table with fall colors and a leafy centerpiece. She turned, smiling. "Look, isn't it pretty!" she said, waving her hand like a magic wand over the table settings.

Jaymie set the salad containers on the counter and strolled over, examining the china dinner service. The pieces were strewn in an airy leafy pattern of fallish colors, delicate gold and sage green with gilt decoration. "Gorgeous. What is it?"

"Haviland Limoges Autumn Leaf," Becca said, clasping her hands in front of her and admiring her work. Gold-plated cutlery picked up the light from the chandelier and glinted, while ruby crystal wineglasses glowed.

Jaymie eyed the coffee and tea service sitting on a sideboard waiting to be placed. "This is the same china pattern," she said. The pots flared out at the bottom and had scalloped bottom and top edges. "I love the shape!"

"I know, beautiful, but sturdy, too." She stood staring at the table, tilting her head with a dreamy expression.

Jaymie smiled. Her sister's enthusiasm for her work was infectious. She had run a china matching service for years, sourcing rare and hard-to-find china pieces for clients. Becca adored crystal and china as much as Jaymie loved vintage kitchen wares. "I brought lunch, salad from the inn."

Becca, her sturdy figure clothed in a leaf-patterned cardigan and beige skirt with tan pumps, perched on the stool behind the cash desk while Jaymie pulled up the visitor's chair, a wooden barstool. They ate as her sister delicately probed how she was feeling after what had happened far too close to home.

Jaymie admitted she was shaken. "I keep beating myself up over it — if only Alicia had told me what was on her mind. Maybe I should have pushed harder or . . . I don't know." She stabbed a cherry tomato.

"What good would that have done?"

"Maybe I'd have a clue as to who killed her." She sighed and shook her head. "I know better. I know there's nothing I could have done differently. Alicia made her choices and it ended in tragedy." She paused and frowned. "That sounded cold. I didn't mean it was her own fault."

"Honey, I know that," Becca said, leaning across the counter and touching her arm. "Do you have no idea what she wanted to talk to you about?"

"Not a clue. I got dragged into it in the first place by Detective Vestry, but now, of course, she wants me to back off."

Becca made a sour face. "She knows she messed up."

"Maybe," Jaymie said slowly. "If the detective hadn't spooked Alicia by calling her and asking her to come in, maybe she would have opened up to me. That call sent her into a tailspin."

"A tactical error?"

"Detective Vestry is smart and cautious, usually, but yeah, I think it was a mistake."

"Maybe because you only know your side of the story?"

"I guess. Vestry couldn't have known I was about to get something important."

"Do you know that?"

"Alicia was going to tell me something, I can feel it in my bones. She was scared and ready to talk but Vestry's call panicked her and shut her up. She felt like the police were going to pin Jace's murder on her. She didn't know who she could trust." She sighed. "I don't suppose the detective could have foreseen that."

"We all make mistakes," Becca said.

"If Alicia had lived I may have been able to find out why the police thought she might be involved in her husband's death. If Jace's death was murder, it might matter who she was seeing on the side. And why was she cheating on her husband? Was she striking out against Jace, angry that he had caused Mia's injury?"

"You think her cheating on him was revenge?"

"It's possible. Probable, even. How could any marriage survive what Jace did?"

Becca twisted her lips, then forked up more of her chicken Caesar salad. After munching she said, "That only makes sense if you don't think she had anything to do with Jace's death. She couldn't have her revenge cheating on him if he was dead."

197

"I don't think she did anything to Jace, but I've been wondering if she knew something, or figured something out."

"What do you mean?"

Jaymie thought about it for a few minutes, eating her salad. "When I was doing research I stumbled on a clip of Alicia being interviewed by a reporter from the Detroit TV station news. It was shortly after his death . . . like, the next day. Watching her, I could see that she was shaking. She was genuinely shocked. But she didn't look afraid, like she would if she suspected it was murder. You know?" In frustration, she shook her head. "It's a feeling I have. I'm not sure that even in the months afterward she thought it was murder. Heck, the police even now aren't sure, unless they have information they haven't given out."

"Which is possible," Becca said.

"Which is possible," Jaymie agreed. "Anyway," she said, setting her empty container aside and taking a deep bracing breath, "I wanted to ask what you remember about these people. You and Val were in high school the same time as Kim — whose last name then was Ellsworthy — and Franklin Vance. And even Russ Krauss." She shuddered. "That guy creeps me out." She wasn't about to tell Becca about his confronting her at Alicia's home. She'd go into big sister mode and forbid Jaymie from doing what she wanted. Becca thought she still had that power, despite Jaymie being in her thirties. "Do you remember Krauss? He's with Kim now. For quite a while, as I understand it, spanning back even to the time of Jace's death. Maybe before."

"I do remember Russ from back then. He was always trying to get into the group, some group, *any* group, you know?"

"Meaning . . . ?"

"He tried out for sports teams and never made it. Same with the chess team. He even tried to get on the debate team, but he was argumentative, not a debater. I know, because I was second string on debate back then. When none of that worked he started hanging around on the periphery of the bad-boys group."

"A wannabe."

Becca nodded. "A wannabe . . . anything to fit in. But Krauss never fit in."

"You mean he hung out with people like Franklin Vance and Clutch Roth?"

"Exactly, the guys who congregated in the smoking pit."

"Smoking pit?"

Becca chuckled. "Yes, they had a smoking pit at the high school back then." She closed her salad container, having picked through and eaten the chicken and romaine, leaving behind the assorted items she wouldn't eat, pine nuts and croutons. "You know what high school cliques are like. There are the ones in the group, and the satellites who circulate on the outer edges, trying to fit in. Why the curiosity about Russ?"

Jaymie explained what Clutch had told her about Russ's criminal past, even as she wondered why he hadn't told her the whole truth, that Russ was, or was trying to be, one of their gang. Was he trying to disavow someone he saw as a bad dude because of the manslaughter? That didn't fit with what she knew of Clutch, who usually didn't care what others thought of him. "Are you saying Russ Krauss ended up on the wrong side of the law by default? Looking for acceptance?"

"I don't know. I saw him as a hanger-on, not one of the tough guys."

"People can surprise you. What do you remember about the others?"

"Besides Franklin Vance and Kim Ellsworthy totally being the 'cool couple' in our school?"

"That's not what she said to me. She downplayed their whole relationship."

"She was lying."

"I wonder why?"

Becca shrugged. Jaymie wasn't sure what to think. Kim had dismissed the notion that she and Franklin were a regular couple, but here was another person who had witnessed it. Everyone had parts of their youth they weren't proud of; maybe her relationship with Franklin was Kim's.

Becca told Jaymie what she remembered. Kim and Franklin were the scandalous talk of the school. Kim's parents did not approve of the relationship so they snuck around, but by graduation their relationship had died and she attended prom with another guy.

"Do you know why they broke up?"

"Rumor had it that he cheated on her." Becca waggled her eyebrows. "He was a player."

Kim had said as much. He had cheated on Kim with Lew and Jace's mother, among others.

Lunch done, Jaymie said her goodbyes to Becca and headed to Queensville Clean 'n Bright. She couldn't just drop in and start asking questions about Alicia. Maybe she'd say she was pricing cleaning help for the historic house. She could ask for quotes at least.

The cleaning company office was in the

garage of a side-split ranch. The garage door had been replaced by an aluminum panel, a glass window and double glass doors with the company name on it. Jaymie entered. A dark-haired woman leaned over the desk of an employee seated at one of the two desks. The younger, seated woman looked up with a professional smile pasted on her face.

"May I help you?"

"I hope so. I'm looking for information right now, and since I was in the area I thought I'd drop in."

The other woman straightened and smiled. She was probably in her thirties: serious expression, no makeup, thin lips, with dark streaked hair pulled up in a high ponytail. She wore slacks and a shirt with *QCB* stitched on the breast pocket. She looked familiar to Jaymie, who stared at her, trying to recall where she'd seen her before.

She stared back at Jaymie for a moment with the same expression, then said, "Welcome to Queensville Clean 'n Bright. I'll be out of here in a second and she's all yours." She turned her attention back to the younger woman and said, "Look, I have to go. I know you're overwhelmed right now with both jobs, but I'll take over the scheduling. I've contacted job recruiters and will start interviewing for a new coordinator.

Everyone is out in the field and no one is scheduled back today. I'm taking the van for the rest of the day until it's time for crew pickup, okay?"

The younger woman nodded and took a deep breath.

The older of the two put one hand on her colleague's shoulder and squeezed. "Wenda, it's okay. Take it easy, we'll get through this. Put the phone on voice mail if you need to." She turned and retreated down a hallway, disappearing, the echo of a slamming door attesting to her exit.

Jaymie had let a critical gaze wander over the place, which was clean and smelled of industrial-grade cleansers. "Hi again . . . you're Wenda?"

"Wenda Puchala, sales coordinator for Queensville Clean 'n Bright," she said. "Why don't you have a seat?" She motioned across the desk from her. "How I can help you?" The phone rang. She glanced at her computer screen and punched a button, then turned her attention back to her prospective client.

Jaymie set her purse down on the floor and sat on the steel and vinyl chair. "I'm on the board that looks after the Queensville Historic Manor. Until now we have hired our own staff, but occasionally our cleaner

203

isn't available." All true. "I was wondering two things: do you do occasional jobs, and can I get a quote on your service?"

The young woman asked about the size of the house and special requirements. Jaymie replied that there were many vintage and antique items, so the cleaner would have to be exceptionally careful. As the young woman punched numbers into her computer, the two got more chatty. Wenda, with long spiral-curled hair pulled off her lightly freckled face with two barrettes, was newly married and looking to buy a house. She had a dog, and didn't like cats, and agreed that dog fur was hard to get out of the carpet. Finally, they discussed numbers.

Jaymie nodded at the price per hour quoted. "That's not bad. I'll have to discuss it with the board. Unfortunately, the men on the board seem to think the 'ladies,' " she said, sketching air quotes around the word, "will take care of the cleaning." She sighed. "Also unfortunately, they're mostly right."

"Like my dad, he knows my mom will take care of things so he doesn't have to. I'm lucky my husband was raised right. He cooks and does dishes and cleans the bathroom."

Jaymie smiled. "Sounds like my husband.

He was a single dad for a long time so he's a better housekeeper than I am . . . more organized, at least. I tend toward clutter." She hesitated, then said, "Being a single parent is hard. I knew Alicia Vance, her daughter and mine are in the same class at school. She must have struggled to balance the two, work and parenthood. I know she worked here. I'm sorry about the loss of your coworker. This must be hard for you," she said, waving her hand over to the empty desk on the other side of the room.

Wenda nodded, her red-rimmed eyes welling. "It's been unreal," she said. "I don't quite believe it yet. I've covered her job for her before when she was on vacation. I keep expecting her to walk in, tanned and smiling, back from a trip."

"You're the second person to say that! I was talking to her mom earlier. Kim said the same thing, that she and Mia feel like Alicia is away on vacation and is due back any day."

The young woman brushed tears away, snatched a tissue out of a box by her keyboard and mopped her eyes. "I've been a basket case," she said, her voice quivering. "I'm trying to keep it together, but . . ." She turned in her chair, blew her nose, and deposited the tissue in a wastebasket at her feet. "Whenever I think of that poor darling child I lose it."

"Mia is in my daughter's class, as I said, and they're both in ballet, too. My little girl, Jocie, made her a card and bracelet. We're going over this afternoon to take it to her." Jaymie felt a moment of shame: was she using the little girl's name to establish a connection? Taking a deep breath, she folded her hands, leaned forward and said, "I'll be honest, Wenda, I'm the one who found Alicia. I'm the one she was coming to see." Her voice caught and she held back a sob. As much as she tried to ignore it and say she was okay, she wasn't. She pressed her hands together until her knuckles turned white. "I wish I could figure out who did that to her, who killed her! I feel . . . responsible. She was coming to see *me,* to talk to *me.* She was worried about something."

Wenda stared across the desk at her. "I *knew* I recognized your name!" Her phone rang. She glanced at the computer screen and then answered it, focused, and pulled up the information needed, relayed it — it was about a client in the field — then hung up. Taking a deep breath, she said, "I wish I could help. Alicia was a friend. She was in my wedding party, for heaven's sake! I'd do anything to expose whoever did this."

"Me too."

Wenda stared at her for a moment, tears drying on her cheeks, her gaze more calculating. "How can I help?"

"I'm trying to get a picture of her life, to see if I can find any . . . any cracks, you know? Any plausible threats. Did you two talk about your lives?"

"We were together all day most days. We talked."

"Was she seeing anyone?"

Wenda nodded. "I don't know who. She was secretive. She never said it directly, but I got the feeling that she didn't think her mom would approve."

Interesting. Who was the mystery man she was hiding? "Speaking of Kim, I understand her boyfriend works here? Russ Krauss?"

Wenda made a face. "Yeah. Some of our workers have cars, others don't. We pay mileage for those with cars and provide transport for those without, especially the ones who live out of town."

"I've seen the van, it's black, with *Queensville Clean 'n Bright* on the side in yellow letters."

"The boss took it. She likes to drive it when Russ doesn't need it."

"Why the face at the mention of Russ

Krauss?"

She glanced toward the door and behind her. Lowering her voice, she leaned forward and said, "I'm not a big fan of his. I don't trust him, he's shifty. Russ has this habit of sneaking up on you. He caught me and Alicia talking smack about him once and blew a gasket."

"What was she saying?"

"She was trying to get her mom to break up with him."

"Why?"

"She said Russ creeped her out, that he was always trying to be nice to her, but in a weird way, you know? Her mom wouldn't listen to her." Her expression clouded. "Alicia thought he had something over Kim."

"Like what?"

"I don't know. Alicia and Russ argued often. She thought he was a crazy driver."

"Was he?"

"He got cited a few times by police."

"Wasn't that an insurance liability for the company?"

"He did some driving courses and cleared it all up. He's been more careful since. But he *was* almost fired."

"Did he blame Alicia in any way for that?" Jaymie asked, thinking about motives, why

208

Russ might be angry enough to kill Alicia.

"How could he blame her for him getting stopped by cops? No, he only got mad at Alicia — well, kind of mad — about what he overheard when we were talking about him. It was weird, almost like he was more hurt than angry. It blew over. He kept trying to win her over, being sucky sweet to her and Mia. Alicia tried to keep the peace for Kim's sake."

"Did she and her mom get along?"

"Sometimes yes, sometimes no. It was complicated."

She had no other information about Russ. Jaymie asked, "Were you working here when Jace died?"

"Lord, that was an awful week! I was new . . . started on Monday of that week, learning the ropes of my job. The next Monday was supposed to be Alicia's first day as service coordinator — she had been promoted from being a part-time cleaner — but that weekend Jace died, so Alicia didn't come in and I had to figure out her job *and* mine all at the same time. There were some unhappy customers that week, let me tell you! The schedule was a mess, customers screaming at me on the phone, me in tears half the time. It was traumatic."

"A friend told me that Jace and Alicia

were having marital problems. Was that true?"

"I didn't know her that well then. She was one of the cleaners and like I said, I had just started at QCB, so . . . I had no way of knowing. Not back then, anyway."

"But you became friends since then and you've talked. How did she speak of Jace, about his death?"

Wenda watched her eyes. "Why are you asking about Jace? It was an accident, right, his death?"

"Wenda, there have been so many accidents, starting with the one that took Mia's leg. It's either a long string of coincidences or something is very wrong."

This was a new thought for Wenda, and her eyes widened in bewilderment, then she shook her head. "No, it can't . . ." She stopped and clapped her mouth shut.

"What?"

"Alicia said to me once that if she ever turned up dead, to tell her mom to look for *the note.*"

"The note?"

"I guess she wrote a note. I can't believe I just thought of this now!" She ran a hand through her spiral curls, where it caught her ring. She detangled it as she said, "My brain has been frazzled ever since I heard she was murdered, but yeah, she said that."

"Where *is* the note? What did it say?"

"I wish I knew! She said her mom would know."

"She told her mom, or she assumed her mom would know?"

Wenda shrugged.

"Didn't you ask what she meant? Or what was in the note?"

"I thought it was a joke, you know, *haha, just kidding*? Like a movie . . . *If I die the killer is . . .* I guess that's why I didn't think of it 'til now. It seemed melodramatic at the time. I probably rolled my eyes and ignored it. That was, oh, three years ago? Maybe a little more? That's why I had forgotten about it until now."

"Three years ago." This was seriously alarming. Jaymie knew Vestry would have to hear about it. "What was going on in her life three years ago?"

"It was . . . spring. Yeah, spring," Wenda said. "Almost the time of the Tea with the Queen event. Over three years ago, I guess. There was something in the news about a suspicious death locally, or a murder — a guy found on someone's back porch, or in their house?"

Jaymie held back a gasp. That would have been the body she found on her very own

Queensville back porch, the first time she faced murder.

"We were talking about it and she said if anything ever happened to her, she'd want people to know who did it. I . . . honestly, I didn't think she was serious. Who would?"

I would, Jaymie thought. So, as long ago as three years Alicia feared for her life. "And she told you about a note."

Wenda nodded. "Do you think I should call the police?"

"That is up to you." Jaymie didn't press it, she'd be telling Vestry about it herself. "Wenda, how did Alicia feel about her father-in-law, Franklin, and her brother-in-law, Lew?"

"As far as I know she got along with them fine. She liked her sister-in-law, Debbie. You know . . . *Debbie Vance,*" she said, flapping her hand. "They went out to lunch sometimes, even after Lew and Debbie split up. I know she trusted Lew. He is who she would call if she was stuck, or if she had a problem with her car."

"A problem with her car?"

"It kept breaking down on her."

"I've heard Alicia was in a car crash. When was that?"

"That was . . . three and a half years ago. Come to think of it, it was around the time she told me about the note. She had a string of bad luck for a while — her garage burned down, and there was the hit-and-run car crash."

"She'd call Lew for help? When? Why?"

"When the car broke down. He would pick her up and tow the car. The family runs a tow truck business, you know."

"I have heard of Vance Towing. But he wouldn't fix the car for her?"

"Lew isn't the mechanic in the family, Jace was."

"What about Franklin?"

"I think they were all close while Jace was alive, but drifted apart." Wenda blinked. "I always wondered, did Franklin blame Alicia for Jace's death?"

"What do you mean?"

"She never went out to the garage and checked on him when she got home that day. I think I'd blame her. Not that Alicia did anything wrong. She didn't. I mean . . . she *wouldn't*." She dashed away fresh tears. "Alicia was a good person."

Jaymie already knew but asked anyway. "Did she say why she didn't go out to the garage to check on Jace?"

"They weren't on speaking terms. She told me later she was on the verge of kicking him out."

"Why?"

"She didn't think he'd taken responsibility for what happened to Mia. She was still angry about it long after he died."

That accorded with what Jaymie had already heard. "Wenda, Kim said that Alicia was talking about leaving town, moving away. Did she say anything like that to you?"

Wenda looked conflicted, but then nodded. "It was supposed to be a secret but I guess there's no point in that now. She was talking about moving to California. She was going to start a Clean 'n Bright–type business there."

"Start a different one, or franchise this?" Wenda shrugged. "Who owns this business anyway?" Jaymie probed.

"Didn't you know? It's owned by Debbie Vance. What did you think I meant, me flapping my hand like that when I said her name? That was Debbie you saw when you arrived . . . Debbie Vance . . . you know, Lew's ex."

THIRTEEN

Jaymie drove back to the cabin considering the implications: Debbie Vance, Alicia's ex-sister-in-law, owned Queensville Clean 'n Bright. She employed both Russ *and* Alicia. Alicia was thinking of heading to California and starting her own business along the same lines, and it was supposed to be a secret. But Wenda knew about the planned move and so did Kim, so who was it a secret from? Debbie? Russ? And did it matter that there was an air of secrecy around it? Kim had not been happy that Alicia was planning to leave, but who else may have been upset? And why was Alicia planning to get out of town? Was she afraid?

So many questions — as usual — and so few answers.

Home again, Jaymie took a pasta dinner out of the freezer to thaw, washed and dried the morning dishes and wiped the table, all while avoiding looking across the road to the woods. It had been her favorite view in the world, the woods she was looking at when she realized she loved Jakob. She had been over for dinner on Valentine's Day, and as he put his daughter to bed, she stared out at the woods and acknowledged that she loved him, and she wanted to be with him forever, that he was the love she had been seeking. That evening he asked her to marry him a few short months after meeting.

And she'd never looked back, never regretted it for a single second. But now she couldn't look out at those woods without shuddering. She slapped the counter in irritation. Hoppy, startled, yipped. "Sorry, pupkins," she murmured. That — her residual fear of the woods — had to change. She *must* figure out who killed Alicia, or she'd never sleep soundly again. She whirled away from the counter. "C'mon, Hoppy. Let's go."

She took her little dog back into Queensville and walked him along the river. In that infernal autumnal pull between summer and winter the weather had again closed in, dark-lined clouds scudding uneasily over the river, a rumble echoing ominously as she stood staring at Heartbreak Island. Leaning on the railing, she watched the dark gray and green water of the St. Clair river slip by, little whitecaps breaking as wind rippled the surface, movement on the island barely visible as mist rose and drifted.

Hoppy looked up at her and waggled his tail, impatient to move on. "Okay, let's go," she said. By the time they approached the Queensville Inn he was weary and she had to carry him the rest of the way, but he was overjoyed to find they were about to visit one of his favorite humans, Mrs. Stubbs, who always had bits of scone or cookie to share. Jaymie tapped on the sliding glass door on her private terrace and she yelled "come in." She was in front of her television, enthralled by one of her murder shows, as she called them, the true crime TV that she watched when she wasn't reading mysteries. She held up one hand in greeting, and Jaymie set Hoppy down and went about making tea while the program finished.

Finally the show was done. The forensic evidence proved that the suspect did, indeed, kill her husband. After taking a mechanics course in community college, she loosened the lug nuts on his car tyres (*tyres*, because it was in England) and sent him off drugged with sleeping pills to fetch her something in the village down a long windy road. A wheel came off on a sharp turn, he crashed his car over a cliff and died. It was her carelessness that did her in. She claimed to never go near his tools, but her fingerprints were on the wrench, her blonde hairs were in his toolbox, and a fellow she had flirted with remembered her from the mechanics course.

Jaymie absently wondered how much forensic evidence the police had collected at the scene of Alicia's murder. She would never be privy to it, nor should she. Her favored methods were ones not open to the police: making friends, gossiping, guesswork and jumping to conclusions. The official police investigation would then have the evidence to support her conclusions, or not. She had never yet been wrong in her ultimate uncovering of a perpetrator, but it could happen.

"If Jace Vance was still alive I'd say it was him who killed Alicia," Mrs. Stubbs said, clicking the TV off with her remote and turning her mobility chair toward the small table. "It's usually the wife or girlfriend, or husband or boyfriend."

"That would make it easier to figure out," Jaymie said. As she poured tea into pretty china mugs she told her friend what she had so far learned.

"Are you going to tell the detective about

the note Wenda Puchala mentioned?"

"I am. But I'm going to see Kim this afternoon when I take Jocie over there. I don't think it would hurt to call Detective Vestry after, do you?"

Mrs. Stubbs winked. "No harm at all." She drank her tea and broke off bits of a cookie for Hoppy, who gobbled them up. "You know, I've been thinking of this all day. Trying to figure out whodunit."

"Did you come to any stunning realizations? I could use a few right now," Jaymie said.

"I wish I did." She frowned and moved uneasily. "I don't imagine I have anything to add that you haven't already thought of. My dear, I am troubled. Even as I watch these shows, true crime TV, I wonder . . . how disgraceful is it that true-life crime has become an old woman's entertainment? It's caused me sleepless nights wondering about the morality of it, and yet I can't seem to stay away. Every day I vow not to watch, but each day at two I get antsy and turn on the TV. It's an addiction." She sighed. "I'm going to talk to my pastor about it. I don't feel easy in my conscience."

Jaymie sat down in the guest chair and looked up at her friend, tracing the blue veining across her sagging eyelids, and the

219

deep grooves under her rheumy eyes. "It's tough to figure out, isn't it? You know my reading tends to be romance novels. I *love* love stories. There's not enough love in the world. And yet I keep getting caught up in these murder cases. I wonder . . . why don't I step back and let the police take care of it? In almost all cases I think they would have gotten there."

"Eventually."

Jaymie nodded. "Each time I feel like I have a connection that allows me to see the case from a different perspective. Sometimes I worry that I'm getting a big head over it. But what is true is that often the different perspective comes from you, or someone else who has something to add, some way of seeing things that I don't notice."

"Are you trying to make me feel better?"

"I don't think you have anything to feel bad about, but I understand. I suppose if viewers stopped consuming true crime stories they would stop making them." She frowned down at her hands then looked up and smiled, as Hoppy, curled up on Mrs. Stubbs's lap, snuffled into sleep after his long walk. Her smile faded. "It wouldn't stop the crimes from happening in the first place. I do feel that your mind — so sharp, always — gives you insight. Talking to you helps me make my way through all the lies and mistakes that allow people to get away with killing. I don't take it lightly. Killing another human being is wrong. The thought of anyone getting away with murder makes me angry.

"You read mysteries and watch true crime. Maybe it's helped you see underlying patterns. I only know that talking it out with you helps me get there, and that solving the murder perhaps saves another life. Maybe there *is* an ethical problem with true crime TV; that's for others to judge. If a show profiling the crime is made with a focus on the victims and the justice people seek for them, I believe it helps. I *do* know that you help me figure things out, and that is seeking justice. When I'm stuck, I come to you."

"My dear, did you know that you give me a reason to get up many mornings? I'll continue my Ironside ways, shall I?"

"Ironside?"

"Good heavens, you're young . . . too young to know about wheelchair-bound Chief Ironside. It's an old TV show, dear. Anyway, enough maudlin weepiness. I've been having one of those days, my joints hurt, I didn't sleep . . ." She waved one hand, whisking it all away. "Never mind. How can I help?"

"I've been thinking about it a lot, and it's possible that this whole mess goes back to connections from the past. I don't know yet, but I think I need to understand all of that before I go forward. It may go back as far as when Becca and Val were in high school, along with Franklin Vance and Kim Hansen . . . Kim Ellsworthy, she was then. You volunteered there all the time. Do you remember them?"

"I do indeed remember Kim Ellsworthy. A little blonde *tramp,* she was."

"Mrs. Stubbs!"

"It's true." Her tone was strongly indignant and she glared at the memory. "She wore low-cut tops and short shorts guaranteed to distract the boys. She wiggled her bottom and flirted with the male teachers. *Everyone* knew Kim Ellsworthy. That girl had not an ounce of self-respect. I heard she slept around."

Restive, Jaymie jumped up and paced, taking her cup and rinsing it out. She dried it and put it away, then turned away from the little sink in the corner. "I don't mean to check you, or be disrespectful, Mrs. Stubbs, but . . ." Jaymie fretted: How could she say what she felt to her friend without it being harsh? How could she respect her elder and still stand up for what she believed? "You don't know firsthand that she slept around, do you?" She returned to her chair and sat. "And even if she did sleep with guys —"

"I guess you think I'm an old out-of-touch lady," Mrs. Stubbs said, a querulous tone in her voice.

Jaymie was silent. The silence stretched into minutes.

"Times have changed," the woman mused, her arthritic fingers, joints like knots, still stroking the little dog snoozing on her lap. "I suppose I *am* out of touch. I should bite my tongue, or at least think before I speak."

"We all make snap judgments, and sometimes say things we don't mean."

"I'm tired. I'm crabby. If you'd be so kind, you'll attribute my peevishness to that." Mrs. Stubbs sighed. "I remember how women suffered if their halo slipped even a bit. Double standard back then. I suppose there still is one today, as far as men and women and sex go. Truth be told, I'm every bit as judgmental as others. I can think of a few instances . . ." She drew herself up and sighed. "Never mind. Jaymie Leighton Müller, I may not agree with *everything* going on today, but times change. Maybe I need to as well. We'll let that rest and I won't criticize the girl. Woman. I suppose she'd be in her fifties now."

"She is, and she's been left with a daughter dead and a granddaughter she'll have to raise."

Acidly, the woman rejoined, "Now that I am properly shamed, can we move along?"

Jaymie stifled a smile. "As if I'd ever dare shame you, Mrs. S. Becca told me that Kim and Franklin Vance were a hot item. Do you remember?"

"Certainly do. Caught them in the library stacks canoodling many a time. He was trouble, that young fellow. Good-looking as the devil and that *always* makes a boy troublesome."

Jaymie thought about Franklin Vance as he was now; he hardly looked the heart-throb. Time marched on. "I've heard that whatever she and Franklin had going it was over by the time graduation came around."

"Maybe. I'm sure your sister and Valetta Nibley remember all of that better than I. It was an unsettling time at the high school. There had been a rash of thefts from teachers' vehicles, and those boys, Vance and Charlie Roth —"

"Who?"

"Oh, I know he has some silly nickname now, but the Roth boy was given the perfectly good name Charles as a baby, and Charlie Roth he will always be to me. Charlie and Franklin were suspected of the thievery, but I always thought that Franklin Vance was far too smart to do that. If they were involved at all it's more likely that they got their little toady to do it for them."

"Toady?"

"Lackey. Minion. Someone toadying to another perceived to have more power or social cachet. Vance was popular despite his outlaw image, and Charlie Roth too. They had some little fellow following them around. What was his name? Kraut?"

It was too much of a coincidence. "You don't mean Russ Krauss?"

"That's who I mean! Insignificant little insect."

"You think Russ Krauss did Franklin's dirty work?"

"I can't be sure of that. Krauss was a sneaky boy and could have thought of it all on his own . . . maybe even trying to be a bad boy so the others would respect him. He was a troubled youngster. I caught him once under the bleachers trying to look up girls' skirts."

"He still seems creepy to me," Jaymie admitted, thinking of his threatening behavior at Alicia's property.

"Leopards, my dear, do not change their spots."

"I don't think that's always true," Jaymie protested. She saw the look in her old friend's eyes and held up one hand. "Don't call me naïve. I hate when people call me that. I simply think that people are capable of change. Sometimes they choose a different path than the one they seem set on."

"I think we must agree to disagree, my dear. I believe they simply get more careful over time."

With lots to think about, Jaymie said her goodbyes and took Hoppy home, where he promptly retreated to his basket, wiggling himself in beside Lilibet and falling asleep almost immediately. It had been a long day but she had promises to keep. Jaymie slipped Jocie's bracelet and card into her purse and went to pick her up at school. Kim was picking Mia up at the same time, and told Jaymie to follow them home. She'd put on tea. It sounded like it had been a wearying day for her as she murmured of having to juggle lawyer appointments, a visit with the detective, and trying to find paperwork necessary for a death certificate. Death is accompanied by too much paperwork, someone once said. For Kim the distraction of company might not be a bad thing.

When Jaymie and Jocie arrived at Kim's house in Wolverhampton she let them in.

Mother and daughter followed to the kitchen, where Jocie gave Mia the sparkly card and gift, a pink and silver bracelet with one silver star.

The little girl read the card, sniffled, and then smiled through tears as she slipped the bracelet on her wrist. "I like the colors," Mia said. She touched the star with one delicate finger. "I like the star . . . up in heaven." Her lip trembled.

"Pink is my favorite color," Jocie said. "I thought it would go with your leg."

Kim surreptitiously wiped a tear from her eye and smiled at the two girls.

There was a moment of awkward silence, but then Kim said, "What do you say, Mia?"

"Thank you," the little girl said shyly, still staring at her bracelet. "I live here now. Want to see my room?"

"Okay."

The two girls headed off, Jocie's thumping gait and Mia's uneven one echoing up the stairs. Kim smiled at Jaymie, her eyes watering, one tear overflowing and trickling down her cheek. She swiped at it with one finger and turned away, filling the kettle from the tap. She cleared her throat and said, "It's good to see her with friends. It hasn't been easy for her, being different. I think that's what worried me the most

227

about Alicia wanting to move away. Would Mia be able to make friends?"

"Jocie and her are ideal friends, in a way . . . both unique. Jocie was having a problem with a bully last year. I hope Mia hasn't suffered from that?"

"Alicia never mentioned it. I hope . . . I *think* she would have told me. We didn't agree on everything, but we both only wanted the best for Mia."

According to Wenda, Alicia was not fond of Russ. That was likely one of their main disagreements. Another area of disagreement was certainly Alicia's tentative plans to move to California. Jaymie sat where her hostess indicated. "It must have been especially hard after the accident. I understand Jace was driving when Mia was injured."

"Driving *drunk,*" Kim snapped. "Yes, he was. I never forgave him for . . ." She shook her head, then took in a long, shaky breath. "I *never* forgave him. I know Jace wasn't legally impaired and that he was under the legal limit, but still! And Alicia had the nerve to criticize Russ's driving! I could not believe the hypocrisy. Russ may have been reckless once or twice and has a couple of speeding tickets, but he has never had a DUI."

"It must have been hard for Jace's father,

Franklin, to know his son was guilty of such an awful thing?"

"I wouldn't know," she said stiffly. "I don't have anything to do with that family." Kim set the kettle on the stove and turned on the burner.

"How did Alicia get along with her father-in-law?"

Kim whirled and glared at Jaymie. "What do you mean by that? What are you insinuating?"

Taken aback, Jaymie stuttered, "N-n-nothing. I . . . was making conversation." Why the aggressive reaction to what seemed like an innocuous question?

"Hey, Kim? You here?"

"In the kitchen!"

Lew Vance entered, glanced at Jaymie, and did a double take. "Hey, you were at the farmer's market on Saturday with Clutch."

Kim turned back and glared at Jaymie. "Clutch Roth? What do you know about him?"

"He's a friend," Jaymie said, trying to ignore her palpitations and sweaty palms. "I told you that."

"No, you didn't."

"Yes, I did, Kim, while we were having tea at Wellington's Retreat."

"Clutch Roth is *your* friend," she restated

in a flat tone, unable to conceive of it, it seemed.

Jaymie's anger rose. "Yes, he is my friend. His daughter had disappeared. I helped find her body and convict the young woman's killer and we became friends. Why is that a surprise?"

Lew glanced back and forth between the two women. "Hey, what's going on here?"

"Nothing," Kim said, subdued. "I think I'm going crazy is all. I'm sorry, Jaymie. Maybe you did tell me. I swear, I hear things and they go right out of my head."

"That's grief," Jaymie said in a soft voice. "And it's okay to feel that way. You're not going crazy. You'll get through it."

She nodded wearily. "What do you want, Lew?"

He hesitated and glanced toward Jaymie, then turned his attention back to Kim. "Dad wanted to know if we can use Alicia's garage for storage."

Kim shot a look toward Jaymie. "I . . . guess it's okay. Just . . . be aware — Russ is storing tools there, in the garage."

Lew nodded. Jaymie looked back and forth between the two, noticing the unspoken words; it was a warning. Did Lew, Franklin and Russ not get along? Was there danger if the men confronted each other?

"You know the combination on the lock and the garage door opener code hasn't changed. Don't let Russ know for now. Let me handle it."

"Okay, Kim."

The front door slammed shut. Russ Krauss tromped into the kitchen and stopped dead at the door, looking between Lew and Jaymie, and sending a questioning look to Kim. "What's going on?"

Kim wearily turned away and began running water in the sink, squirting dish detergent over a stack of mugs and bowls. "Nothing, Russ. What are you doing home so early?"

He plunked a fast-food bag down on the table and slipped off his jacket. He slung it over a chair and said, "I got dinner. I thought Mia might like her favorite, chicken tenders with plum sauce, and thin French fries. You know the kind she likes, thin and crispy?" He sounded almost uncertain. "I got extra plum sauce."

Lew, who had been shuffling his feet, said, "I guess I'll take off, then."

"What did you come here for?" Russ said, his tone belligerent.

As Lew shuffled his feet, not knowing how to answer, Kim looked undecided, then with an exasperated sigh she said, "Russ, Lew asked if he could store a car or two in Alicia's garage. I said okay."

Russ nodded. There was no explosion and Kim appeared relieved.

"We'll be moving a couple of cars in tomorrow or the next day. Thanks for letting us . . . for letting me . . ." His voice had choked and Jaymie looked up at him, surprised. There were tears standing in his eyes. He swallowed. "Kim, I . . ." He didn't finish whatever he was going to say, shook his head and turned away. "I'd better go." He stopped at the kitchen door and said, over his shoulder, "Maybe . . . maybe I can take Mia out for an ice cream? Not now, but . . . sometime?"

Kim didn't answer and he left, his shoulders sagging.

"What gives him the right to ask that?" Russ said, pointing after the departing Lew. "Hey, Kim? What gives him the right to use Alicia's garage and ask to take Mia anywhere?"

Interesting that he waited until Lew had left before voicing his displeasure, Jaymie thought.

"Shut up, Russ," Kim said, giving a significant glance in Jaymie's direction. "I'm Alicia's executor and Mia's guardian and I'll decide who gets to do what. Everyone else can drop on their heads." She sighed, then said, her voice softer, "Mia is Lew's niece, Russ. Let it go."

"I'm going to take a shower." He flung himself from the room and clomped up the stairs.

There was an awkward silence, almost a vacuum in the room left as the aftereffect of such tension. Jaymie was at a loss for words, but talking from the heart was the best way to break through and overcome such tension. "Kim, I want you to know, my heart goes out to you. I've been thinking about you ever since we had tea this morning, about you and Mia and Erin, how you must be feeling. I'd like to do something for you, if you'll let me."

The woman turned from staring out the window over the sink. Her eyes were full of tears and she looked weary. She slumped down in a chair at the table and buried her face in her hands. "I don't know what anyone can do for me right now."

Jaymie bent toward her. "I can figure out who killed your daughter. Who followed her into the woods and took her life." Jaymie's voice was trembling and choked. "I'm *angry* that poor Alicia, walking through the woods to come speak to me, was killed. I'll do what I can to help find out who did it."

Kim looked up, and there was hope in her eyes. "If we knew . . . if that person would pay . . . I think I could start to move on. Move ahead. Not get over it but . . ." She made an impatient gesture.

"I can't fully understand, no one ever will, but I imagine it's like living through a nightmare every day for you and Mia. If you knew who that person was, if you knew they'd go to jail, it might help. Infinitesimally, but some relief is better than none."

Finally Kim appeared to relax, to breathe. She nodded. "Right now I'm dealing with so much: paperwork, and the police and the fear that whoever killed my Alicia is out there, watching Mia." With one swift look to the door through which Russ had departed, she said, in a low tone, "I'll do anything I can to find out who did that to my daughter. I know you've done this before but I haven't, and I'm scared. What if whoever did it comes after us? How can I protect Mia? The police aren't doing a damn thing."

"I understand you feeling that way, and I'm nervous too. After all, she was coming to me to confide something."

Kim looked startled and stared into Jaymie's eyes. "What?"

"I don't know what. I wish I did. But Kim,

234

as for the police . . . I know it seems like they haven't made any progress, that they aren't doing anything, but they are. Much of what the police do, we don't see. They are working hard behind the scenes to catch the person who did this."

She paused. How could she approach this next subject without Kim becoming angry at the police? Their investigation of Alicia was what sent her into a fearful tailspin, resulting in the walk through the woods that ended in her death. The law of unintended consequences, Jaymie had heard it called.

It was probably best to not raise the issue of police involvement and how they had used Jaymie at all. "That being said, I am coming at this from a different angle than the police, and from time to time I've been able to help. I'm not a detective, but I am resourceful."

Kim took in a deep quivering breath. She was still in the fragile shattering first few days after losing a loved one. "How can I help?"

A tight knot of fear released in Jaymie's chest. Her one worry was that Kim would tell her to take a hike and leave them alone. "First, do you suspect anyone? Anyone at all."

Kim wove her fingers together on the table

in front of her and stared at them. She wore no rings and her nails were blunt and short and unpolished. She was a long way from the high school temptress of Mrs. Stubbs's stories. She had grown up, as women do, and perhaps grown past the need to garner the admiration of men. "Alicia was seeing someone, but she wouldn't tell me who."

"Why do you think that is?"

Kim shrugged. "She thought I wouldn't approve? That's all I can think of."

"And do you suspect this guy, whoever he is?"

"Don't they say it's usually the husband or boyfriend?"

"True. But I never think it's wise to focus on one person to the exclusion of others. What do you know about the guy?"

"I think I know who it is."

"Oh?" Jaymie's heart thudded as she remembered Nicki's assertion that it was Russ Krauss. What would she say if Kim mentioned him? "Who is it?"

Kim looked up and met Jaymie's steady gaze. Thunder rumbled, shaking the house. "Lew Vance."

FOURTEEN

It made sense, and given the tears in Lew's eyes minutes before, seemed likely. Why would she hide that from her mother? It would be unusual but not unheard of to date or even marry a late husband's brother. Alicia and Kim's relationship was complicated. Jaymie understood complicated mother-daughter dynamics firsthand — she and her own mother had a complicated bond. It didn't mean you didn't tell your mother stuff. There was a thud in the hall, and then a thump overhead. Jaymie started, and so did Kim.

"Mia? Is everything okay?" Kim called as she got up and went out the kitchen door to the bottom of the stairs.

"Everything's okay, Grandma," the girl called down. "I was getting my rag doll down for Jocie to see."

Kim came back to the table and sat down. "She loves that rag doll. My mom made it for her before she passed away two years ago. She loved Mia."

Probably the grandmother whose kitchen tools Alicia had been bringing over to Jaymie. "You were saying that you thought Alicia was seeing Lew Vance. Why do you think that?"

"Partly because I can't imagine anyone else she'd be dating that she would hide from me. And Lew was spending a *lot* of time with them. Also, Lew has been selling off his stuff lately, like he's planning on going somewhere."

"Harkening back to Alicia's tentative plans to move to California," Jaymie mused. "Did Alicia ever express any fear to you?" Jaymie asked, thinking of the note Wenda mentioned, trying to find a way to bring it up.

"Fear? Of what? Or who?"

"Anyone." Jaymie hesitated, watching Kim, then went on, "Alicia told a friend that if anything ever happened to her, to tell you to find the note she'd left."

"To tell *me*? About a note?" Kim blinked rapidly but remained still otherwise. "Who said that?" Her expression quickly shifted from mystification to realization. "I'll bet it was that girl at QCB." She watched Jaymie and nodded. "It's that ditz queen, Wenda. She's a gossip and a drama queen and I wouldn't trust her as far as I could throw her."

"Oh?"

"Sure. Russ tells me all the stories about her. She makes herself important by inventing things."

Jaymie was interested in that take on Wenda and that it came from Russ, but for the moment she let it go. "Kim, do you ever wonder if any of this goes back to Jace's death?"

"Why do you ask?" Her expression was guardedly neutral.

Nothing but the truth . . . "Alicia was afraid she was going to be arrested. I heard that directly from her. She was *really* scared. But we know she didn't do it," Jaymie said, though she wasn't completely confident of that. "What did she have to be afraid of?" Not wishing to influence Kim, she didn't ask yet if Alicia may have known something about Jace's death, maybe even who had murdered her husband.

Kim bit her lip and stared at Jaymie for a long minute. "After it happened there was a lot of gossip going around. You don't know how many people on social media kept saying things like, *What wife wouldn't check on her husband? Or, What kind of woman leaves her husband outside all night long? It doesn't make sense. She* must *have had something to do with it.* I got so sick of it! I'd be scared too if people kept looking at me with suspicion. You know the old saying . . . no smoke without fire. People kept quoting that, like they'd made it up."

"It got around that she and Jace weren't getting along. Someone said to me that they weren't even sleeping in the same room anymore."

"People have got nothing better to do than spread rumors and lies," Kim muttered. "Vicious! I *hate* all this social media stuff. She had to lock hers down."

"I understand your feeling," Jaymie replied. "As unfair as it is, that may be the kind of gossip that started the suspicion against her." Plus the knowledge some had that she was seeing someone else while she was married. Jaymie couldn't think of a tactful way to approach that topic, so let it alone for the moment. "What do you know about the day Jace died?"

"Do you honestly think Alicia's murder is tied up with that? Why? Couldn't her killer have been . . . oh, I don't know, some lunatic who followed her into the woods?"

Jaymie hesitated a moment to find the right words, and then said, "It's always possible, but nine times out of ten in cases like this — not a robbery, not a home invasion, not a drug crime — the victim knows their attacker. This was not a crime of opportunity, no robbery, or . . ." She shied away from saying sexual assault. "It was personal, using a tool Alicia was carrying. If we can figure out if anyone had a grudge against her, or what was going on in her life . . . Kim, I think we *need* to go back that far. The start of much of this seems, to me, to be Jace's tragic death. First . . . do you think Jace's death was murder?"

Kim frowned and glanced away. "Let me check on the girl."

"Do you want me to go up and check on Jocie?"

"No. I'll be right back." She was gone only a couple of minutes. Some of the tension had eased out of her when she returned, and she had a half smile on her face. "They're playing with Mia's rag doll and her stuffed animals. Jocie is such a nice kid."

"Her dad has been a wonderful father, and I'm trying to do my part now."

Kim got serious. Keeping her voice low, she recounted that day, most of which Jaymie already knew. She had spoken to Alicia twice that day, once around noon and then later; she had sensed tension in Alicia's voice. That wasn't unusual, Alicia and Jace were having marital trouble. As Jaymie suspected, Alicia was still angry over Mia's injury.

"He hadn't, in her opinion, taken responsibility," Kim said, echoing a common phrase concerning the couple's troubles. "Oh, he apologized, and I think he was deeply hurt. He did love his daughter. But that family . . . Franklin raised those boys to never admit they were wrong and a lot of that was in Jace. The angrier Alicia got, the more stubborn Jace became."

"Sounds like they were at a marital impasse."

"By the time of his death they were in a deadlock," she confirmed. She met Jaymie's gaze. "You asked me, do I think Jace was murdered? Truthfully, I don't know. Sometimes I think yes, sometimes I think no. More important to me is, how would Jace's death help my daughter? It didn't, and I made damn sure the police knew that at the time when they danced around that question with me. Those two would have worked it out or divorced, but she had no reason to kill him. I'll *never* believe Alicia had anything to do with it."

"She told me despite an insurance payout from the accident, medical bills for Mia almost bankrupted them."

Kim nodded.

"And that Jace didn't have any life insurance at the time of his death."

"He had a policy once but cashed it in for mortgage money. So shortsighted. Life insurance is cheap, but I guess when your electric is being shut off every dollar counts. Mind you, he didn't have the guts to tell Alicia that," Kim said contemptuously. "She didn't find out until . . ." She stopped dead and froze, her eyes wide.

"Until . . . ?"

Kim shook her head.

"Until Jace was dead and she tried to collect?"

Kim, stony-faced, gave a slight tilt of her head. "Alicia didn't kill Jace. I know that in my bones," she said, one hand flattened over her breastbone.

"That day she said she was going to Port Huron with Mia to shop for the start of school. But she wasn't, was she? I have reliable information that she was going to meet a lover."

Kim's lined face spasmed and she nodded, wiping the corner of her eye. "She was seeing some guy on the side. I tried to stay out of it. Alicia and I . . . we argued too often, and I was trying, at that point, to be supportive. She had enough on her plate."

"Do you know who it was?"

She nodded. "Lew. I think she was seeing Lew Vance. Then and still. She never told me, but that's who it was. And is."

Alicia had been working for Debbie Vance and five years ago Debbie and Lew were still married. If Alicia and Lew were having an affair, did Debbie know about it? How much better revenge would that be if she killed Jace and framed Alicia?

That was a devious way to get revenge, though. Why not just kill Alicia? Unless . . . Jaymie considered the thought. Would she kill Jace, then wait five years and kill Alicia? It would certainly be a long time to hold a grudge, but maybe the point was to make Alicia suffer before killing her. Jealousy can take hold, planting a seed to grow a fury that burned deep. Maybe Debbie had planned to let it go. Maybe she had gotten over it in the intervening five years, but perhaps Alicia figured out recently that Debbie killed Jace and was about to report her suspicions to the police. In that case, killing Alicia would simply be self-preservation, not long-burning jealousy. She needed to speak to Debbie Vance now that she knew who she was and decide if her hypothesis was even possible.

There was a more likely scenario that

could explain Jace's death, the oldest murder tale ever written, Cain and Abel. Did Lew Vance kill his brother to get him out of Alicia's life? Had Alicia started to suspect it?

She sighed and regarded Kim, who had covered her face with both hands and was scrubbing her eyes with her knuckles. Instead of homing in on suspects for Alicia's murder, she seemed to be gathering new suspects, ones she hadn't anticipated. Still . . . she couldn't forget Nicki's guess that it was Russ who Alicia was having an affair with. If that was true and Kim knew about it and yet still stayed with the man, maybe she would divert suspicion from Russ by putting the attention on Lew. "Are you sure it was Lew she was seeing?"

Kim shrugged. "It's what I believe. I've told you why. I think he's been in love with her since her and Jace first got together."

Family gatherings must have been complicated if that was true. "I only remember the tragedy — Jace's death — vaguely. Did the police come to any conclusions? How did they leave it with you?"

"Jace's death certificate says what medically caused his death, but it leaves how it happened — accident or homicide — open, or 'undetermined.' " Her eyes took on a

245

misty look of remembrance. "I recall that day clearly. I was working then at the school district office, a temp position. I got off at noon and called Alicia to see if she wanted me to pick up lunch and bring it to her. It was supposed to be her last day cleaning. I thought I'd meet her wherever she was, take her lunch, and we'd celebrate her promotion. She told me she had the day off and was shopping with Mia, but when I asked her to put Mia on the phone, she brushed me off, said she had to go. I know now it's because Mia wasn't with her. I got . . . I don't know how to describe it, this weird feeling," she said, hand on her chest. "I couldn't breathe. Something was up."

Kim's expression, bleached and fearful, was mesmerizing. "What do you mean by that?"

"I thought she was making arrangements to divorce. I believed that she was at a lawyer right that moment."

"Were you happy about that?"

Kim frowned and pursed her lips in thought. "I was . . . I guess I was hopeful."

"Hopeful?" Whatever Jaymie had expected, it wasn't that.

Kim shook her head in dismay. "You don't understand what that family had been through, how they'd suffered, when Mia was

246

injured. We thought my beautiful grand-daughter was going to die." She grabbed a tissue from a box on the table and dabbed at her eyes. "I was hopeful that Alicia was finally moving forward. Hopeful she could move on. Looking back . . ."

Tears ran down her cheeks. "I didn't like Jace. I was angry. So was everyone who loved Mia . . . angry that he had almost killed her." She glanced toward the door leading out to the hall. Her voice clogged, she said, "If she left Jace I was hopeful that it would be a clean break and I wouldn't have to see him every stinking day." She blinked and swiped the tears away, then tossed the sodden tissue. She ripped another from the box on the table and again dried her red-rimmed eyes. "Looking back I wonder . . . could I have done things differently?"

"What do you mean?"

"Could I have . . . I don't know. Pushed more, interfered more. Demanded more of Alicia. I was worried . . . fearful. Uneasy."

"What do you think caused that feeling?"

"I think I had a premonition."

"A premonition Jace was going to die?"

"No, not that specifically. But that something was going to go horribly wrong. I had it before Mia's accident too."

Jaymie watched her for a moment; the woman clearly believed what she was saying, that she had a sense of impending tragedy. "Did you get one before Alicia died?"

She shook her head.

"Why do you think that is?"

The woman's eyes again filled with tears, the red staining around her eyes rimming them in swollen sorrow as they dampened yet again. "How could I imagine I would lose a daughter?"

"You talked to Alicia twice that day, the day Jace died?"

"She called me later in the afternoon about . . . something unimportant, I don't remember what."

"When and how did you hear about Jace's death?"

She dabbed gently at her eyes. They must be stinging by now, made delicate and raw by the repeated tears gathering. Salt crusting in the corners dried in white flakes. She licked the tip of her finger and swiped at the salt crust, then dabbed again with the tissue. "That was the next day. Alicia called me, hysterical. She told me to come get Mia, that Mia couldn't see her dad that way. I asked how, what way, but she couldn't talk. I guess Lew found Jace. Terrible for him." After a pause she added, "Look, I don't want you to get the wrong impression. Lew's not a bad guy, but . . . that family!" She sighed gustily. "So much drama!"

Another possible solution occurred to Jaymie. With a shock to her system and a wide-eyed glance at Kim she considered: if Alicia and Lew were having an affair, did they conspire *together* to kill Jace? Did it seem easier than divorce? They only had Alicia's word for it that her lover did not meet her at the motel. Were Alicia and Lew actually together that day killing her husband? It was all too possible. Or, if she thought about it a different way, maybe Alicia was telling the truth; she had been stood up at the motel (as Nicki related) because Lew took the opportunity to kill his brother. "What did Alicia tell you about it all . . . Jace's death? Did she think it was an accident?"

"At first, yes. She was shocked when the police started questioning her about her whereabouts the day before. It never occurred to her it was anything but an accident." Her expression darkened. "I could tell by the questions they asked me, the cops were ready to pin it on my Alicia. I told them she'd never do anything of the kind. It wasn't in her, to take away her little girl's daddy."

"That garage . . . it's pretty big. Was that where he worked most of the time?"

Kim nodded. "He had worked in garages in Wolverhampton, but after the accident he went through a period of unemployment. Working in his own garage brought in money." She sighed and looked down at the tabletop. "He was a good mechanic. That whole family . . . they understand cars. He was good about fixing my old beater. I could always rely on him: he always said, *Mom, you and Erin come to me and I'll make sure you're safe.* He checked over every vehicle I was thinking of buying and advised me on whether it was a good buy or not."

"It sounds like he did his best for you."

Kim nodded. "Looking back, I see that. I guess at the time . . . I was so angry." She left it there, that her anger at Jace had over-ridden any memory of the good moments with him as a son-in-law.

"He worked for anyone who asked?"

"People took to dropping in and he'd look at their car, tell them what was wrong."

The million-dollar question . . . "Whose was he looking at that day, the day he died? As I understand it Jace already had another car up on jack stands. Whose pickup was he

250

working on that killed him?"

"I . . . have no idea."

Jaymie frowned and eyed her. That hesitation . . . she was almost certain Kim did know who the truck belonged to. Why wouldn't she say? Was it worth it to press her on it? Someone had to know. "Kim, do you think Alicia knew who killed her husband, or suspected someone?"

Kim started to shake her head, but then stopped, her mouth slowly opening and her head tilting. "Maybe."

"Who may she have suspected?"

Clumping footsteps echoed down the stairs. Russ Krauss, wearing flannel elastic-waisted pants and a T-shirt stretched over his belly, his thin hair damp, entered. "Can we eat early?" he said, ignoring Jaymie.

There was silence for a moment, then Kim sighed deeply. "Why?"

He sat heavily in a chair and glared past Jaymie. "I went to the trouble of getting Mia's favorite dinner. I thought you'd be happy." There was a whine in his voice.

Kim glanced at Jaymie. "Uh . . . I'll get the girls so that you and Jocie can head out."

And that was that. Russ was present and even walked with Kim to the door. There was no chance for further conversation.

■ ■ ■ ■

At home she put dinner in the oven. Jocie and Jakob were out walking Hoppy in the Christmas tree field, so Jaymie called Val. They chatted, then Jaymie said, "I'm so tangled up in all of this, Val. I'm confused. I don't know who is telling the truth and who is lying."

"Talk to me, kid. Who are your suspects?" Val was the ideal sounding board.

"Let's start with immediate family. I have to admit, Alicia could have killed Jace. She lied to her mother where she was that day, probably because she was meeting up with her lover and was ashamed, or because her lover was Lew and she didn't want anyone to know, or because her lover was Russ Krauss and she didn't want her mom to know for obvious reasons."

"Russ Krauss? Are we actually considering him as a possible lover for Alicia?"

"That's who Nicki thinks she was seeing. It's unlikely, I guess, but it would explain why she never told her mother who she was seeing. And it's possible that either alone or with a co-conspirator Alicia set up the accident that killed Jace."

"So . . . Alicia and Russ, or Alicia and

Lew? Are we speculating that Alicia talked Jace's brother or Russ into killing him?" Her tone was powerfully laced with skepticism.

"I get that it feels far-fetched, but it's not the weirdest thing I've ever heard. Alicia had motive — she was furious with Jace — and, listen to this, she thought that Jace still had life insurance at his time of death. She only found out later, after he was dead — I got this from something Kim said — that Jace had cashed in his life insurance."

"Ah, money! She expected an insurance payout. With Alicia dead, how are you ever going to know? Do you suspect Kim at all? Because Kim could have implied that to throw the suspicion on Alicia. Though, on second thought, why would she do that? She doesn't know you're investigating."

Jaymie was silent for a moment. "Well, actually . . ."

"You didn't tell her that?"

Jaymie's stomach dropped. It had been a mistake, the kind she didn't make often anymore, the mistake of freely letting it be known that she was snooping, aka looking into a murder. "I kind of did."

"Oh, Jaymie! You were the one freaking out that someone might know you were in possession of information!"

"I know, I *know,*" she said, irritated.

"Don't make it worse than it is. At that point I didn't suspect Kim at all, and thought she wanted to find out who killed her daughter. I told her I wanted to help. But you're right, Kim certainly had a reason to kill Jace. She was so angry still she was shaking, all these years later and with Jace dead, that he had been responsible for hurting Mia. And yet shortly after, she was saying how helpful he had been to her, checking her and Erin's vehicles for them."

"She wouldn't have killed Alicia, though . . . would she?"

Jaymie thought about it as she leaned on the kitchen counter and stared through the gathering gloom into the woods. She shivered. "Who knows? Val, Alicia was thinking of moving to California — possibly with her boyfriend, who may or may not be Lew Vance — and taking Mia. Kim has said she'd die without Mia."

"That's a powerful motive, but strong enough to kill her daughter?"

"If you add in that maybe she found out Alicia had been fooling around with Russ? Or had known the identity of Alicia's lover all these years but let it ride rather than end up separated from her granddaughter?"

"You could be on to something," Val said. A loud meow and a purr echoed in the phone. "Denver knows I'm speaking to you."

"Oh, come on!"

"It's true! He ignores me on the phone unless I'm talking to you. Something about your voice . . . cats have extraordinary hearing."

Jaymie smiled and listened to the purr. "Hey, Denver! How are you, buddy?" Sobering, she said, "Val? There are other suspects, though. Listen to this: if it's possible that Alicia was having an affair with Lew Vance five years ago, his wife may have known."

"Even if that's true, why would she kill Jace?"

"Maybe she wouldn't, but . . . hear me out." Jaymie repeated what she had thought through, about Debbie hypothetically killing Jace to set Alicia up on a murder rap, and then killing Alicia as final payback, or because her employee had figured out her culpability in killing Jace. It sounded weaker out loud than it had in her head. "If she knew that Alicia and maybe Lew together killed Jace . . ." Jaymie gathered her thoughts. "No, to be rational I guess Debbie Vance doesn't have much of a reason to kill Alicia."

"Unless . . . Jaymie, what if she was still hoping to get Lew back? Maybe Alicia figured she and Debbie were friends, and she and Lew have been divorced for years so she told Debbie that she was planning to move to California with him. Maybe Debbie snapped?"

"Weak, but possible. A stronger possibility is Russ Krauss." Jaymie explained all she had learned about him, and all she felt about him from meeting him a couple of times. "And Alicia, unless she suspected him in Jace's killing, wouldn't have thought anything of him walking through the woods with her. I keep thinking she was walking with whoever killed her, like . . . she trusted them."

"Couldn't it have been someone following her and attacking her?"

"No, it can't be. Listen, she had that bag of whisks. An attacker wouldn't stop and take the time to damage the whisk to make a weapon. The killer had time with the whisk. It wasn't a spur-of-the-moment attack. She was walking with her murderer."

"Okay, you make a compelling argument, Counselor, now . . . who else is on your list?"

"Erin Hansen and Franklin Vance."

"Whoa. One victim's sister and one victim's father? Make your case."

Jaymie set the phone on a stand and

tapped the speakerphone button, then started assembling dishes for dinner. "Okay, could Franklin Vance have killed his son? He likely had the capability, he knows jacks, he's strong enough. Did he have a motive? I don't know. Maybe. How did he feel about his granddaughter being injured? Or there could be other reasons we don't even know about at this point. I'll have to snoop around. Why kill Alicia? I have no clue, unless she knew about him killing Jace?"

"Okay, now Erin . . . ?"

"Kim says the sisters did not get along at all. But . . . really, I can't imagine a strong enough reason. I mean, Erin may have wanted to kill Jace for what happened to Mia. But then to kill Alicia? Doesn't make sense."

"So . . . both Franklin and Erin are low on the suspect list."

"I guess. I'll keep them in mind, though."

"Kim, Lew, Russ and Debbie," Val said. "Those are your primary suspects, at least in the killing of Alicia. What do you need to find out to figure out whodunnit?"

Jaymie reached up to get cups for dinner. "Ideally, I'd figure out both crimes and see if they are tied together. I keep going back and forth on that. I mean, it all changes if Alicia actually killed her husband; then I could make a case for Franklin killing Alicia. He'd have a powerful motive. My immediate priority is to find out two things: who was she cheating on Jace with five years ago, and who was she going with now? Are they the same person? Different people?"

"How can I help?"

"I don't know yet. How about thinking back to high school . . . oh, *ah,* I've had a brainstorm!"

"What is it?"

"I met Debbie Vance the other day and I couldn't figure out why she looked so familiar. I knew her in high school. Her name was Debbie Kouris then! She was class president in our senior year. We were in the same year, though she is a little younger than I am. I wish I'd remembered that the other day when I met her in the QCB office, I would have chatted her up."

"Does that get you anywhere?"

"Not really."

They both laughed then agreed to talk the next day. Val would get out her high school yearbooks to see if they triggered any memories of Kim and Franklin.

Jakob, carrying a weary Hoppy, and Jocie came in smelling of pine and fresh cool air. Both washed up while Jaymie fed the animals. Dinner came out of the oven, and then it was homework — more work on Jo-cie's presentation — pajamas and bed. Jakob and Jaymie crawled into bed and lay in the dark talking about their day.

Conversation turned to what Jaymie had so far discovered.

"I bought a car from Lew once," Jakob said, turning on his side. "For Mom and Dad. Good car, great deal." He hesitated, on the edge of saying something.

Jaymie could feel him tense. "What's wrong?" she whispered.

"Uh . . . Gus came to me today. He told me Tami would like to talk to you."

Jaymie drew in a quick breath. "I don't . . . I can't —"

"It's okay, honey," Jakob said, rubbing her arm. "I told him there was no way you were going to go to see her. She's going to write you a letter. She remembers the day Jace died and wants to try to help figure out who did it. Is that okay?"

"Okay. All right. A letter is good."

Jakob was soon sleeping, but Jaymie lay awake for a couple of hours, reliving events of almost two years ago and the last time she saw Tami, not a good memory. She finally turned her mind to pleasanter thoughts: Canadian Thanksgiving coming, then American, and then Christmas. Only then did she drift off to asleep.

FIFTEEN

Phone to her ear, Jaymie tapped her fingernails on the tabletop and, restless, got up and paced to the window. She turned her back on the woods view and paced back to the trestle table, where her tablet was open beside her notebook. Finally, Vestry answered.

"Detective!" Jaymie said. "How are things going?"

"Ah, Detective Jaymie, how are you this morning?"

A witticism from Vestry, how unusual. As irritating as she found the woman's joke, she did her best to play along. "The game is afoot, Detective."

"Please tell me you haven't been investigating," Vestry said.

The detective likely knew she had been snooping and asking questions. She had to tread carefully. "Of course not," she said, fingers crossed. "People do tend to talk to me, though. I can't help that. I saw the department's statement online. You have a person or persons of interest that you are not free to talk about at this moment and ask the community to come forward with any tips. I'm the public, and I have tips."

"Okay. Shoot."

As concisely as possible, Jaymie summed up all she had heard, including about the note Wenda Puchala had mentioned, and Kim's dismissal of it. Vestry interjected occasionally and finally said, referring to the purported note, "I can tell you we have searched Alicia Vance's house and have come across nothing of that sort. We have her home files in our possession, and someone is going through them for pertinent information."

"I appreciate you listening to me, Detective. You did, after all, enlist me for my help." She paused then said, "Is it okay if I run past you some of my thoughts?"

There was a sigh on the other end, but the detective said, "Could I stop you even if I tried?"

Jaymie was silent.

"Okay, sure. I've got nothing better to do."

Whether it was meant as jest or irony, Jaymie didn't care. "Okay, first, I know you'll have considered most of this . . .

maybe all of it. I do appreciate you listening."

"I have five minutes, Jaymie. Shoot."

"I have a couple of people in mind, and it comes down to whether you think Jace's and Alicia's deaths are linked. I had to consider that it's possible that Alicia killed her husband. She did hold Jace responsible for Mia's injury and was still angry at him to the point of dissolving the marriage. I believe she was having an affair with someone at the time of his death, perhaps with someone close to her."

"Close to her?"

Jaymie took a deep breath; if she was going to do this, she was going to do it completely. "Yes, close to her. You'll have all of this in your files, I'm sure, but I think unless she killed Jace herself — which I doubt — then she was at a motel waiting for her lover, who never arrived. I think that's what you were talking about when you told me there were discrepancies in her story of what she did that day. Two names have been mentioned to me as possible lovers: Lew Vance, whose name has been mentioned by more than one person — including Kim Hansen, by the way — or Russ Krauss. Both would likely have the knowhow to set up an accident with a jack.

But I don't know . . . Jace wouldn't have let the guy anywhere near his garage. No one in the family seems to have any use for Russ Krauss. It's possible that Alicia suspected him of killing her husband but was unsure. She may have been trying to decide if she should turn him in, knowing how it would damage her relationship with her mother. Maybe that's what she wanted to talk to me about. That's all true whether Alicia and Russ had an affair back five years ago or not."

"Alicia and Russ . . . okay, go on," Vestry said.

"If it was Lew Vance she was having an affair with five years ago — if she was angry enough at Jace, cheating with his brother might feel like payback — he may have used the opportunity of having Alicia safely out of the house to kill his brother."

"Why would he kill his brother, though?"

Jaymie frowned down at the tabletop. "Jealousy, to get him out of the way so he could marry Alicia?"

"If that's the case, what has stopped them from marrying in the five years since?"

"Maybe she suspected he'd killed Jace?" Jaymie paused, and thought about the next name on her list. She took a deep breath and let it out slowly. "I hate to say this, but

I've considered whether Kim may have killed her daughter."

There was a swift intake of breath on the other end.

"I know it sounds crazy, but there *is* a motive. Alicia had been preparing to leave Michigan to move to California. Kim loves her granddaughter deeply, profoundly, more than she loves anyone else on earth. Would that be enough motive? Especially if . . . if Alicia had, indeed, had an affair with Russ. Would Kim, in anger, jealousy, and a determination to keep her granddaughter close, kill Alicia?" She paused and sighed. "I don't think so, and I sure don't want it to be so, but I had to put it out there.

"There are two more names on my list. First, Franklin Vance. If he believed Alicia was responsible for Jace's death, would he kill her in retribution? That feels weak to me because he doesn't seem like the type to stew for five years before taking revenge. And it's the same for the last name, Debbie Vance. If she found out Alicia and Lew had been having an affair, would she have killed Alicia out of jealousy? Now, she might wait five years in one case." Jaymie explained her theory about Debbie setting Alicia up to take the fall for Jace's death, and when that didn't work, killing her.

Vestry was silent for a moment, then said, "That's . . . comprehensive."

Jaymie scratched the surface of the table. "I can't help thinking about it, and this is the result. You have access to more than I have — like people's alibis at the time of Jace's and Alicia's deaths and forensic clues — but I thought I'd run it by you in the interest of full disclosure."

"Full disclosure, yes. I *have* asked you to keep me in the loop. So thank you."

"Do any of the people I've mentioned have alibis for either murder?"

"Jaymie, you don't honestly expect me to share that information with you?"

"Okay, I get it. Overstepping the boundaries. If I find anything else out —"

"Jaymie, stop! I did ask for your help initially, and I get that you're like a bloodhound — once on the trail it's hard to call you off. However, I would appreciate it if you would *stay out of it* from now on."

"I'd love to but I'm having trouble with that." She rested her head in her free hand and stifled a sob. "I'm worried for my family. I know what you said, but I can't let it go, you must understand that. I won't get in your way, I promise, but Detective, it happened so close and Alicia was on her way to see me and I feel so terrible about

266

poor little Mia and I can't help feeling responsible . . . *she was on her way to see me.*" It all came out in a rush. She wiped away the brimming tears. "I'm not sleeping. I see poor Alicia every time I close my eyes. I'm still uneasy about the woods across the road."

"Maybe it will help if I tell you that the Brouwers have allowed us to place cameras at strategic places on the property."

Homely sayings about barn doors being closed against horses that had already escaped occurred to Jaymie.

"In fact, that's how we know you were at Alicia's, and that Russ Krauss showed up."

Taken aback, Jaymie was silent for a moment then said, "True. Once I realized that her path was through the woods I had to see it from the other angle. Russ seemed . . . hostile." She paused, debated her next words, then said, "I know about his past, Detective, that he was in jail for manslaughter. Is he one of the persons of interest from the police press release on the *Howler* site?"

"I'm not telling you that, Jaymie."

"He seemed vaguely threatening and I don't know why," Jaymie mused. "His hostility is why I started wondering about him, why I put him on my list. Look, I didn't call to pick your brain. I did call to tell you what I know, and now I've done that. If I find anything else out, I'll let you know." Even as she said it she heard the irritation in her own voice, and recognized it was anger fueled by a feeling of helplessness.

"Good to know," Vestry said, her tone crisp and abrupt. "I have to go."

Sixteen

Wolverhampton was quiet on a drizzly fall-ish morning as the wind whipped rain in sheets across the street. Jaymie parked the SUV in the lot behind the newspaper building and ran along the side wall of the building to the front reception doors, scooting in and shaking herself.

Erin Hansen looked up from her computer, ready with a smile to say hello, and recognized Jaymie. "Oh . . . hi. How are you? Nan isn't in her office yet, she's back on the printing floor talking to the production manager. Will you wait here?"

"Sure," Jaymie said. She leaned on the high counter and watched Erin tap away on the keyboard for a moment, then went to the front window that overlooked the street. She traced a raindrop on its path down the window, thinking of all she had learned, and all she needed to learn if she was ever going to help figure out who killed Alicia. She turned to find Erin watching her, a troubled expression on her pretty face. "Are you . . ." Jaymie stopped and shook her head. It was silly to ask if Erin was okay. Her sister had been murdered; of course she wasn't okay. She approached the counter again and looked down into Erin's eyes, clouded by sudden tears. "I'm sorry, Erin," she said softly, knowing there was nothing else to say to someone grieving so profound a loss.

Erin shook her head and swiped at the wetness in her eyes. She had slender white hands and long nails painted an imperfect pale pink, one ragged edge ruining the symmetry. "I feel . . . empty. I keep thinking, why am I so upset? Alicia and I never got along. *Ever.* Sometimes I even thought I hated her. Why am I heartbroken?"

"She was your sister, and despite whatever came between you, you love her," Jaymie said, thinking of Becca and how she'd feel if she was suddenly gone. "She's a part of your life, your story. She is your mother's daughter, your niece's mom, woven into your life like a thread that leaves a frayed hole when it unravels."

Erin nodded her head eagerly, her breath catching on a sob. "That's it! It's like . . . like a hole I'll never fill." She sniffed back the tears. "An Alicia-shaped tear in my life," she moaned, her voice choking. "I can never make up for the nasty things I've said, the fights we had. I always thought there'd be more time." She took in a ragged breath as her computer blooped and she checked the screen. "Nan's ready for you," she said, then met Jaymie's gaze and stared at her for a long silent moment. "You know, I keep trying to fill in the last few days of Alicia's life. Something was bugging her, something big, but I don't know what it was and I can't let it go. You were one of the last people to speak with her. Can we meet somewhere and talk about it?"

"I'm free for lunch today. Meet me at Wellington's Retreat?"

"I take my lunch at noon."

"I'll see you there."

Jaymie and her editor mapped out her weekly columns until the new year, then chatted. Nan pressed Jaymie hard about what she saw when she found Alicia Vance's body. Jaymie had, over the years, learned how to push back and resist. "I can't tell a reporter what I saw, Nan, that's not . . . it could interfere with the case."

Nan stood, shaking out her creased trousers. "I understand this was personal, finding Vance's body as you did. Our investigative reporter is looking into things, though, so . . . if you have any info you feel you could share, we would welcome it."

They said goodbye amicably. Nan never held a grudge.

Erin was busy with a walk-in ad customer but nodded to Jaymie as she passed. Outside, the rain had let up, but it was cold . . . colder than it had been, maybe even in the fifties. The skies were still gray, the pavement wet, and rain threatened any second. Jaymie huddled into her jacket, buffeted by the wind as she hustled to the restaurant and the promise of hot tea. What did she want to know that Erin could tell her? It was the same questions over and over again, seeking answers from different people. What was the truth behind Jace's car accident that injured Mia, and how did Alicia feel about it? How did Kim feel about Jace really? That was hard to grasp, because on the one hand Kim said he was good about taking care of her car and that she trusted him, and on the other there was a white-hot rage just below the surface. She had never forgiven him for his carelessness. How much did Erin know about the tangled web of relationships between her family and the Vances?

The cafe was warm and steamy, the aroma of soup, coffee and muffins wafting to her the moment she entered. It was busy but two women at a window table had stood and were donning heavy sweaters. Jaymie hustled to grab the table and sat after slinging her coat and purse over the chair back. A waitress approached and cleared the dirty dishes. Jaymie ordered a pot of tea, telling the young woman that she would be joined by a friend in a moment, and would order lunch then.

The low murmur of voices was soothing, a babble of indistinct chatter. The window was covered in vapor so Jaymie cleared a spot with a napkin, watching the traffic and pedestrians on the street beyond the glass. She had been through this so many times before, and every time she wondered why? *Why* was she in the middle of it? The truth was, one event snowballed upon another. Alicia knew she was adept at solving mysteries and wanted to enlist her help, leading to her terrible murder on her way to discuss things with Jaymie.

Not that she believed Alicia's death was her fault, it wasn't. If Alicia had made one choice differently — if she had stayed with Jaymie and told her what was worrying her — she may have come out of it alive, but that was not to be. Alicia knew or suspected something about Jace's death, something

she was considering revealing to the police
— that was Jaymie's inevitable conclusion.
The killer murdered her to shut her up.
Jaymie now had the choice she always had:
she could walk away and let the police
handle it, as Vestry would clearly prefer, or
she could use her knowledge of the partici-
pants and circumstances to help the police.
There must be justice for Alicia and for
Mia, who had lost her father *and* her
mother. Jaymie would do her best to ensure
it.

Erin entered and glanced around as the
tea came. Jaymie waved to her around the
waitress's back, and she approached, removing her heavy sweater and draping it over
the chair opposite. "It's frigid out there! Fall
is coming," she said as she sat.

"The weather is catching up with the calendar."

Erin swept her long hair off her face and
tied it into a ponytail with a scrunchie she
had in her hand. "Hair kept getting in my
lipstick. I should have tidied it before I left
the paper."

"What do they do while you're gone to
lunch?" Jaymie asked.

"Put the phone on message and lock the
front door," she said with a wry half smile.
"Most people use our online ad order form

anyway. It's only the older folks who come in to the ad desk in person."

They ordered from the fast lunch menu and their soup arrived swiftly. They ate, then Erin checked her phone as she pushed her bowl aside. "I've got fifteen minutes," she said.

"Okay, I'm listening."

"Like I said at the office, Alicia and I never got along. We had different fathers —"

"Who is Alicia's father?"

"Mom would never say. When we were little she said he was a bad dude and she didn't want him anywhere near us. She hasn't talked about it in a long time."

Jaymie stored away that bit of information; surely someone knew? Not that it mattered. "And your dad?"

She shrugged and looked sour. "No mystery there, he's a jerk. He married Mom but took off right after I was born. I'm in contact with him — he lives in Alaska now and he's remarried and has two more kids — but he can drop on his head as far as I'm concerned." She drained her tea, took a deep breath and settled herself. "Alicia and I had different lives. I was pretty young, just out of middle school, when she got married. I was a junior bridesmaid . . . wore a hideous dress, uncomfortable shoes, carried a smelly bouquet, wilted in the heat."

"Did you like Jace?"

"Sure. He made a fuss over me, especially at first, when they were dating. He'd buy me things, and I'd go places with them. Jace was cool, from a kid's point of view. I think Alicia was a little jealous of how close we were." She paused and scratched at the table surface with the ragged fingernail. "I had a bit of a crush on him. He was good-looking . . . dark eyes, dark hair, really sexy."

Jaymie let that revelation pass without comment.

"It's only later that you figure out that things aren't always what they seem."

"Meaning . . . ?"

"Things change. I got older, grew up . . . Alicia resented me. I had nicer clothes, more friends, a social life. I was prettier, younger, more popular. Meanwhile, she was stuck at home with a kid. She was *always* jealous of me."

Jaymie wasn't sure how to take that.

"Looking back, I think I was a bit of a pain. I didn't always treat her nice and we fought like cats and dogs at times." Erin faltered as she said, "Still . . ." She cleared her throat. "She was my sister. I see what pain Mom is in, and poor little Mia . . . I love that kid. And for Mom, Mia is the sun

276

and the moon and the earth." She stared into Jaymie's eyes. "I can tell you're looking into it. Alicia said she had been talking to you about Jace. What did she tell you?"

"About Jace?"

Erin nodded.

Why was she fishing for information? "She didn't say much," Jaymie replied, then changed the subject. "People keep telling me that Alicia was seeing someone on the side five years ago, when Jace died. Was that true? Who was she seeing?"

"I don't know. Mom thinks it was Lew."

"You said you felt like something was bothering Alicia the last few days before her death. There was, she told me so herself."

Erin sat up straight, her attention riveted on Jaymie. "What was up?"

"I know some but not all of it," Jaymie said. "Are you up for sharing information?"

Erin nodded.

Jaymie relayed as much as she thought was safe to tell Erin about Alicia's worries that she was going to be arrested for Jace's murder, if that's what it was. Alicia had already told her mother her fears, so this was not new information for them. "Do you think Jace was murdered, or do you think it was an accident?"

Erin frowned and sat back in the chair,

glancing around, then saying, her voice quiet, "At first I was sure it was an accident, but then I was like . . . I'm not so sure."

"What changed your mind?"

She leaned forward. "Did you know Jace accused Russ of stealing stuff from his garage?"

An accusation of theft against Russ was serious, especially with his background. He was more likely than someone with no record to go to jail if he was found guilty, and that might be motive enough to kill Jace. And then there was that shadowy suggestion that it was Russ that Alicia was dating at the time of her husband's death; this accusation complicated things immeasurably. "What was he supposed to be stealing?"

"Something called . . . gosh, I can't remember the name . . . cata-something?"

"Catalytic converters?"

"Maybe." Erin shrugged. "Anyway, it was more than one taken off cars in Jace's garage. He said it was Russ, but Mom says that's garbage, that Jace didn't know what he was talking about."

Catalytic converters are valuable because of the metals used in them, and so are often the target of thieves. Jaymie knew that from reading of local thefts in the *Howler.* One parking garage in Wolverhampton had been the target of thieves who had removed seven in a single night. Given his past history, it was possible that Russ had done it, but he'd be taking a heck of a chance. "Was Jace going to go to the police?"

Erin nodded. "He said something to Russ about it and they got into a huge argument. Russ complained to my mom and Jace held off, but there was another theft after that so . . ." She shrugged. "What else could Jace do but report his suspicions to the police?"

"Did he do it?"

"Nope. He died."

It was out there, those words, stark in their implication. "Erin, who do you think killed your sister?"

The young woman met her gaze. "I'd like to ask you the same question." Her tone was accusatory.

"If I knew anything for sure I'd be on the phone to the police," she said, alarm thrumming through her.

"Would you? Would you really?"

"Erin, I don't know anything. And anything I suspect or have learned I've told the police." Jaymie stared at the younger woman. Erin seemed suspicious, accusatory. "What's going on? Why did you ask me that?"

"It's so weird. I mean, Alicia's going along fine, and then all of a sudden she starts talking to you and *bam,* someone kills her. Why is that?"

"The killer was afraid of what she was going to tell me," Jaymie said promptly. "What do you think that could be? What did she know that she was about to divulge?"

Erin, her gaze troubled, shook her head.

"Maybe you can tell me this: who was Alicia going out with?" Jaymie asked, testing the waters. How would her sister answer?

Erin shrugged. "She was always secretive and she'd gotten more so lately."

Okay, so the sisters didn't confide in each other. Or did Alicia not trust Erin? "I did have one more question, going back to Jace: whose vehicle was he looking at the day he died? I understand he had one up on jack stands. When another came in he put it up on a jack, which is why it could be toppled on him. Who owned the second vehicle, the truck that fell on him?"

Erin's eyes watered and she dashed away the moisture. "It was . . . it was a pickup I was going to buy."

"It was *yours*?" Jaymie gasped.

"Not yet. I had a car . . . a real beater, my mom's old Chevy. It had been stolen by

280

joyriders. The police found it torched in the woods at the site of a bush party." She cleared her throat, staring steadily out the window, not meeting Jaymie's gaze. "I was using the insurance to buy another vehicle. I mean, I was only eighteen and I thought a pickup would be cool. I was looking at it — Lew hooked me up — and was driving it for a day or two before buying it. Lew's dad said a girl like me couldn't handle a truck. Made me so mad! Lew said I'd be fine, that he'd vouch for the truck being good, but Jace knew I was worried. When his dad said I shouldn't buy it because the brake pads were old, Jace said he'd take a quick look at it."

"I didn't know you had to remove the wheel to check the brake pads."

"Neither did I. Apparently you don't always, but sometimes you do. Anyway, I was thinking of buying it and left it there the night before."

"You didn't stay while he checked them? It wouldn't have taken long." Jaymie eyed the other woman critically.

"Jace didn't have time right then. I was babysitting for a friend of Jace and Alicia's, my sister was giving me a ride over there. I was staying overnight. I didn't know . . . I'd never have . . ." She bit her quivering lip and shook her head. "I didn't know he'd have to put it up on jacks, or that it would be unsafe."

Jaymie was going to have to think about this long and hard. She had not foreseen that the truck was a family member's. Along with the accusation against Russ — leading to the bad blood between him and Jace — there was a strong familial thread through the whole tragedy. And yet the way information had flowed from Erin was suspect. It wasn't usually so easy to get people to open up. She chastised herself. Erin was hurting and wanted to know who had killed her sister.

The young woman leaned across the table and stared directly into Jaymie's eyes. "You spoke with Alicia a couple of times before she was killed. What did she say to you? She was scared of something, but what?"

"I don't know a whole lot," Jaymie said slowly. Erin had asked a version of the same question earlier. "Like I told you, she was afraid the police were trying to pin Jace's murder on her. Alicia had asked me about how the police operated, whether they're honest. I think she wanted my opinion on information she had, if she should take it to the police, but she was hesitant about talking to me. I believe she had finally made up her mind to tell me and that's why she was on her way to see me. I'm assuming, I don't know for sure."

"Oh." Erin looked pensive. "Okay." She glanced down at her cell phone. "Crap, I'm late. I gotta get back to work."

"I hope you and your mom and Mia are doing all right. Please, if you need anything, let me help. If you need someone to take Mia any time, we're available. Jocie loves your niece!"

Erin, standing and slinging her purse over her shoulder, looked down at Jaymie, her eyes watering. "Thanks. I'll let Mom know." She exited.

Jaymie sat for a minute, finished her tea, and considered what she had learned. She had expected a big mystery about whose truck was up on the jacks the day Jace died, but it was just his sister-in-law's about-to-be-purchased vehicle. It was the kind of thing a friend who understands vehicles does for another. Jaymie was fairly confident about purchasing a car for herself, but still, she had taken Valetta with her. Her friend was a shrewd bargainer.

That was different, though, from actually examining a vehicle. Was it odd that Erin had dropped off a truck for Jace to check over before purchase, or was that how things were done when it was a sale between friends? And what was Lew's role in the truck purchase? Was he selling it to her, or facilitating a sale between Erin and someone else? Something more to check out.

She paid her bill, left a tip on the table, slipped on her jacket, grabbed her bag and headed outside. She had left her car parked at the newspaper so she started down the street but saw, some ways down, a sight that stopped her cold. It was Erin and . . . Franklin? They were engaged in conversation that looked intense. He took her arm and they walked to the parking lot of the donut shop and got into a pickup.

Jaymie stepped back to hug the building, not wanting them to see her. It struck her as odd, but there was no reason why they shouldn't be talking, Jaymie supposed. Her cellphone buzzed. Jaymie checked her messages. Valetta's text asked Jaymie to come to Queensville. Something had come up.

SEVENTEEN

Valetta was outside the Emporium waiting. When Jaymie parked and got out of her SUV her friend motioned her to follow. A picnic table sat under the big oak tree outside of the store; she and Val took lunch breaks there in nicer weather. Queensville had not had as much rain as Wolverhampton, so it was not soaking under the tree but the breeze was still chilly. A woman was seated there. When Jaymie approached she could see that it was Debbie Vance.

Val grabbed Jaymie's arm, stopping her a ways away from the table. "She came in to pick up a prescription and had a meltdown. Go easy. She's had a rough day."

"What's going on?"

"You'll see," Val said tersely.

They approached and Jaymie greeted the woman, then said, "When I saw you the other day I didn't recognize you until I thought about it later. We went to high school together."

The woman had tear streaks still on her cheeks tightening into dried trails. Without makeup she looked older and tired, like she had been through the wringer. "Jaymie, sure. I didn't get the connection until I thought about it. We had homeroom and American history together." She tried a smile. It faltered and died.

"I have to get back inside," Val said. "I'll close up and come back out with hot tea."

Jaymie nodded and climbed over the bench, sitting opposite Debbie. As the other woman struggled to get her emotions under control, she said, "I'm not sure why I'm here, Debbie. Did you want to talk to me?"

The woman nodded, sniffed, took a tissue out of her windbreaker pocket and blew her nose. She balled up the used tissue, stuffed it back in her pocket and took a deep breath. "Something's come up, and I heard you were snooping . . . uh, looking into the murder. I figured out something today that I suspected but hoped wasn't true."

"And that is . . . ?"

"That Alicia and Lew were having an affair."

Jaymie hesitated. "Do you mean . . . now? Or before?"

"For five years, as far as I know. Then.

Now." She sobbed, covered her mouth, then dropped her hands to the wood tabletop. "*Damn!* I've got to stop this weeping. I don't know what's wrong with me lately. I mean, Lew and I have been divorced for four years. Alicia and I were friends. Or at least I thought we were. That's what hurts, I guess, her betrayal. I hired her because she was my sister-in-law and my friend. Didn't know she was banging my husband." Her voice was guttural, choked with bitterness.

It was hard to know what to say. "Are you sure it's true, and not hearsay or gossip?" Jaymie asked, curious about the woman's sudden revelation.

She nodded.

"How do you know?"

"Looking back, I should have known all along. I was told they had been seen together, but stupid, naïve me . . . I defended her. I didn't want to believe it."

"Who told you they had been seen together? And where?"

Debbie looked undecided. "Her sister said a friend saw Alicia and Lew going into a motel."

"Erin said that?" Jaymie was taken aback. "Let me get this straight: Erin told you Alicia and Lew had been seen together . . . five years ago, I'm assuming. How did that

287

come about, that you would be talking to her and she would say that to you?"

"She was going out with a friend of my younger brother. I was giving them a ride to the movies, or . . . a concert, maybe? Erin sat in the front seat with me. We were talking — I can't remember what about — and she asked me, did I know that Alicia and Lew were hanging out at a motel."

Erin had admitted to having a crush on Jace, and to fighting with her sister. Was her revelation a teenager's spiteful attempt to sabotage Alicia's frail marriage? "What did you say?"

"I didn't say anything, I don't think."

"No response at all?"

"I didn't want to get into a discussion with Erin. I don't know what she's like now but she used to be prickly. She and Alicia didn't always get along. I remember thinking that if it was true, why would she do that to her sister, tell on her like that? That's what made me doubt her." She sighed. "Then my brother said something from the backseat, and the conversation turned."

"You didn't ask Lew?"

"To be honest, I had other things on my mind," she said slowly.

"You broke up shortly after Jace died. Why?"

She shrugged and her eyes watered. "He was a mess after it happened. I mean, I sympathized, but Jace's death was the final nail in the coffin of our marriage. We'd been having trouble for a while. Same old story, I wanted more from him than he was prepared to give."

"What Erin said couldn't have helped," Jaymie mused. "Can I ask you, Debbie . . . how did Lew and Jace get along?"

"Okay, I guess. Competitive with each other, always trying to get Franklin's approval."

"How did you get along with your father-in-law?"

"Franklin?" She smiled. "He can be totally charming when he wants. I had a bit of a crush on him back when Lew and I were dating. When he talked to you, you felt like you totally had his focus." Her smile died. "And he stood up for me when I needed it. He told Lew in no uncertain terms that he had a good wife and he ought to be better to me." She rolled her eyes and sighed. "Of course, all that did was set Lew's back up. We had a ginormous fight afterward."

"Debbie, why did this strike you now? That Lew and Alicia were a couple, I mean."

"I read the piece in the paper, the article about the police saying they had a person or people of interest. I wondered . . ." She bit her lip and looked away.

Jaymie stared at her. "You wondered if it was Lew?"

She met Jaymie's gaze, nodding.

"Why would that make you think of Lew and Alicia cheating, and why did you wonder if Lew killed her?"

She frowned and tightened her lips into a firm line. She was the ex, Jaymie thought, and as such her opinions and information had to be considered carefully. Did she have an ax to grind against her ex-husband? Enough to maliciously peg him for murder?

"Debbie?" she prompted. "Did Lew ever do or say anything that makes you think he could be capable of murder?"

She blinked and her eyes clouded with tears. She shook her head, tears sprinkling to the tabletop. "No. I can't imagine him stalking her through the woods and killing her." There was more, Jaymie could hear it in her voice. "But if he loved her — and I believe he did, I believe he loved her the whole time we were married — and something happened between them, he could have . . . have lashed out. In pain."

Unconvinced, Jaymie tapped her fingers on the picnic table and watched the other woman. She had doubts about Erin's motive in suggesting to Debbie that Lew and Alicia were having an affair, but that was five years ago. A lot had happened since. Still, she wouldn't discount the information completely. "Debbie, do you still care about Lew?"

She nodded with a trembling smile. "He'll always be my husband. I don't love him the same way, but . . . he's such a good guy, Jaymie. I don't actually believe that he killed Alicia. But if she got her talons into him and convinced him that they could be together if Jace was dead . . ." She shrugged. "I don't know for sure that he wouldn't . . . help her out."

"Are you suggesting that they conspired to kill Jace?" Jaymie asked. If he killed his brother with Alicia's knowledge, and if she was going to spill her guts to the police, it would be a powerful motive for murder.

"I don't know what I'm saying," she admitted. "This has been running through my head all day until I'm ready to go right around the bend."

"First, how sure are you now, looking back, that they were lovers five years ago? I mean, with what Erin said, how did you just figure it out now?"

"I went back in my calendar."

"Your calendar?"

"I keep a paper calendar on my desk. I note every single thing that happens, along with the time. Whenever Alicia would ask for a day off Lew had business 'out of town,' and he'd be unavailable all day. It was a pattern I should have seen then. Willful blindness, I suppose."

Jaymie waited for more but she was done. "I'm confused. You mean . . . five years ago?"

She nodded.

"Do you mean you went through your calendar then?"

"No, this morning."

"You can't be sure, though. Couldn't that be a coincidence?"

"I feel it in my gut," she said, fist over her stomach. "That day — the day Jace died — was one of those days. Alicia said she needed to go shopping for Mia. She didn't go, though, did she?"

Jaymie stayed silent. Mia had been left with Tami, but she wasn't about to acknowledge it or she'd have to reveal her source.

"Lew told me he had business in Rochester Hills," she said, naming a suburb of Detroit. "A car auction to buy some inventory for his used car lot in Wolverhampton. It's small, kind of a side business to the towing business with his dad. He was going to the auction with his brother, his dad and Clutch, but Clutch called me looking for Lew. I logged that call like I log every call I receive, business or personal. I told him what Lew told me, that they were all going together. Clutch said maybe there was a mix-up and hung up. Those guys — Clutch, Lew, Franklin — have always been tight. So . . . if Lew wasn't with Clutch, where was he that day?"

That was troubling. Clutch had said that he and Franklin were no longer close, but that he still dealt with Lew. And yet he and the Vance men were heading off together to a car auction? "Still . . . what makes you think Alicia and Lew were together that day?"

"That's the thing . . . I don't think they were," she said with a troubled frown. "I think Alicia *thought* they were going to get together."

"Why do you say that?"

"Little things. Female things. She got a Brazilian wax the day before at the Queensville Inn day spa." She crossed her arms over her chest and nodded.

Jaymie waited. She vaguely knew what a Brazilian wax was, but wasn't sure what it meant for Alicia to get one.

"Oh come on!" Debbie said, leaning

across the table, her eyes dark with fury. "No woman gets a Brazilian for her husband. Besides, her and Jace weren't sleeping together. It had to be for a lover!"

Val came back and set down a tray that had a thermal carafe, cups, sugar, milk and spoons on it. Glancing back and forth between the two, she said, "How's it going?"

"She doesn't believe me!" Debbie said, throwing up her arms.

"I didn't say that, Debbie, but what you said, that's not proof of anything." It didn't prove who killed Jace and how and why, or who killed Alicia and how and why, and those were the only questions Jaymie was interested in, not who slept with whom. Alicia having a long-term affair with Lew may have bearing on one of the two crimes, but it wasn't evidence.

There was silence for a long minute. Val poured tea into the three mugs and pushed two toward Jaymie and Debbie.

Jaymie fixed hers up and took a sip, relishing the warmth on such a chilly day. "I'm not saying I don't believe you, Debbie," she said, setting down her mug. "It's possible they were having an affair. It's possible they were having an affair recently." She had reason to believe that Alicia was considering

294

moving with Lew out of state, but she wasn't going to share that with Debbie. However . . . "If you're right, how long do you think their affair had been going on before Jace died?"

Her gaze turned inward and she paused, then said, "When I think about it now, Lew had been acting weird for a while and so had she."

"Weird how?"

"He was . . . absent, I guess. Like I said, I knew our marriage was on the rocks even if I didn't want to admit it."

"Had they always been friendly?"

"Mmm . . . not really. Just casual, like relatives, you know? I mean, he was her brother-in-law, and the husband of her boss, too. I guess it was a weird dynamic. Jace and Lew were competitive. They were both always trying to get their dad's attention. I wonder if Lew wanted Alicia because she was Jace's?"

"Could they have started seeing each other after the accident that almost killed Mia?"

Her eyes widened. "That would be about the right timing. If I was Alicia, I'd sure be looking for a way to hurt Jace. Hooking up with Lew would do it!"

"Debbie, can I ask you something else?

This is going to come out of the blue, but . . . why did you hire Russ? Did he work for you before you hired Alicia or after?"

"About the same time. He actually used to work for the Vances, but there was trouble of some sort. It was Lew's idea that I hire him." She frowned. "I think I hired Russ first, and then Alicia. I'd have to look at my records to be sure because it was around the same time. Does it matter?"

"Probably not. What do you think of Russ?"

"He's . . . steady," Debbie said in a neutral tone.

"You've never had any trouble with him?"

Debbie cocked her head to one side. "Why do you ask?"

"I'm trying to get a larger picture of the whole family, I guess." It had occurred to her just then that Russ seemed to have a lot of autonomy in his job. If Alicia was meeting a lover that day Russ was still in the mix as a possibility.

"He's okay. We've had minor issues, nothing huge. Actually, when you get to know him, he's a decent guy." She leaned forward again, as Val watched with raised eyebrows. "I'll tell you this, there is something going on with that family."

"What do you mean?" Val asked.

"The Vance family?" Jaymie said.

"Not just the Vances, all of them. There are so many accidents! Doesn't that seem odd to you? What happened to poor Mia; Jace's death; the garage burning; Alicia's accident; Kim's accident; Erin —"

"Wait . . . what? I knew about some of this, but Kim? And Erin?"

"Sure. Kim got rear-ended last year, and Erin had her car stolen a while before Jace died. It was found torched."

"Car stolen," Jaymie echoed. Yes, her old beater had been stolen then found torched in the woods. That was the incident that had necessitated the purchase of a new vehicle, the very one that collapsed on and killed Jace. Jaymie sighed and shook her head. Her mind was teeming with ideas, suspicions, possibilities. To sort them out she would need time and solitude, but she had access to Debbie right now, so . . . "Was Erin buying a vehicle from Lew?" she said carefully, not mentioning what she already knew. Erin had said Lew "hooked her up." Did that mean he was directly selling her the truck?

"You mean back then, five years ago?" Jaymie nodded. "Maybe. Everyone buys cars from Lew. It's what he does, aside from the tow truck business him and his dad run.

He goes to auctions, buys cars, and sells them from his lot in Wolverhampton."

"So I've heard. Does he have his own garage to work on them? Or to examine them?"

"No, he always used Jace's. He's not the mechanic, though, it was always Jace or Franklin who checked out and fixed the cars Lew sold. Jace was hard to replace. After he died, Lew went through several mechanics before he found one who worked out."

A few random ideas were starting to pull together, like magnets. Among the jumble, strands were sorting into distinct shapes. While she had Debbie in front of her she had two more questions. Maybe three. "Did you think Jace was murdered when it happened? And do you still think the same way now?"

"At the time I thought it was a tragic accident, you know? Awful." She shuddered and shivered, pulling her windbreaker close around her. "But now . . . I mean, with Alicia dying and everything? I do think Jace was murdered."

"You now think Jace was murdered because Alicia has died too? You believe the two must be tied together?"

"If not it's an awful coincidence. Could she have known something, maybe about

Jace's death?"

"It's possible," Jaymie said, not wanting to confirm or deny her thoughts. It was unavoidably true that Lew and Alicia's affair, if it was going on five years ago, gave them both a good motive for killing Jace. Interesting as that possibility was, she was not about to share her thoughts. Instead she asked, "Debbie, the day Jace died and Alicia was supposed to be with Lew, where do you think he was, if not with her?"

"I don't know."

Who would? she wondered. Who would?

Late at night she lay in Jakob's arms. Lovemaking had soothed her fretfulness, and they lay naked under the covers in the blissful quiet of the house, with Hoppy snoring in his bed by the window, the wind creaking the glass, a soft rain pelting. They discussed the day in whispers as the house settled around them. She could talk to her husband about anything. It was a relief to have someone in whom to confide. As much as she loved her parents and sister, she had never been able to share all she thought with them. She was closer with Val, but still . . . there were barriers. With Jakob nothing she thought or felt was out of bounds.

Silence fell between them, finally. She

thought maybe he was falling asleep; his breathing was rhythmic, his chest rising and falling. But then . . .

"Tami sent the letter," he murmured, his voice rumbling in his chest.

"Okay. How . . . how is she doing?"

"Better, I guess. Gus doesn't talk about her much."

For good reason. "Jakob, how do you think Jocie's doing with all of this? She's been awfully quiet the last few days."

He was quiet for a moment, then said, "Jaymie, this is not a criticism."

She held her breath, trying to quell her trembling. "Yes?"

"I think she senses your tension about the woods across the road. She watches you, you know."

Jaymie turned her face into Jakob's chest. "I don't know how to hide it."

"I don't think you should. Jocie needs to see you dealing with your feelings. Maybe we can talk about it tomorrow."

"Okay. I'll try to be more careful how I act."

"Don't change your behavior."

"I don't want her to be afraid of the woods, or get . . . I don't know . . . an aversion to it."

"Jocie needs to know that adults are afraid

of things but that we find ways to deal with our fear. I don't want her losing confidence in her ability to handle things that upset or scare her. She has to see us being vulnerable, or she'll feel alone when she's scared, like she's the only one in the world who gets frightened. I've never hidden my feelings from her, even when I was worried."

"You're so wise," she whispered.

"Honey, we'll get through it together," he said, holding her close, wrapped in his arms. "I have a couple of ideas how to handle Jocie's wariness of the woods. But I don't think we should do anything until they get whoever did it."

A tightness squeezed at Jaymie's chest. She had probably already talked to or seen the killer. That was unnerving. But she was determined and had a few ideas already on why Jace died and perhaps even why Alicia died. There was still a ways to go before she had a working theory.

But there was a light at the end of the tunnel, hopefully not a freight train.

EIGHTEEN

It was one of those moments, those times when you wake up in the middle of the night with your heart pounding, a nightmare fresh in your mind. Jaymie crept from bed, sweat beading on her forehead, chills racing through her body. Hoppy looked up from his little wicker basket by the window, a question in his eyes and his black button nose wiggling. She tapped her leg and he followed as she tiptoed downstairs and made tea.

The nightmare had been specific: Jocie was trapped on a train track, her foot stuck, and Jaymie couldn't get to her. A train was roaring toward them. With it rushed a sense of impending doom. Jakob was there. Because of the roar of the approaching train he couldn't hear her calling for him so she was on her own. She dove for the train tracks to free Jocie and awoke as the train screamed past, her heart pounding and a headache coming on.

Taking her tea to the sofa, she picked up her tablet and checked her email, then the news of the day as Hoppy joined her, curling up in the crook of her knees. She read reports of robberies in Wolverhampton, a string of car thefts, and an accident on the main thoroughfare. All minor stuff. Insurance would take care of financial losses. No one had been seriously hurt, and that was good news.

None of it could distract her from the problem at hand. Why did a skilled mechanic like Jace, who was so careful, put the truck up on a jack and crawl underneath? And if it was murder, how had it been affected? Had the jack been tinkered with? Or the vehicle shoved off it? His death horrified her still, the thought of him suffering and then lying there dead. It was a nightmare, a shocking way to die.

She stilled as an idea came to her . . . an appalling idea. Diabolical. But it *would* tie up loose ends and explain inconsistencies. *And* would implicate one of her suspects. Or maybe more than one. And . . . it would explain behavior that was otherwise inexplicable. She tapped her fingers on her thigh and frowned, then grabbed her notebook and began jotting down her ideas. Now she had to decide if she should she tell Vestry her ideas or wait until she knew more. She curled up on the sofa, pulled an afghan Valetta had made over her, and fell back to sleep with Hoppy snuffling at her side.

Jakob was making coffee and the smell woke Jaymie. He brought her a cup and kissed her nose as he set it down on the coffee table.

"I've fed Hoppy and Jocie took him out to the tree field for a little walk. I'm sorry you didn't sleep," he said.

She sat, stretched and yawned, took a long drink of excellent coffee and stood. "It's okay. I'm better this morning."

He cocked one thick dark eyebrow. "That must mean you've figured something out."

"You know me so well!" she said with a laugh. "Let me run it past you." She sat at the table and picked up Lilibet, cuddling the sweet cat while Jakob made Jocie's school lunch and breakfast. She told him her nighttime musings and how the pieces were starting to fit together, but stopped when Jocie came in with Hoppy and washed her hands. Jocie sat at the table, kicking her legs and eating breakfast while watching Jaymie with concern.

"Why the long face?" Jaymie asked.

"Why were you sleeping on the sofa?"

The truth or a comfortable lie? The truth; Jakob met her gaze and nodded.

Taking a deep breath, she turned to her daughter and said, "I had a nightmare and couldn't go back to sleep. Instead of lying there awake I came downstairs, made a cup of tea and sat on the sofa. After a while I felt better and was sleepy again. Rather than wake up your daddy, I curled up with Hoppy and fell asleep."

Jocie nodded, a relieved look on her face. Jaymie stored that thought away for later, and once the child was off getting dressed for school she asked Jakob, "Does Jocie have any old memories about her mother?"

Jakob nodded as he filled the sink with soapy water. "She didn't sleep well and often wandered at night. She even went out driving. I found her asleep in the car more than once. Jocie probably has memories of that. I helped my wife all I could, but . . ." He shrugged. Jaymie joined him at the sink, tea towel in hand, and put her arm around his waist, head on his shoulder. "I'm glad you told her the truth," Jakob said, putting one soapy hand around her shoulders and squeezing. "It's what we talked about last night."

"You're right." As she dried the dishes he

handed her, she told him the rest of what she had been thinking concerning Alicia's murder and Jace's death.

"It's horrible, but it's logical. Are you going to tell Detective Vestry?"

"Not right away."

"Why wait?"

"I'd like to be a little surer, first. I have questions."

Jakob looked concerned — worried, even — but he stayed silent and nodded. She appreciated that he never tried to tell her what to do. In return, she had promised herself not to take any stupid risks. They finished the dishes and he left for the day, ferrying Jocie to school. Jaymie got out ingredients for potato soup, peeled, chopped, diced and seasoned, and piled the food in the slow cooker, turned it on, then tidied up.

Finally, she stood and stared through the kitchen window at the woods. "I'll figure it out, Alicia," she vowed. "For you, but also for Mia; that darling child deserves answers. I'll figure it out and we'll get justice."

She made one more cup of coffee then sat for a while at the table with her laptop and notebook and made a list of people she needed to talk to. Mrs. Stubbs. Kim Hansen. Val. Maybe more. She drew a string of question marks beside the names. She then called Brianna Sheridan, who had left a message that she had information for Jaymie. They chatted for a few minutes, then Jaymie asked why she had called.

"I was looking through my old notes and came across a question I had that was never answered. I underlined it. It was about insurance. I remember that Jace didn't have any personal life insurance. Is that true?"

"As far as I know, yes," Jaymie replied. "He had let his policy lapse when he and Alicia ran into financial problems after the accident when Mia lost her leg. Why?"

"There's more than one kind of insurance, you know." She explained what she meant. If she was right, it was the final piece to the puzzle . . . or it was *almost* the final piece.

The picture was becoming clearer, though much was still a mystery. However, Jaymie was determined that by nightfall she would have all the information she needed so Alicia's killer could be brought to justice. She thought she knew who did it, but police detectives would have the kind of information she could not access. They held the proof in their investigation, if only they put all the pieces together.

She now knew whose pickup was up on jacks — Erin's — and why it was there, and how that related to Jace's accident. She didn't know a crucial detail that might prove it truly was murder, and who was responsible, nor was she sure how to get the information she needed.

She also knew why Alicia was stood up by her lover on the day her husband died, and thought she knew what Alicia was coming to tell her, who accompanied her, and how she ended up dead. If she was right it was a betrayal of trust so monumental it seemed impossible. Her brain hadn't yet fully processed how someone who professed to love Alicia could deceive her so foully and kill her. It all came down to Lew.

If Jaymie was right, Lew Vance, afraid that his murder of his brother was about to be revealed, accompanied Alicia across that lonely darkening field trying to figure out what she knew. Alicia may not even have suspected Lew. Alicia actually suspected Russ Krauss, Jaymie thought; it explained her dislike of the man and her tension with her mother over Kim's relationship. By the middle of the woods, as Lew fashioned a makeshift weapon, he had heard enough from Alicia to convince him that what she was about to tell or say would expose him on purpose or by accident. Lew decided to save himself and killed her to keep her from revealing his crime.

It was senseless and a profound treachery. Lew was a part of her family and she was planning a future with him before he murdered her to save himself. However . . . as much as it made sense, it was all merely a working theory at this point. She needed proof before saying anything to Vestry, and she was still investigating other angles, other possibilities.

First, a phone call. "Val? Hey, can I ask you a question?" Val agreed, and Jaymie said, "Brock was studying to get his license to sell insurance, right?" He was. "Does he know anyone who sells policies locally?" He did, and when Valetta heard what Jaymie wanted to know, she promised to enlist both her brother's help and his silence.

Jaymie wasn't sure how much she trusted Brock's ability to be reticent, but by the time he told anyone she would already have given Vestry all she knew, laying out the case at the detective's feet, and if she was right, Lew would be under arrest. She hoped. It was perhaps precipitous to think she had that much sway with the detective — was she getting ahead of herself? — but she had to think once Vestry saw the evidence, she'd agree.

Then she called Clutch. What he had to

say was key to her theory. "Clutch, I have a question: I heard that you were supposed to go to a car auction on the day Jace Vance died, with Franklin, Jace and Lew. Is that true?"

His tone cool, he said, "Why you asking me that?"

She paused; he sounded suspicious, distant. Maybe she should have done this face-to-face. "I'm asking to clarify a point. You said you and Franklin were not so close by that time. Is *that* true?"

"Yup. But you got it wrong. Don't know where you heard it, but that trip to Rochester Hills was never planned to be with Franklin, it was going to be me, Jace, Lew and Russ."

That surprised her. "Russ Krauss?"

"Can't stand that guy. Never could, even when he was tagging along behind us at school. But he wanted to come along for the ride. Don't know why Lew said yes. He knew Jace hated the guy as much as I did."

"So . . . wait, Clutch, are you telling me that you and Lew did go that day? And with Russ?"

"Lew and I did, but Lew couldn't get hold of Jace and Russ flunked out on us. Why do you ask?"

Her heart thudded and she stared at noth-

310

ing. It appeared she was wrong about a lot. "I . . . I've . . ." She marshaled her thoughts. "But Clutch, I've been told that you called Debbie Vance that day looking for Lew. Why would you do that if he was with you?"

"You've never called around lookin' for someone who's not answering his phone? Crossed wires is all. I was driving and had mixed up where we were meeting. I told her as much."

"But not quite in those words. She said you clammed up when she asked why he wasn't with you."

"I didn't clam up, I told her there was some mix-up. I didn't have anything more to say to her. Never liked the woman. She always was the suspicious type. Lew couldn't move without her asking him where he was going. Anyway, Lew finally answered his phone — he'd been on the road when I called him — and we met at the donut shop in Wolverhampton. He told me Jace wasn't answering his phone and Russ wasn't coming . . . some fool excuse. Guy had a tummy ache, prob'ly," he said dismissively. "Lew wanted to go over and see why Jace wasn't answering his phone, but I said if we were going to make the auction we needed to get on the road." He paused. "That haunts me to this day. If I'd said yes to Lew, we mighta saved Jace."

"Maybe. Or maybe not."

"Anyway, we headed off to Rochester Hills. Bought three cars that day, two for Lew's lot and I bought one to fix up for Gabby." He paused, then said, "Jaymie, what the hell is going on? Why all the questions about that day and Russ and Lew?"

Jaymie tried to calm the wild spinning of her thoughts. She thought she had it all figured out and she was wrong. Time to rethink. "I must have things the wrong way round."

"What's going on, kiddo?" he asked, his tone gentler.

"I thought I knew what happened, but it turns out . . ." She let out a shaky sigh. "I feel like . . . you know how something seems wildly improbable until you find out it's true, and then it all falls into place and makes sense and you wonder why you ever doubted it?"

"I can't say that's ever happened to me."

"Well, it just did to me."

"You mind sharing?"

"I . . . can't right now, Clutch." Everything was shifting and, in the process, clarifying. It was like a crazy kaleidoscope and each turn of the wheel showed a different pattern. Lew, Franklin, Russ, Jace, Kim, Erin,

Debbie . . . all players in a bigger game. She kept getting the combination of players wrong. Was this new version she was thinking of the real deal or another wrong direction? She still had questions, things to figure out, but she had a familiar sense that now, finally, she was on the right track. With this new information she realized there was one possibility she had dismissed before, one monstrous plot that included every bit of information. The image changed from hazy suppositions to clarity.

"I don't wanna have to worry about you, kiddo. Tell me what's on your mind," Clutch urged with increasing concern.

"I can't. Not yet." It was a monstrous, diabolical, unnatural plot, one she never would have imagined. If she was finally right, it did explain it all, but her recent mistakes made her cautious. "I'll be able to tell you more soon, but right now —"

"Right now you're playin' it close to your chest. I get it." He was silent for a moment, then said gruffly, "Be safe, kiddo. There's a killer out there, and you're irreplaceable."

"I'll be careful, I promise. Clutch, one more question: you say you don't like Russ. Why is that?"

"Weasel," he said. "The guy's a weasel and a weakling."

"Weakling?"

"Always getting shoved around in school. Always taking the fall for some other dude's prank. Afraid of his own shadow." Jaymie was quiet for a moment. "Why do you ask?" he said.

She didn't want to think of Clutch as a high school bully, however . . . maybe he was. Even good people aren't always wholly admirable. "How does him getting shoved around in high school make him a weakling? Clutch, if he was bullied . . ." Bullies become abusers, but sometimes the reverse was also true and the victims act out in devious and violent ways. She thought of Russ's manslaughter conviction.

"Some guys ask for it. Don't suppose you understand, Jaymie. Your generation . . ."

She braced for criticism that her generation was marshmallow soft, unable to stand up to a little push and shove, expecting everyone to be nice and kind and sweet. She had an argument ready; it wasn't political correctness to abhor cruelty.

But he didn't finish the thought. "I'll leave it at this: I never liked the guy. Wouldn't trust him as far as I could throw him."

"Okay, I guess that's honest enough. I'll admit that having met him a few times I'm not a big fan of his either. I'd better go."

"You be careful, kid," he repeated gruffly. "Don't take no chances."

"I won't."

Hoppy and Lilibet had finished a rousing game of got your tail, then collapsed in a love puddle in their shared basket by the fire. Jaymie hung up the phone, gave both animals a kiss on the head, gathered her things, and headed out the door. First, she collected the mail from the box, sorted it, and noted with alarm an envelope with the stamp of the prison where Tami now resided. She stared out the vehicle window, gulping deep breaths, calming her heart. She set the other mail aside on the passenger's seat with her purse, holding and turning the letter from Tami over and over. Should she open it now, or later? Later, she decided, tossing it in her purse and starting the SUV.

Morning tea with Mrs. Stubbs was always an event. Edith, her daughter-in-law, brought in for them a "tasting" array of new desserts the talented pastry chef was trying out for the autumnal holiday season teas they would be putting on. They partook, compared notes, and decided that all of them were too good to choose.

Jaymie drank her last drop of tea and sighed, hand on her stomach. "That's what

I needed, five pounds of sugar and pastry." She sobered as she caught a glimpse of the letter sticking up out of her purse and remembered what she had meant to ask her friend. "Mrs. Stubbs, remember our last conversation? We spoke about Kim Ellsworthy, now Kim Hansen?"

The woman had closed her eyes as a rare beam of autumn sun found its way to her chair, but her eyes snapped open again and she had a rueful expression on her face. "I offended your delicate sensibilities by calling the girl a tramp."

Jaymie held back a sigh. "I'm not about to argue with you again," she replied.

"I also told you I'd thought better of how I spoke of Kim Ellsworthy. Let's leave it at that."

"Mrs. Stubbs, you remember that time when your kids were in high school. Do you know anything about the lives of the others, like Kim, Franklin, Russ and Clutch, *after* high school?"

"Until the last few years it was only Valetta who I saw with any regularity. Maybe she'll remember what you need to know."

"That's a good thought and I'll be asking Val, but a different perspective may help. You do remember that Kim and Franklin were a hot couple in school. Do you know if they broke up before school was over?"

Squinting through her glasses, Mrs. Stubbs said, "Why are you asking about Franklin and Kim?"

"I'm gathering information. Their lives are so tangled together still. His first son, Lewis, was born — either before or shortly after their graduation — from a relationship he had with an older woman, the one that broke up his connection with Kim. His second son married Kim's oldest daughter. Alicia was apparently going to move out of state with Lew." She frowned and shook her head. "I'm sorting it all out. And I guess I'm trying to track down the anger Kim still harbors toward Franklin's sons."

"That doesn't necessarily go back to their high school days. Let me tell you it is not always easy navigating your sons' and daughters-in-laws' relationships. I try to stay a neutral observer of my sons' relationships —"

Jaymie snorted in laughter, knowing Mrs. Stubbs was not one to stay out of anything that interested her.

"— but it isn't always possible. But to answer your questions . . . though I didn't keep track of all the love affairs among students, when it came to Kim and Franklin, even the teachers were gossiping."

"Was it Franklin's cheating that broke them up?"

"So I understand. The guidance counselor at the time was a particularly gossipy fellow. He said that a 'friend' of one of them had snitched about his other girlfriend and it broke them up. Both were going with others by the time graduation came."

"A friend snitched," Jaymie mused. "What friend? Could it have been Russ Krauss?" she asked, thinking of Clutch's assessment that the man was sneaky.

"The peeping Tom?" she said, referring back to her mention of discovering him under the bleachers. "Nasty creeping fellow. Not a stupid boy, but his intelligence was visceral . . . feral, like a rat that figures out the trap and steals the cheese without triggering it."

Jaymie thought over her new theory. Russ did seem to thread his way through the lives of the principal players in the drama that ended in Alicia's death, there at every vital juncture.

"Why all these questions about things that happened thirty years ago or more? You don't imagine any of this mess is related to years gone by?"

"Maybe, maybe not. The connections among them all are tangled: Franklin and

Kim were dating; Russ was always on the periphery, wanting to belong; years later Franklin's son married Kim's daughter; Russ is now Kim's live-in partner . . . it's so —"

"So small-town," Mrs. Stubs said. "The high school was not large . . . not back then anyway. And among people their age there were only so many couplings and re-couplings. One tends to marry within one's peer group."

Jaymie took a deep breath, looked down at her purse, and said, "Speaking of people from that peer group . . . Tami Majewski knew them all. She was involved with the families back when Mia had her accident, and the day Jace died she was looking after Mia while Alicia was going to meet her lover. Tami sent me a letter."

"Why a letter?"

"She has information, Gus told Jakob."

"What information?"

"I haven't opened it. It makes me a little shaky."

"It's a letter, dear, not a shark. It won't bite you."

Jaymie nodded and grabbed the letter. Mrs. Stubs handed her a letter opener, and she slit the envelope open and pulled out the sheet, then handed the opener back to

319

her friend. She unfolded it. The handwriting was neat. She read through it once, her hands shaking, then took a moment to assess the information it contained.

"Well?" Mrs. Stubbs said.

"It may have changed everything. Vestry needs to see this." She handed it to her friend, who peered at it, then handed it back, asking Jaymie to read it aloud.

Jaymie complied, skipping over the early part of the letter and adding significant emphasis when she got to one line. "Listen to this part . . .

a couple of hours after Alicia dropped her off at my place we realized that Mia had forgotten her special dolly . . . a rag doll that she carried everywhere, one her grandma made for her. She asked if we could get it and I said sure. We went back to the house and I unlocked the door for her. She went and got it. When she came back she said she had looked out her bedroom window — it faces the back and you can see the garage from there — and asked why there was a black truck parked around back. I didn't think anything of it at the time . . . I knew Jace was back there in the garage working. Mia wasn't allowed anywhere near the garage; too dangerous, Alicia always said. I figured maybe Jace had someone there . . . a customer. That was at noon. I remember because we went home and I made chicken noodle soup for lunch.

Jaymie looked up and met Mrs. Stubbs's gaze. "A black truck. There are two black trucks that I know of. One is the Vance family's tow truck."

"What's the other?"

Jaymie took in a shaky breath. "Queensville Clean 'n Bright's passenger van."

"What are you thinking?"

"So *many* thoughts. They're like ferrets chasing each other around and around."

"Then you need to box up the individual ferrets," she said with a smile.

NINETEEN

Jaymie left the inn and sat in her SUV, thinking about black trucks and how they fit into her working theory of the day Jace died. Maybe she had to alter her theory yet again. Maybe she had to abandon it altogether. Or maybe she was letting all of this about black trucks distract her. The Vance tow truck was black, but now that she thought about it, there was likely more than one. Lew might have one. Franklin, maybe. But Mia would have recognized one of their trucks, wouldn't she? She would have asked why was her grandpa there, or her uncle, rather than talking about a black truck. Did Mia see the Queensville Clean 'n Bright van, black with yellow lettering? Very eye-catching. Russ Krauss drove it in his professional capacity as driver for the cleaning company, ferrying workers to their clients' homes.

But . . . Debbie Vance drove it too.

However, Russ Krauss had the more compelling motive to kill Jace, who had accused him of stealing catalytic converters off cars in his garage. Russ was in a precarious position, close to losing everything. He could have gone back to jail, maybe for a long time as a repeat offender, and he would most certainly have lost Kim all over again. And he had canceled his plans to go with Clutch and Lew to the car auction with some excuse.

Jaymie sat and stared at the letter Tami had written. The whole first part had been an aimless protracted apology for what had happened between them. It was a year and a half ago, but Jaymie hadn't forgotten it . . . not one second. It was weird to think that five years ago Tami had been going about her business, trusted to guard a precious child like Mia, and now she was in prison. Five years ago; so much had happened since. And yet, some things were still the same. The Vances still ran a tow truck company. Kim Hansen still lived with Russ Krauss. Erin still lived with her mom and Russ.

Erin. What had she been doing that day in Wolverhampton with Franklin Vance? No time like the present to ask. She called the newspaper.

"*Wolverhampton Weekly Howler,* Erin speaking. How may I help you?"

"Erin? It's Jaymie. How are you today?"

"I'm okay."

"Look, I won't keep you but I have a question. It's bugging me, and I have to know. The other day after we had lunch I saw you get into a truck with Franklin Vance. What was going on?"

"What's it to you?"

Jaymie stared at the letter and pondered. Say something in the face of the young woman's confrontational attitude or let it go? Say something: "It struck me as odd that you were with him. I didn't think you two would be close."

The line beeped. "I have to go." The phone clicked and buzzed, the connection gone.

Jaymie was torn: on the one hand, there was no reason why Erin should answer her. On the other . . . why wouldn't she? Her phone rang, it was Jakob. "Hey, hon," she said. "What's up?"

"Just checking in to make sure you're okay," he said.

"I got Tami's letter today."

"I thought you might when Gus said she sent it on Monday. You okay?"

"I'm fine," she said.

"Do you want to talk about it?"

"Not right now. Maybe later. How is your day going?"

"Good. Hey, I've got a shipment coming in later this afternoon and it might be late. Can you pick up Jocie from school today?"

"Sure."

They said sweet and naughty things to each other, made kissy noises and signed off. She appreciated that he took her at her word that she was okay and didn't press her. She drove to the Emporium, parked on the street and went in. Valetta was closing her pharmacy window and suggested they go to her house for lunch.

Valetta's cottage was a nineteenth-century bungalow painted dark green, with a wide porch. Inside it was cozy and comfortable, happily cluttered with Val's much-loved mid-century kitsch: ceramic poodles, old paint-by-number paintings and shabby braided rugs, along with comfortable furniture. Lunch there meant that Jaymie could visit her onetime pet, Denver, the crabby tabby, who now lived the life of a feline king as Val's companion.

Val disappeared into the kitchen to put on the kettle, yelling through the connecting arch that Brock had not yet gotten back to her about the insurance question. She reappeared with a steaming teapot and cups. Jaymie refused lunch, groaning that her stomach was full of the inn's pastry chef's creations, but she did accept a cup of tea, which she sipped as she visited with Denver on her lap while Val ate her tuna fish sandwich. "Val, I'm wondering, you knew Franklin Vance and Kim Ellsworthy in high school."

"Mhmm. I told you, she was my lab partner."

"They went together for a while and were the hot couple. Do you know why they broke up?"

"As a matter of fact, I do. Hold on." She ate her last bite, then cleared her lunch. Once done and tidied, she checked her watch and said, "I have something to show you. Wait here."

She came out with a dark blue, slim hardbound book. It looked familiar. On the cover was emblazoned *Wolverhampton High — The Wolf Pack.* It was bookmarked with hot pink sticky notes. Jaymie opened to those pages. First was a photo of senior Kim Ellsworthy. She was pretty, with her hair spiral-curled and pinned up on each side of her head, an exaggerated swoop of curly bangs, and the fixed toothy smile of the teen queen. She wore a pale pink shirt, collar popped, pearls around her throat . . . perfectly coiffed and made up. The next marked photos were of Russ Krauss and Franklin Vance. Krauss was as nerdy as he had been described — Jaymie examined him closely, trying to imagine him and Val on their one date to the movies — and Franklin as good-looking, in an eighties John Hughes bad-boy way. Lew looked just like his dad.

She looked up. "Okay. High school photos. Are you going to answer my question?"

Val held out her hand and took the book back, then flipped to another page, where there were random photos of groups out at sporting events and club meetings. She pointed and handed the book back to Jaymie, who eyed the picture Val had pointed to. It was of two lovers, tightly embracing, and another boy staring at them with . . . anger? Jaymie squinted and got close to the page. Was that . . . ? It *was*. Kim Ellsworthy was in the tight embrace of Russ Krauss. Franklin Vance was looking on with an expression of tight anger, a moment of raw emotion captured, a sliver of time when rage had simmered close to the surface.

It told her two things: Franklin and Kim's relationship was, indeed, over by senior year, and she had taken up with Russ. "Are you saying it was Russ Krauss who broke them up?"

Val shrugged. "Maybe. I know it got around that Franklin had been seeing some other girl."

"It 'got around,' as in, was purposely told to Kim? By Russ?"

"I'd bet on it. Russ was a sneaky jerk even then."

Jaymie hesitated, then said, "Val, you say he was sneaky. I've heard he was considered a weakling, a coward, and was bullied by the other guys, and that he was even used as a scapegoat, blamed for things he didn't do."

"That sounds about right. You know what high school is like: *Lord of the Flies* meets *Breakfast Club*, all those cliques and rivalries."

"But this," Jaymie said, pointing at the picture. "This would take a lot of guts, to embrace Kim in front of Franklin, one of the toughest guys in school."

Val tipped her head to one side. "I never thought of it like that. You're right, though."

"So . . . why?"

"Given that they are together all these years later, I have to say . . . overwhelming love on Russ's part?"

Jaymie nodded. "I agree. But what does Kim see in Russ? I mean, the guy is kind of a jerk, and he's been in jail for manslaughter. He has an unsavory past, to say the least."

"She wouldn't be the first woman to be with a guy no one else can stand. There must be something about him, I guess."

Jaymie pondered that and shook her head. "Either he's got something we don't see, or . . . maybe he's holding something over her?"

Val looked incredulous. "Does Kim Hansen strike you as the kind of woman who would knuckle under to a blackmailer?"

"No, she doesn't."

Val stood. "I have to get back to work. You be careful, okay?"

People kept saying that.

Jaymie gave Val a lift to the Emporium then headed back out to the country. She had two hours before she had to meet Jocie at school and she wanted to check one thing. When she pulled up to Alicia's house, abandoned and forlorn, she hesitated. Taking out her phone, she called Vestry's number but the detective was not in. She was invited to leave a message. "Have her call me when she has a moment," Jaymie said. "Jaymie Müller . . . she has my number."

She sat on the shoulder of the road and stared at the house, turning over and over in her mind her supposition that Jace Vance's death ultimately came down to money: who had it; who wanted it; who needed it. How his death guaranteed it. She swallowed, sickened by her own thoughts, her new theory. But she had come here to salve her curiosity, so . . . she got out of the vehicle. The wind was coming up. She reached back in, grabbed a sweater from the backseat, and huddled into it. She climbed the driveway and circled to the back of the house, looking up to where she presumed Mia's room would be. Then she turned; the child would see the black truck only if it was pulled right up in front of the garage.

The heavy sound of a motor thrummed in the drive and she started walking back, nervous now that someone was about to join her. She clutched her cell phone in her sweater pocket. A white tow truck with *Vance Towing* in black letters on the side door pulled up the lane with a grimy sedan on the hook, but stopped as the driver saw her. Franklin Vance stepped down out of the high cab.

He eyed her as he strolled toward the gate and undid the padlock. He opened the gate, pocketing the lock.

"Mr. Vance, hello," she said.

"Hi. You're . . . who?"

"I'm a friend . . . I'm . . . I knew Alicia."

He looked blank for a moment, and then said, "Are you . . ." He hitched a thumb toward the back of the property, where the woods were.

Jaymie nodded. "I still can't believe it. That she was coming to see me when she . . ." She shook her head and shrugged helplessly, shoving her hands deeper into her cardigan pockets.

Somberly, he looked down at the dirt lane. "I don't believe it either. It makes me angry that someone would do something like that to such a beautiful soul."

"Alicia?"

He looked up and met her gaze. "Alicia was first-class all the way. My son loved her to the day he died. I'll never forgive . . ." He stopped and took in a deep breath.

"Forgive who?"

"Whoever killed her."

"Who do you think that was?"

His eyes darkened and his lips twisted in a grimace. "I'm not sure. Yet."

"Yet?"

He looked undecided, watching her. He shuffled from foot to foot, and then said, in a burst of candor, "Look, to be honest, I thought it might be you."

"Me?" she gasped. "Why . . . how . . . I don't understand."

"Look, I don't wanna be rude, but lady, you're in the news . . . a *lot*. And you know, where there's smoke —"

"Sometimes where there's smoke there's just a smoldering pile of nothing," she retorted. "I would never —"

"Okay, okay!" he said, holding up his hands. "You didn't kill Alicia. Who else knew she was coming to see you?"

"I don't know," Jaymie admitted.

"And you found her in the woods, even though you say you didn't know she was on her way to your place through those woods."

"Yeah, that's right. I did not know she was on her way to my house. She was supposed to call me."

"How do I know she didn't? How do I know she didn't tell you she was coming through the woods and you met her there and killed her?"

"This is ridiculous. What motive would I have to kill Alicia?"

His expression clouded and he squinted his eyes. "I don't know. I can't think of anyone who would want to kill my daughter-in-law. Alicia was a good woman and a great mom. We're all devastated."

"And I had my daughter and dog with me. Even you must be able to see what you're saying is ridiculous. I'm in those woods a couple of times a week. Mr. Vance, were you and Erin trying to find out what I knew? Did you tell her to question me? Is that why she got in your truck the day I met her at Wellington's Retreat for lunch?"

Shamefaced, he nodded. "Like I said . . . I thought maybe you knew something you weren't sharing."

"Your connection to Kim and her family goes way back," Jaymie said. "My older sister Becca and friend Valetta went to school with you and Kim and Clutch Roth. Why did you and Kim break up?" She wanted to hear it from his viewpoint.

"Why are you asking?"

"I heard there was a rumor about you dating someone else during high school and I wondered . . . did that come from Russ Krauss? Did he snitch on you to break up you and Kim and then date her himself?"

He smiled, a grim kind of smirk. "You're a little dirt digger, aren't you? That was a hundred years ago. Russ Krauss was then and is still a piece of work, let me tell you.

And he got what he always wanted, didn't he?"

"Only after years between then and more recently, right? I've heard there was a lot of turmoil in his life, that he even killed a guy once."

His face shadowed with a troubled look. His glance shifted off to the woods. "I'll admit, I've been concerned about him being around my granddaughter. I'd do anything for that little girl, but Russ . . ." He hunched one shoulder and knit his brows. "I don't know how Kim could be taken in by him. And to let him *live* there . . ." He shook his head, a look of disgust on his face. He scruffed his unshaven chin. "Erin doesn't trust him and neither do I."

Jaymie got a shivery feeling down her back. She was close to a solution, she could feel it. Was what she suspected true? "I don't mean to bring up painful memories, but I have to ask . . . do you suspect Russ was involved in Jace's death?"

"*Jace's* death? But . . . that was an accident."

"Would it surprise you to learn that there was a truck here the day he died . . . a *black* truck?"

"A black truck?" He narrowed his eyes. "What are you getting at?"

She took a deep breath; once said, this could not be taken back. "A black truck was seen here. I was wondering if it could have been the Queensville Clean 'n Bright van that Russ Krauss drives?"

He blinked, mouth open, and his gaze turned inward. He tilted his head and a minute passed. "Are you saying you suspect Russ Krauss killed my son?" he said, his voice a guttural growl. The idea was new to him, it appeared. "Why would he do that?"

"Maybe you know?" She waited to see if he raised the motive she did wonder about.

He shook his head and frowned, then his gaze cleared. "Wait . . . do you mean . . . ?" He watched her face, appearing undecided.

"I've heard Jace was about to go to the police about a theft of catalytic converters from vehicles in this garage. He thought Russ was the thief. Russ had been in jail. I'm sure he didn't want to go back. As a repeat offender, his sentence would be longer."

Franklin took in a deep breath and rocked back on his heels, passing one hand over his thick graying hair. "You've sent me reeling, I don't mind saying. To think that all these years —"

"You never suspected?"

"What, that Russ was stealing catalytic

converters? I knew about that, and that Jace was going to press charges. I never considered that Russ may have *killed* Jace." His words rang with the tone of absolute sincerity. "If it's true, and Alicia suspected him . . ."

Jayme nodded at his line of thought. "If Alicia suspected he caused her husband's death, she would have tried to prove it. Maybe she was coming to me to share something, some knowledge." She watched him carefully. Had she said too much? He was taking it in, absorbing it.

"Russ is there living at Kim's house, he would have known what was up. Alicia was over there with Mia all the time. Sneaky son of a . . . he was always a creeper, you know?" He glanced back at the garage and then to Jaymie. "And yeah, he could have done it, now I think on it. He's got the knowhow. I mean, he knows his way around a jack. And he's always around here, always driving that black van up behind the house." He stared at her, his thick brows lowering over his dark eyes. "I gotta think about this. You've knocked me for a loop, lady."

"I'm not sure of any of this, you know," Jaymie warned. "It's just one theory among others."

"But it makes sense," he said with grow-

336

ing urgency. "What are you going to do about it? We can't let that jerk get away with this!"

With grim determination, Jaymie said, "Russ is not going to get away with anything, I promise you that."

"I misjudged you," Franklin said. He strode forward and took her hand, shaking it, his large calloused hand enclosing hers with warmth. "I misjudged you and I'm sorry."

His smile transformed his face. She caught a glimpse of what in his teen years attracted girls. He was charming when he chose to be, with a smile that radiated sincerity. She gave him an answering smile. "I'd best be off," she said, and returned to her SUV. As she started the vehicle she saw him get back into the tow truck and haul his load around to the garage in back. Talking to him had helped her solidify her suspicions. She felt fairly certain she was right, but . . . how to prove it?

TWENTY

There was still a lot to do with her day. She bought groceries and took them home, checked on the soup in the slow cooker, stirred it, then turned it down and got out the ingredients for cheddar biscuits, which she would throw together at the last minute. She took Hoppy for a walk down the road to the property they had bought, to check on progress. It was taking longer than they had anticipated to get zoning changed and permits allowed, but work was finally starting on what would be the site of a Müller family farmer's market. Land had been cleared, a section leveled. Footings had been poured and were curing. It was too late this year to start building. In spring they would be ready to get down to it, and by the following autumn they would be open.

After a game of fetch Jaymie returned to the cabin, tidied, did a load of laundry, checked her email and her blog, answered questions and then shut it down. She was trying to avoid thinking of the letter from Tami and how she felt about the contact. Her last encounter with the woman had been unsettling and she still wasn't over it. She should be after a year and a half but nope, it was still there waiting, like a coiled venomous snake poised to strike when least expected. Normally if something was bothering her she would go for a walk in the woods to calm herself, but now she couldn't even look at the woods without thinking of Alicia, and that took her back to where her suspicions were straying and who she thought was guilty. It was a vicious circle.

Everything pointed to Russ Krauss. Her own sense of him as someone she could not trust; no one had a good word to say; he had the violent past and motives for both deaths. He made sense as the killer of both Jace and Alicia.

And yet . . . she thought the killer might — just *might* — be someone else entirely. She jumped to her feet. She needed to get moving. It was almost time to pick up Jocie. She was grabbing her keys when her phone buzzed with a text. It was from Erin, sending her Kim's number and asking her to call her mother, please.

Puzzled, Jaymie called the number and

Kim answered, sounding distressed and breathless. Jaymie explained the text from Erin.

"Oh, Jaymie, you're a lifesaver. Or . . . you could be. Are you or your husband picking Jocie up from school today?"

"I'm actually setting out to do that right now."

"Could you . . . oh, I *hate* to ask this." She sounded near tears, desperate.

"Kim, I offered help and I meant it."

"Erin can't get away, she has a class at the college this evening. Could you pick up Mia from school and keep her for me for an hour or two? Or . . . maybe more?"

"No problem. What's up?"

"Russ thinks he's having a heart attack."

"Oh *no!*"

Kim spoke to someone in the background, and there was a jumble of noise. "We're at the hospital in Wolverhampton right now getting him checked out. He got a phone call an hour ago and collapsed. He got up again, but he started feeling chest pains. Look, I have to go. I'll feel ten times better if I know you've got Mia."

"Kim, do not worry about it one little bit. How about I keep her for the night unless you tell me otherwise? The girls can have a midweek sleepover. We'll make it fun. Is there anything I need to know about the prosthetic?"

"Mia knows how to take care of herself. And she has keys to Alicia's house if you need PJs for her, or anything else," she said, her voice breaking on her late daughter's name. "I'll call you when I know more but . . ." Her voice faded and she again talked to someone else over beeping and the noise of a loudspeaker. "I don't know how much more I can take. I have to go," she said, a sob in her voice.

"Kim, it's okay, stay strong. Call me when you can, but if you can't, please, *don't worry!* We can look after Mia."

"I know she'll be okay with you and Jakob. Thank you, Jaymie. I have to . . . Russ looks so gray! I have to go." Kim loved Russ, that much was clear from the fear in her voice. This could get complicated. Jaymie checked the time. Better get a move on.

It was fortunate that Jocie had decided to take Mia under her wing and was standing with her outside the school door waiting. Jaymie got out of the SUV and went to the girls. She crouched down, unsure what to say or how to refer to Russ. "Mia, your grandmother's friend, Russ, was feeling ill. She took him to the hospital in Wolverhampton."

"Grandpa Russ is sick?" Her pale narrow face twisted in worry, and her blonde brows lowered.

"They're not sure what's going on, but he's not feeling well."

"Is . . . is he gonna be okay? We're supposed to go horseback riding this Saturday."

"Just you and him?"

She nodded. Jaymie was surprised. Kim trusted Russ to take Mia out like that? "Do you often go out with your Grandpa Russ?"

"Sure," Mia replied, fidgeting with her knapsack. "He likes doing stuff. We go out on the river in his boat. And we go fishing. I caught a sunfish, but we let it go. Grandpa Russ took it off the hook and it swam away." She frowned and looked worried. "Is he gonna be okay?" she asked again.

Jaymie hugged the girl close. "We'll think good thoughts. Your grandmother is with him and they're getting him checked out. You'll come home with us for now. You may even sleep over if your grandmother is late getting home."

Jocie said "Yay!" but then said, in a small voice, taking Mia's hand, "I hope your grandpa is okay."

The girls played with Lilibet and Hoppy for a while, then Jaymie sat them down at the kitchen table and brought out the craft supplies. Mia wanted to make a card for Russ. Jaymie provided the craft paper, markers, glue and assorted bits and pieces. Mia drew a nice rendition of a horse, and then glued googly eyes on it, and wrote *Get Better Soon, Grandpa Russ!*

Jaymie mixed the biscuit dough, then rolled it out and cut it into squares, lining them up on a parchment-lined baking sheet. She turned on the oven to preheat and glanced out the window as Jakob pulled up the drive. She grabbed a sweater and went out to greet him as she pulled it on. After a hug and a kiss, she told him that Mia would be with them for dinner and possibly overnight, and explained why.

He put his arm over her shoulders as they strolled back to the door. "Russ is having a heart attack? That's terrible!"

"We don't know if it's a heart attack yet. I hope not."

"And you say Mia seems fond of him?"

She paused with him on the doorstep. "When I was at Kim's one day he came home early from work and had brought Mia's favorite fast food. He seems to care for her. I don't know what to think. I guess I didn't peg him as a kid-friendly guy, especially after hearing that he . . ." She glanced around and lowered her voice, continuing, "*Killed* someone. Even if it was an accident. Is it weird that I felt that way?"

"Honey, it's not weird. You were going off your feeling from meeting him, but I suppose if Mia is fond of him . . . he's probably a different guy when he's relaxed and doing something he likes, like fishing. We never see all sides of people we meet so briefly. Let's go in."

They ate dinner, cleaned up, and the girls retreated upstairs to investigate Jocie's bookshelf. And still no word from Kim. Jaymie had been pacing anxiously, phone in hand. It was getting late. "I think we need PJs for Mia. Kim said to get the key from her and go over to Alicia's house to get whatever we need."

"I can go, if you like."

"I already know the house," Jaymie replied. "It will only take a half hour at most."

Mia told Jaymie where her room was in the house, and asked for a couple of other things. Jaymie made a list: PJs, the books Jocie had let Mia borrow from the Junk Stops Here — she had already read some of them — her cat-shaped nightlight, and her unicorn-hooded bathrobe. Jaymie grabbed a shopping bag to take over to carry things back in, got her keys, Mia's keys, donned a light jacket, and headed out.

Alicia's house was dark, but a motion detector light mounted on the front corner came on as she drove up the drive and around the back. She didn't want her car to be seen from the road. She wasn't sure why, but it felt safer to park behind. As she approached the back door she imagined Alicia coming home with a sleepy Mia, climbing those steps, unlocking the door, throwing the keys aside and turning on lights. She tried to imagine the mother and daughter's lives in this house.

She took a deep breath and entered, shoving the keys in her pocket and searching around for a light switch. She found it on the wall and flicked it on, taking another deep breath and letting it out, looking around the kitchen. Covering her mouth, she choked back a sob. It was heartbreaking to witness the detritus of a life cut short: crusted dishes on the kitchen counter; scummy coffee cup set on the table on top of a stack of flyers; school bulletins and bills; the bag of knobs and drawer pulls Alicia had bought at the Junk Stops Here.

The police had been here and searched the home, evident in fingerprint powder on surfaces, but since the crime hadn't happened in Alicia's home, not much else had been disturbed. Resisting the urge to tidy and clean, Jaymie set to the task at hand, finding Mia's room and the items she needed for the night.

And yet . . . it came back to her in that moment, Wenda's insistence that Alicia had left behind a note in case she was ever hurt. Three-plus years ago she had suspected she was in danger, but from whom? What would the note say? No one else but Wenda had ever heard of it . . . or admitted hearing of it. Kim dismissed Wenda as a drama queen. Did the note even exist? Or was it only there in the fevered imagination of a coworker prone to exaggerating or dramatizing? That had not been her impression of Wenda, but she didn't know her well enough to be sure. Detective Vestry had said that they had searched. If there was a note, they would have found it.

Still . . . they could not have searched every book, every corner, every place one might hide a note, especially a note of that sort. Where would Alicia leave a note if there was one? She'd hide it, certainly, so the casual observer would not come across it, but where? Did she have time for a quick look? Jaymie patted her pocket and realized that moment that she had left behind her cellphone. Darn. She couldn't call Jakob and tell him she'd be a few minutes longer. She'd better hop to it, because if she was gone too long he'd worry, and she didn't want to put him through that. There was a clock on the wall; she had only been gone ten minutes. She would go get Mia's items, then, if she had time, she'd have a quick look around.

The house was startlingly still, nothing but the *tick tick tick* of a wall clock. She climbed the stairs, her steps silent on the carpeting, switched on a hall light and found Mia's room. It was messy, as a kid's room often is, with the bedcovers pulled up roughly and toys scattered over surfaces. There was a coloring book on the floor, crayons strewn about, and a pile of books by the bed. Were those the books from the junk store? She had to assume they were. She gathered and stacked them on the bed then found the colorful robe hanging on the back of the door — it had a hood with a unicorn horn on it. So cute! She folded that and set it by the books.

Now . . . pajamas. She wanted fresh ones, not the ones that had lain on the bed for the last few days. She checked the dresser and found a neat stack in what was the pajama drawer. She chose a comfy pair warm enough for the cabin, then thought

347

she'd better get Mia a change of clothes in case she did spend the whole night. Finally, she had everything gathered. She picked it all up, piled it at the head of the stairs and checked — quickly — Alicia's room.

It felt like an invasion of privacy checking the book she was reading, the medications she took, the journal she wrote in. But the dead have no privacy, not when something in their life might provide a clue to their murder. She steeled herself to the task; she was doing this for the right reasons. There was nothing in the bedroom. She checked one other tiny room with slanting ceilings, Alicia's home office. If she had left a note about her fears, it might be in here.

She flicked the light on and approached the desk, looking around with amazement and concern. It looked like a blizzard of paperwork. She stood stock-still for a moment taking in the mess. It did not look organized, it looked like someone had been searching. The police? Maybe this was how they left it when they took her files away to sift through, but Vestry hadn't said anything about this pile of paperwork. Not that the detective was forthcoming about extraneous details. Maybe someone else was searching for the accusatory note? She crouched down and leafed through some of it, but acknowledged that if the note had been in this room, the searcher would have found it. It was a waste of more time than she had to go through all of this.

Something banged below. She started, flicked off the office light and crept out the door and into the hall. A door slammed. Should she hide out or acknowledge that she was there to whoever it was? Maybe it was Kim. She took a deep breath, grabbed the stack of books and clothes from the top of the stairs and started down, as a male shouted, *"Who's there?"* Her heart pounding, she descended the rest of the way and paused at the bottom of the steps. "Hello?" she called out.

Lew Vance charged toward her but stopped as he recognized her. "What are *you* doing here?"

"Mia is spending the night at our house. I'm getting her PJs and a change of clothes." She paused a beat, blinking and looking at him. "What are *you* doing here?"

"I . . . I was bringing stuff to the garage and saw the light on and thought . . ." He stopped and shook his head. "I thought someone had broken in."

"As you can see, I'm not a burglar," she said, jingling the keys in her free hand. She moved to go past him but he grabbed her arm. She whirled and tugged her arm out of his grasp. "Hey, don't grab me!" Her heart was again pounding with a sickening *thud thud thud,* her stomach roiling.

Lew stared at her with mistrust, his dark eyes under thick brows clouded with anger. "I want to know why you're here, what you're looking for."

"Exactly what I said." Suspicion flooded through her and she tried to control her breathing, which had quickened, and her heart, pounding still with panic. Why was he being so confrontational? He wasn't Alicia's killer . . . was he? "Kim called me," she said, her breath short, her words gasping. "She took Russ to the hospital. Erin was tied up and she didn't know what else to do. Mia and my daughter Jocie are good friends, so . . . I picked her up and she's staying with us." She was babbling.

"She could have called me."

"Well, she didn't." She took a deep breath. With shaking hands she shifted the pile of clothes to her other arm and pointed to the canvas bag nearby. "Can you hand that to me so I can put this stuff in?"

He stayed still, his hands at his side, his fists clenching and unclenching, his jaw tightening. He appeared undecided and he looked terrible, his eyes bloodshot, his beard coming in scruffy, his clothes rumpled. Was this the demeanor of a guilty man? Or a man in pain and grieving? She was not going to stay in this house and find out. She snatched up the bag and shoved in the clothes, the books tumbling to the floor in a clatter. She was not going to stop to pick them up, but he blocked her way and bent, gathering them.

"I cared for Alicia, deeply," he said, his voice thick with tears. "I miss her. And Mia. Now that Kim has her in her clutches I'll probably never see my niece again." He handed her the books.

"Lew, I won't pretend to understand all the dynamics of your family and Alicia's," she said, her voice softer and more in control. "Were you and Alicia a couple?" She worked her way around him toward the door.

He nodded. "I've always loved her. I think I always will."

"Did you love her five years ago, when your brother died?"

He stared at her for a long minute, his expression uncomprehending, but then he appeared to get her implication and anger flooded back. "If you're asking were we cheating on Jace with each other, the answer is *no*!" His expression changed, a grimace of pain squeezing it. "I gotta go." He elbowed past her and flung himself from the house. In seconds she heard the sound of a throbbing motor gunning and raced to the door in time to see his black pickup roaring away into the night.

Hands shaking, her body flooded with adrenaline now that the danger — imaginary or real — was over, she knelt and packed the bag more carefully, thinking about what he had said. He loved Alicia. He had *always* loved her, though he claimed they weren't together five years ago. She stopped and the final truth dropped: if he was telling the truth, he and Alicia were not a couple five years ago. So that left . . . she shuddered, but it was inevitable. It was the last piece of the puzzle, and it had fallen into her hands.

This time she was sure. She now knew who killed Alicia, and why.

The girls were supposed to be asleep but whispers and giggles floated down the stairs from above. It was good that Mia and Jocie had become friends. Maybe it was helping the little girl in a time of turmoil and sadness. Jocie was adept at what the family called seeing the silly, and the laughter from above proved she was deploying her special talent.

Jaymie told Jakob about trying to find the note and about the confrontation with Lew Vance. His grip around her shoulders tightened, but he didn't say anything. They'd had a conversation early on in their dating life that she had been on her own and independent for a long time. Now, in her thirties, while she would take no unnecessary chances, she would live her life as she expected he would, guided by good sense and a refusal to let fear have control. It didn't mean occasions like this didn't alarm him as her husband and lover, but it did keep him from overreacting, and she appreciated it.

Her phone rang; it was Kim. She was home with Russ. He had not been having a heart attack, but a panic attack. "A panic attack? What was he panicking about?" Jaymie asked, puzzled.

"I . . . don't know," the woman replied. She sounded tired. "He's been stressed lately and I think it overwhelmed him."

"The girls are in bed and comfortable here, and you sound exhausted, Kim. Why don't you pick Mia up in the morning, or let me take them to school and you can pick her up there in the afternoon? I can run her extra things over to you after I drop them off."

"Are you sure she's okay? After what Mia has been through, I don't want her to worry."

"I'm going upstairs now to check on them, but Jocie has her laughing, and that's a good sign. She was worried about Russ earlier. I'll tell her he's okay. If she seems like she'd like to come home, I'll bring her to you. How about that?"

"I can't thank you enough, Jaymie. I really can't. And you're right, I'm so tired. I've always had Mia with me a lot, but she was with her mom most of the time. I've forgotten what it's like to have a kid around twenty-four-seven. Now it's just me, and with Russ the way he is . . ." Her voice cracked and she stopped.

Jaymie took in a long shaky breath; the heartbreak in Kim's voice was devastating. Gently, she said, "I hope you'll let us help in any way we can. I'll text you in a few minutes to let you know if Mia is staying here or if I'm bringing her home." She hung up with a sigh.

Jakob hugged her and kissed her cheek. "I love you," he whispered in her ear. "You're a good woman."

"Oh, Jakob," she said, turning to him and burying her face in his neck. "Kim sounds lost. I feel so awful for her. Losing a daughter . . ."

"I know."

She climbed the stairs, leaving Jakob downstairs to turn off lights. She checked on the girls. They were still awake, as she had suspected they would be, and engaged in trying doll bonnets on Lilibet, as Hoppy tried to muscle in on the fun. Mia was fond of the little dog and had said during dinner that he was like her, losing a leg when he was little.

Jaymie noticed the pink prosthetic leg propped up against the dresser in the corner, and looked to the little girl. "Mia, how are you doing, sweetie?"

She looked up and smiled. "I'm okay."

But she wasn't. She looked tired and pale. Jaymie sat down on the bed and regarded them both. Jocie met her gaze and there was a hint of worry in her pretty eyes. Jaymie turned her attention to Mia, taking the girl's slim hands in her own and chafing them.

"I heard from your grandma. Your Grandpa Russ is fine, nothing at all wrong with him. He was upset and it made him feel ill. Taking him to the hospital was a precaution."

The girl sighed in relief, but then looked puzzled. "How can being upset make you sick?"

"You know when you're worried it gives you an upset stomach?"

She nodded.

"It's like that." She paused, but then saw the danger and added, "But you should never dismiss pain or anything like that because you think it's only happening because you're upset. Your grandmother did the right thing to take your Grandpa Russ to the hospital to get checked out. If you ever feel sick, tell someone, don't pass it off."

Mia heaved a sigh and nodded. "Mom got headaches all the time," she said. "I wonder if it was because she was upset?"

"Was she upset?" Jaymie said carefully.

"She worried all the time," Mia said with a solemn look on her face. "She worried about money. And she worried about me all the time. I heard her yelling at Grandpa that he'd never see me again if she had her way."

Jaymie took in a sharp breath. She knew that Alicia didn't like Russ, but to threaten to keep Mia away from him when he lived with Kim? "Mia, if you're ever worried about things you should speak up. Tell your grandma, or your Aunt Erin. Never ever feel that you need to keep things to yourself."

She yawned and nodded sleepily as Jocie took the bonnet off Lilibet.

"I'm going to take you to school in the morning, and your grandmother is going to pick you up later. Is that okay with you?"

Mia nodded, then yawned again and curled up on the big double bed, relief making her sleepy. Jocie put her arms around Jaymie's neck and whispered, "Thank you, Mama. You made her feel better."

"Goodnight, sweetie. We'll see you both in the morning. Mia, Jakob and I are in the next room if you need anything at all." She smiled and turned off the light. "Come on, Hoppy . . . come with me."

TWENTY-ONE

In the middle of the night Jocie came and got Jaymie. Her friend was crying. Mia had awoken from a nightmare. Jaymie sat on the edge of the bed and held the little girl close, letting her tell the whole nightmare as Jocie curled up close to them. It was one of those spooky childhood dreams of being lost in the woods with something or someone chasing her. It wasn't hard to understand the context. She let the little girl babble for a few minutes trying to decide if this was something she should call Kim about.

But soon Mia was getting sleepy again. The girls were too old to be read a bedtime story, but maybe this was an exception. She covered them both up again, dimmed the light and, using her most soothing voice, Jaymie read out loud one of Jocie's favorite books, *The Velveteen Rabbit,* a gift to her from Jaymie's mom. By the time she had come to the end both girls were snuffling softly in sleep.

Jaymie crept from the room, tears in her eyes, and slipped into bed with Jakob, who was also snuffling in sleep. But Jaymie didn't sleep immediately. She made a vow: *Alicia,* she whispered, *I will make sure the monster who killed you pays.*

Morning was the usual jumbled chaos. Jakob made breakfast — chocolate chip pancakes, his specialty — but had to zoom out the door as he had a meeting with his brother to schedule the upcoming Christmas season, talk about the construction of the market, and then go off to do some deliveries for the junk shop. While the girls got ready, Jaymie quickly did the dishes. As they headed out to her SUV she decided at the last minute to let Hoppy join them. He struggled up into the backseat and sat between the two girls, where Mia petted and fussed over him.

She dropped them off at school, told the parent volunteer that Mia's grandmother would be picking her up that afternoon unless things changed, and headed back to the SUV. It had been days since she spoke to Detective Vestry. The woman was no doubt busy. Jaymie had read on social media that the police had conducted interviews with

Alicia's employer, family members, and anyone she had recently had contact with. The town was buzzing with innuendo, suspicion, gossip and rumor, but the police had given no new information to the *Howler*.

In Jaymie's opinion, Alicia's murder had the hallmarks of a difficult case to solve. Her life was tangled and complicated, numerous people had reasons for wishing her dead, and she had been killed away from home. Forensics — fingerprints, blood evidence, material evidence, interviews, security video, public pleas for tips — would be reviewed, but unless something happened soon it would likely go cold. Jaymie was now relatively certain who did it. Would Vestry believe her? It went back so far and was so tangled and unbelievable in the most distressing way, she needed to get it straight in her own mind before she made the accusation. Troubled and gloomy, Jaymie drove into Wolverhampton to Kim's home, parked in the drive, got the bag of Mia's belongings out of the backseat and invited Hoppy to come along.

She tapped on the door. Kim opened it and waved her inside, finger to her lips.

"I have my dog here, is that okay?"

She nodded and held the door open for Jaymie as Hoppy wobbled in and set about sniffing around the house. "Russ is still sleeping," she muttered, pointing upstairs. "I called in to QCB and told them he's not coming in to work today."

"Who takes his place driving the employees on days he's out?"

"Debbie."

Jaymie followed her into the kitchen. "Ah, Debbie Vance. I knew her as Debbie Kouris. We went to school together. Is it ever awkward, Lew's ex-wife as Russ's employer, while Lew was dating Alicia, your daughter?"

"Coffee?"

Jaymie nodded.

Kim flicked on the coffee maker. The scent of coffee filled the kitchen. She sat down at the table, where a tablet was propped up against the sugar bowl. "I don't think Debbie cared. It's been years, after all. She was over Lew a long time ago."

"I'm not so sure, Kim, that Debbie is over Lew."

Kim shook her head but said nothing. She brought over mugs of coffee and both women fixed up their beverage. Jaymie shared Mia's nightmare with Kim. "I thought of calling you, but she calmed and got sleepy. I read them Jocie's favorite story and she went back to sleep. Russ being sick upset her, especially after . . . after losing her mother in such a tragic way."

Kim's red-rimmed eyes brimmed with tears.

"She and Russ seem to get along. He cares for her."

Kim nodded. "She's his granddaughter, after all."

"Birth relationship, adopted, step . . . none of that matters, does it? Love is love. My in-laws love their grandkids and step-grandkids equally."

"But she's his natural granddaughter."

"What?"

Kim hesitated. She then took a deep breath and said, "I'll tell you. I may as well, he's been wanting this for so long and now I feel bad I waited, but it's so complicated. All this stress has made him anxious. I blame myself for what happened." She met Jaymie's gaze. "After high school Russ and I stayed together for a while. I got pregnant with Alicia, and then . . ." She bit her lip and looked away.

"Then he had the trouble that sent him to jail."

She nodded.

Alicia's father was a bad dude, Erin had said. So that's what that meant. "Kim, what happened? What led to his arrest? I want it from your perspective."

"The same thing that has always happened to Russ," Kim said, a bitter tinge in her voice. "I know he's not perfect, but that man has put up with more than anyone I've ever known. Everybody's scapegoat . . . caught in a web of *lies*."

Jaymie watched her. "Do you mean Russ didn't do it? That he didn't kill that guy?"

Tears streamed down her cheeks and she shook her head. "But nobody's ever going to believe him. Not now." She grabbed a tissue out of a box in a basket on the table and blew her nose. "He *tried* telling the truth, but his past arrests . . . it's like everything that has been put on his shoulders for so long snowballed." She shook her head. "When he went to prison he told me to forget him, to raise Alicia not knowing he was her dad. I was stupid and so, *so* angry."

"He didn't do it?" Jaymie asked again.

"He's no angel, Jaymie, but no, he didn't do it. However, he knew the score. There were people . . ." She sighed and buried her face in her hands, scrubbed her eyes and put her hands down on the tabletop. "He pled guilty to the lesser charge of manslaughter. At the time I didn't understand what he was doing. I was like, *why won't you fight the charge?* It took me a long time to

363

realize that he was trying to protect me the best way he knew how. That was so long ago now . . . twenty . . . six years? Twenty-seven? Alicia was a toddler. He spent ten years in federal, got out, moved around a little, and then ten years ago we met up again. I still loved him." Defiantly, she lifted her chin. "I know you won't understand that, but no one sees the Russ I know. He loved Alicia. He loves me and he adores Mia."

"So you and Russ got back together. But you never told Alicia he was her father."

She shrugged helplessly. "Russ was working on her. Or trying to. She was a tough cookie. I was trying to figure out how to tell her. He and Mia get along like a house afire, and I think Alicia would have come around eventually."

Jaymie frowned, puzzled. "So . . . Alicia didn't tell Russ that he was never going to see Mia again?"

Frowning, Kim shook her head in puzzlement. "Of course not."

"She *was* planning on moving away."

"Maybe," Kim admitted. "It wasn't set in stone. Russ and I would have moved too if she left. Alicia knew that."

There was stirring upstairs and the flush of a toilet. Kim's glance shifted and she

364

listened. "I have to check on him. His blood pressure was through the roof when they hooked him up. He could have a heart attack for real."

Jaymie drained the last of her coffee and rose. "I'll let you go, Kim. Thanks for confiding in me. Hang in there. I think things will turn out all right. Or as right as they can be."

"I hope so. I don't think I can handle any more. I feel like I'm on the verge of a nervous breakdown."

Impulsively pulling the older woman into a hug, Jaymie murmured, "I'm sorry for what you've been through! I know we haven't known each other long, but if you need to talk or a shoulder to cry on, call or text me."

Kim sniffed and nodded as they parted. "I will. Thanks."

"One more thing," Jaymie said, pausing mid-turn. "Who was the phone call from, the one that sent Russ into a panic?"

Kim wasn't sure — Russ wouldn't say — but she suspected. Jaymie nodded at the name. She should have known. "I may have more questions. Is it okay if I call or text?"

"Text, that way if Russ is sleeping it won't ring and wake him up. I have text on vibrate."

"Okay. I'll go now."

She had a lot to do, including a long walk with Hoppy along the St. Clair. During the walk she tried to figure out how to explain her hypothesis to Vestry. The detective was resistant to Jaymie's theories, but usually fair. If Jaymie included all she knew, all she suspected, the woman would hopefully see it her way. After her walk, she stopped at the Emporium, where she got the final bit of information she felt she needed. It came to her from Val by way of her brother Brock, who had spoken to a friend and insurance professional in Wolverhampton. The insurance agent had been able to expound on the various types of insurance and who would receive benefits in what event. Her theory was complete except for minor details she had to surmise, without the resources of the police department behind her.

That evening, after talking about it with Jakob, she decided: the next morning she would go to Vestry and tell her all. No phone call would do . . . she'd visit her in person. She called and left a message for Vestry that she would be coming in to talk.

It was late, but Jaymie was restless. The next day was a professional development day for teachers, so Jocie was staying over at her grandparents with her cousins. Jakob tried to get Jaymie to sit on the sofa with him to watch a movie, but she was pacing. Until she could see the detective she was antsy, unable to settle. Jaymie fretted aloud and at length, fortunate to have a husband who would listen to her worries and fears.

"I get why you're apprehensive," Jakob said. "You like to feel fully prepared. You know how you always write notes before you go in to talk to your editor? Maybe you should do the same before you talk to the detective."

"That's a good idea," Jaymie said. She retrieved her favorite notebook and pen. Jakob patted the sofa beside him. Hoppy took it as an invitation and jumped up. He pulled the little dog onto his lap and Jaymie sat beside him.

"Write a detailed account of how you think it happened."

She wrote for a few minutes. "Okay, I've explained how I think Jace was killed."

"And you're sure it was murder?"

"I am." She explained how Val's information on insurance had given her confidence that she was on the right track.

"So who killed Jace?"

Tapping her pencil on the notebook, Jaymie thought for a moment. "I started with two competing theories: one was that Jace, despondent about what he had done to Mia and concerned about money for her ongoing care, set up the accident, killing himself so his insurance could go to Alicia and Mia."

"Except he didn't have personal insurance."

"Exactly. When I heard that, I started to think Alicia had set it up. She was angry at Jace for the accident that injured Mia so badly. Kim let slip that her daughter thought Jace did still have life insurance. She didn't find out it had lapsed until after he was dead and she tried to file a claim. She checked into a motel the morning of his accident, but who's to say she stayed there? She could have gone back and set up the murder, asking Jace to crawl under the truck to check it for Erin. Or maybe she set up the accident before she left with Mia that morning."

"Setting up that murder to look like an accident could not be easy."

"And yet, if it is murder, it was almost categorized as an accident. It's happened before. Mrs. Stubbs's true crime addiction made me curious and I did some online snooping. I've read some cases."

"What made you decide this one had to be murder?"

"Everyone says how careful Jace was. I know, I know," she said, holding up one hand when Jakob was about to speak. "Smart and careful people do dumb things all the time, especially when they are under stress. Though that's often true, I don't think it is in this case." Her stomach churned. "What I started to think was so awful, I couldn't believe it at first. Maybe Jace went along with the 'accident' on purpose to provide for his wife and child. But I kept running into the fact that he did not have personal life insurance and was not reportedly despondent; he didn't want to die. However, there was another possible source of revenue that would leave him alive and yet able to collect ample money. It required the cooperation of someone who would help him set up the accident."

"But he was betrayed."

"He was betrayed. His killer set up the accident and left him to die. I decided that if Jace's and Alicia's murders were connected — and I think they are — then it was clear that Alicia did not kill her husband. Jace's killer worried that Alicia had figured out the truth and was about to tell someone . . . me, in this case, but she was scheduled to go in and talk to the police again and probably would have spilled her guts. She was becoming scared of the killer, frightened that even Mia was in danger."

"That is all unbelievably cold," Jakob said, gently stroking Hoppy's furry head. "I can't believe . . ." He trailed off, sighed, and shook his head. "I can't believe it."

"It all comes down to the day of Jace's murder. Alicia was at the motel awaiting her lover. Mia was at a babysitter. Kim was working. The killer knew all that and chose a time when no one could save Jace's life. If I'm right, the murderer checked back to make sure Jace was dead."

"The black truck Mia saw from her bedroom window."

Jaymie nodded. Her cellphone pinged and she picked it up. "It's from Kim Hansen," she said to Jakob, and read out the text. *"Meat me @ Alicia's house . . . got something 2 show u."*

"It's late, hon."

"Don't worry, I'm not going." Jaymie texted that answer back, asking if they could let it go until morning. But the reply was swift. *"PLEASE come. Im a mess & nede u to c this. Found TRUTH."*

"Poor Kim. She's been a ball of nerves, with Russ being ill." Jaymie sighed and met Jakob's gaze. "I *am* still dressed. Maybe I should go. Maybe she found the note Alicia supposedly wrote."

"Why not take it to the police then?"

The phone pinged again. Jaymie read the text out loud: *"PLEASE, Jamie, Im begging u."*

"We'll go together," Jakob said with an expression that said there would be no argument.

Jaymie nodded. "Good. I'd like that."

TWENTY-TWO

When they pulled up to Alicia's house it was pitch dark except for one light glowing inside in what looked like the living room. "I wonder why the security light isn't coming on?"

"Are you *sure* that text was from Kim?" Jakob asked, undoing his seatbelt.

Jaymie turned off the SUV and did the same. She grabbed her cellphone and checked the message. "It's from her number. I did tell her to text me if she needed me."

"Why meet her here? Why not at her place?"

"Maybe she doesn't want to upset Russ. It has to be the note — she must have found it. I asked her about it, but she shrugged it off at the time." Jaymie sat for a minute and regarded the gloomy house, an ominous huddled mass in the midnight darkness. "I'm pretty sure that's her car over there,"

Jaymie said, pointing.

"You trust Kim?"

"I do. I know she didn't kill her daughter." At that moment, the curtain in the front window twitched and Jaymie saw Kim's face in the window. The woman beckoned, then the curtain flicked back into place. "That's her, she's waiting for us."

"Let's see what she's found."

They got out and approached the front door cautiously. It creaked open. Kim opened it wider, a stiff look on her face. "Come in," she said, eyeing Jakob with alarm.

"You've met my husband. He didn't want me to come over alone and our daughter is at her grandparents, so . . ." She eyed Kim with trepidation as they moved into the entryway. Something was wrong. Jaymie and Jakob exchanged a look. "Kim, why are we here? What's going on?"

"I have s-something to show you, Jaymie," she said in a loud voice that echoed as she closed the door behind them and led the way into the living room.

"What is it?" Jaymie asked, following into the dark room that had been lit moments before. She was grabbed from behind and jerked backward, staggering against a solid body. Lightning bolts of fear coursed through her as she struggled against an iron grip. The room suddenly blazed with light as Kim flicked the switch and Jaymie twisted enough to see she was being held by Franklin Vance, who stank of anger and body odor. Jakob lunged forward, but Jaymie felt a cold sharp blade against her skin and her husband stopped, wild-eyed, staring at the knife.

"He made me do it!" Kim cried, sinking down onto the floor, fingers thrust in her disheveled hair. "He said he'd kill me, make it look like Russ did it, then take Mia!"

Jakob, fists clenched, stared into Jaymie's eyes. As Franklin grunted and growled in her ear, saying something about "taking care of business," she took a deep breath, her chest compressed against his strong arm, but expanding her lungs with air and letting it out. Her husband's gaze calmed her. She could hear her heart beating in her own ears, her blood pumping, the adrenaline coursing through her drowning out every other sound. Jakob's expression showed his grim determination and a rarely seen emotion . . . fury. His dark eyes glistened, anger radiated from him. As she calmed, slowing her breathing, steadying her pulse, the array of sounds became a chorus: Kim's sobs, Franklin's growl, Jakob's steady breath, her own heart pounding.

"You don't want to do this," Jakob said to Franklin, his tone guttural with rage.

Franklin tightened his grip on Jaymie and moved the knife. "You weren't supposed to come. You were supposed to stay home with your daughter. You'll have to die too."

"Leaving another little girl fatherless?" Jaymie said, struggling to worm out of his hold. "Like Mia, when you killed Jace?"

"Stay still!" He let out a string of expletives. "That wasn't supposed to happen," he grunted, his voice hoarse.

"You dumped a truck on him and expected him to live? You trying to convince Kim of that?"

"Shut up!" Franklin yelled.

"It was an accident!" Kim wept, her sobs becoming hysterical.

"Sure, an accident," Jaymie said, her voice quavering with fear. "It was no accident, Kim. Franklin set it up to rip off his business's insurance company."

"Shut up," the man muttered in her ear, his breath hot and stinking.

She struggled but his grip tightened. "I'm sure employee insurance paid you way more for his death than it would have for an injury," she said to Franklin. "If he was injured he'd have gotten the money, but

375

because he died, your business got it. He didn't understand that when you told him not to worry about insurance, that you'd take care of it, did he? He trusted you!" She sobbed in fear and caught her breath.

"What is she talking about, Franklin? What does she mean?" Kim stood and took two tottering steps toward them, her expression bewildered. A floorboard squeaked behind them.

Terror was choking Jaymie, but she had to stay calm, had to think while keeping Franklin off balance. She hoped he'd forget about Jakob, who she could hear creeping across the hardwood floor behind them. "Did Jace crawl under that truck willingly," she said loudly. "The truck Lew was selling to Erin and that you claimed had worn brakes?"

Kim stared at her in horror, her gaze flicking from Jaymie to some point behind her.

"Shut *up*!" Franklin roared, the knife wavering. He jerked her off her feet and she stumbled.

Kim cried out in fear and Jakob yelped, but then went silent. Jaymie couldn't see him, as hard as she tried. Franklin twisted and turned, but kept the knife at Jaymie's throat. Jakob wouldn't dare do anything while it remained there, the point pricking Jaymie's skin. "The truck you tricked Erin into insisting on buying? I'll bet the brakes were perfectly fine, or Lew wouldn't have sold it to her." She was going on instinct. A little voice whispered *keep him talking, keep him off-kilter.* "Erin's easy to manipulate, isn't she? Poor girl . . . she's felt guilty about Jace's death ever since, hasn't she? Felt bad for putting your family though it?" Jaymie felt the nick of the blade and a trickle of warm blood down her neck. But she couldn't let up. *Keep the pressure on.* "Did you tell Jace you'd ease the truck down gently and then call for rescue? He'd be hurt, you told him, but he'd live? You've staged so many accidents he believed you. You told him he could claim a back injury, those are hard to prove. I've seen the insurance stats. For the rest of his days he'd get compensation through your business insurance. Have I got it right?

"Did you then collapse that jack on your own son and leave him to suffer in agony and die? How did it feel, walking away while he shrieked in agony?"

Kim wailed with fresh sobs and stared up at the man in horror. Franklin roared in anger and his grip around Jaymie tightened. She was terrified, but felt in her gut that her husband was planning something. She hoped she'd be able to help when the moment came. Until then, all she could do was keep talking. "Poor guy. What son would believe his father would plot to murder him?" He tightened his grip on her throat, but she went on, muttering in a choked voice, fighting hysteria, "You used his guilt, convinced him that he'd get the nice big company insurance payout to pay off his mortgage and help his daughter, but you won't convince me you didn't decide to kill him and keep the insurance money for yourself."

"Insurance?" Kim said, her sobs subsiding as she finally heard what Jaymie was saying. "There was no insurance on Jace."

"No personal insurance," Jaymie whispered, meeting the woman's gaze. Tears were blurring her vision. She was desperately afraid, but she had to keep talking, give Jakob and herself time to figure out how to overcome Franklin without suffering injury. "But the towing company had employee insurance on Jace and Lew both. I understand it's two hundred and fifty thousand for injury but . . . a million for death on the job."

"Shut up!" Franklin roared, jerking her with his iron grip.

He had hauled her off-balance, but she found her footing and steadied herself.

"Lew is lucky to be alive. He probably won't be for long. But there's no insurance on Franklin, right?" she said, as she twisted to look up at him. She could see every detail of his face: the bloodshot eyes, the individual gray and black hairs of his scruffy beard, the flare of his nostrils, with bristly hairs sprouting out of them like a bush, the pockmarks on his cheeks from old acne.

Urged on by fear, Jaymie blurted out, "You've spent years masterminding the crash-for-cash scams — all those car accidents, Franklin, too many of them — and convinced Alicia to let you set fire to her garage to get her some money. She only went along with it because she was scared and because she'd be away from the scene. She was petrified of *you*. From the moment she figured out how her husband died she was terrified."

"Franklin killed Jace, his own son? I c-can't believe it!" Kim was finally catching up with all Jaymie had been saying. Her voice quivered with fear.

"Kim, think about it! It was Franklin she was having an affair with." She looked over her shoulder at the man. "Isn't that right? You and Alicia? You used her emotional state after Mia was injured. You got close, you sympathized, you demonized Jace,

379

drove a wedge between them . . . did anything and everything to muddle her into thinking you were on her side, that you *loved* her."

"*Shut up,*" he roared again. He was a powerful man and shook her like a rag doll. "Let me think!"

Jaymie was seeing stars and feeling nauseated. She couldn't catch her breath, pain shooting through her spine. This had to stop. At least the knife wasn't at her throat now.

"You seduced my *daughter*?" Kim shrieked, balling her hands into fists and holding them up in front of her, boxer pose, as if she was ready to fight. "You scumbag!" she wailed. "After everything you did to poor Russ, scapegoating him, tormenting him, torturing him relentlessly, through school and all the years since . . . making him take the fall for a death he didn't even cause. You filthy *pig*! And then . . . and then you seduce my poor Alicia? No wonder she was confused!"

Franklin's grip loosened. *Good,* Jaymie thought, they might need Kim angry rather than weepy to fight Franklin. "Shut up, shut up, shut *up,* Kim," he grunted yet again. "Let me *think,* goddammit!"

Kim subsided into moans of horror and anger.

This all seemed to be taking an eternity, though in reality it had been mere minutes. She again heard Jakob's footsteps creak on the wood floor. He was still working toward freeing her. Nothing precipitate for her husband, who planned carefully and then executed his plans with vigor.

Fortunately, though he was strong in body, Franklin wasn't a fast thinker. His plots brewed for weeks and months, they didn't occur suddenly.

Kim's energy surged again and she shouted at him about Alicia, and Jace, and Mia, and Russ, and even Lew and Debbie and Erin. She was babbling, working things out — though she didn't seem to know it — but had not arrived at the actual crime, the fact that Franklin Vance had murdered her daughter in cold blood: hunted her, followed her, and killed her, fashioning a lethal weapon out of a harmless whisk.

When Kim started to slow down again, sobs becoming more frequent punctuation in her hoarse harangue than colorful swear words, Jaymie decided to throw gas on the fire. She twisted her neck, glanced back at Jakob, then to Kim, stilled herself, then said, "He put Jace up to causing the accident that took Mia's leg and almost killed her. Didn't you, Franklin?" That part wasn't true and didn't make sense, since what little insurance there was had barely paid Jace and Mia's medical bills, but Mia was Kim's heart and soul, the most precious person in her life. She reacted as Jaymie hoped, with a flare of anger so violent the air vibrated with her shriek of anger.

"You filthy *bastard,*" she screeched, and let loose a torrent of profanity as she finally launched into motion, picking up a book off the floor and swatting at Franklin's head. He moved the hand that held the knife to fend off the book. Jakob, with faster impulses than one would have thought possible in such a sturdy man, combined with the decisiveness born of anger and fear, lunged forward and hammered her assailant's hand, sending the knife flying.

As Kim continued to shriek and swat, Jaymie kicked at Franklin's leg and twisted out of his hold even as he tried to clutch at her sweater. She pulled her arms out of the garment, and he was left with a handful of bloody fabric. She was no ninja and neither was Jakob — their offense was sloppy and noisy, but it was effective. Franklin, taken by surprise at the three-pronged attack, tripped and fell because of her kick and landed over the sofa, hitting his head on the windowsill and falling unconscious to the floor in a huddled mass, blood streaming from his forehead.

Silence, but for Kim's muffled sobs. Jakob seized Jaymie in a hard hug and kissed her. "Are you okay, *liebchen*?" She nodded against his chest, mumbling that she was fine. "It felt like forever that he had hold of you, but I couldn't risk him hurting you with that knife." She kissed him back soundly until they were both out of breath.

A stunned Kim, weeping and shaking, stood, blood flowing from her nose — she must have banged it — and tears coursing down her face. She glared at Franklin and kicked his leg. He didn't react, out cold. "Did he kill my Alicia?" she asked of Jaymie.

Jaymie met her troubled, confused stare. "He did. First he killed Jace, probably for the insurance. Then he killed Alicia because she suspected that he'd done it and was about to tell the police. Alicia likely never thought he would kill her. They'd been intimate, after all." She stared at the prone figure of Franklin. She could imagine Alicia's tension, her fear as she walked with Franklin, afraid to back away in case it would trigger him to attack, and yet her determination to remain calm and appear unconcerned, certain she'd make it out of the woods to Jaymie's home. "I think she was coming to ask me to go in with her to talk to a detective."

A guttural cry erupted from Kim and she fell on Franklin, hammering his unconscious body with her bare hands, weeping inconsolably.

To keep her from hurting herself in her anguish, Jakob grabbed Kim in a bear hug and held her tight until she dissolved, weeping. "Let's get out of here and call the police." Jakob, with Kim gripped tightly in one arm, had his cellphone in the other hand and called 911 as Jaymie grabbed a tissue and picked up the knife, carrying it away from the scene, not willing to risk Franklin regaining consciousness and having a weapon close to hand.

Vestry arrived at the scene minutes after the police and ambulance. As the paramedic treated Jaymie's nicked neck — only superficial cuts, though bleeding copiously — the detective asked her and Jakob a few questions. Jaymie explained as much as she could, promising a more thorough explanation when needed. Most important was that Franklin was a killer and an insurance fraud and leader of an insurance fraud ring.

Vestry then interviewed Kim. Even at a distance as the night chill penetrated the shiny emergency blanket the EMT had given her, Jaymie could hear the mother babble a confused but complete story of how Franklin had called her, telling her that there was a problem at Alicia's house, could she come right away. Leaving Mia with Russ, she drove over. He led her inside, but would not say what the problem was. She got suspicious and started asking him questions based on things Jaymie had said, which no doubt implied much more knowledge than she actually had at that moment. He then grabbed her, seized her cellphone, and threatened her: if she didn't summon Jaymie to come there he would kill her, then take Mia and escape the country.

A traumatized, scared, confused Kim followed orders. Even then, as much as she hated him for the torment he had caused Russ all these years, she hadn't made all the connections. She had not yet realized that he was behind the murders of Jace and Alicia. Jaymie didn't blame her. She was suffering from her daughter's death, still in that fog of grief and denial and pain that would never fully subside, just gradually get more bearable.

Vestry approached Jaymie and Jakob, who

385

sat in their SUV getting warm after standing out in the chill early October night. She leaned in to the vehicle and said, "You folks okay?"

Jakob eyed her and nodded. He had never been impressed by the detective, given that she downplayed his wife's investigative skills. Jaymie smothered a smile and touched the blood-soaked bandage. "We're good, thank you, Detective. Is Kim all right?"

She nodded and shoved her hands in her blazer pockets.

"How about Franklin? Is he awake so you can question him?"

"Still unconscious. He'll be at the hospital handcuffed to a gurney under police guard, but yes, I'll be questioning him as soon as he wakes up." She paused, then met Jaymie's steady gaze. "I *had* considered him as Alicia's attacker, but I couldn't make it make sense. He didn't exactly have an alibi — or at least not one we could check out — but neither did others with stronger motive. We couldn't find enough to justify keeping Vance under surveillance. I'm sorry about that. It left him free to do this," she said, waving her hand at Alicia's house and Jaymie's throat. "Look, I'm going to need to speak to you both to get the whole story. It can wait until morning. Come in to the station at ten."

She straightened and was about to walk away, but Jaymie leaned out the window and said, "We'll be there. I'll bring donuts."

TWENTY-THREE

Looking back, Jaymie realized that several people she knew suspected the Vance family business of tow trucks, vehicle repairs and sales was a side business to the real money-maker, insurance fraud, but for a variety of reasons never exposed them. Jace knew, even though he didn't take an active role in the scheme like his brother did. Clutch likely suspected, Jaymie figured, and disapproved. The biker was not what he would have referred to as a snitch, though, and would not have turned his old buddy in even though he thought it wrong. Clutch never in a million years would have suspected his old friend of killing anyone, much less his own son. Johnny Stanko may have suspected the insurance fraud, but it was too much to expect someone who had suffered at the hands of law enforcement to turn in friends who had been kind to him.

In her anger and resentment at Jace's

grave error that led to Mia's devastating injury, Alicia had let herself be seduced by the charming Franklin. In the first months of denial after Jace's death she would not have suspected her lover of killing his own son, but she must have made the connection eventually. Jaymie remembered Mia's contention that someone had helped her father put the vehicle up on a jack and did it wrong. If she had said that to her mother, and Alicia realized it was Franklin, she would have lived in terror, unable to confront him and afraid to turn him in. Her and Lew's plan to move to California, seen from that aspect, was an escape plot, one that had taken too long to carry out.

Franklin had, Erin admitted to Vestry — the detective told Jaymie in their debriefing interview — ingratiated himself with her, trying to use her to find out what Jaymie knew. He feared Jaymie was onto him, and she was eventually, though his paranoia had overstated how much and how early. There were other more likely suspects. Russ had begged off the auction trip the day of Jace's death, making it possible that he had killed Jace to avoid being turned in to the police for the theft of catalytic converters. Lew, Jaymie thought, could have set up his brother's death before meeting up with

Clutch, one explanation for why he was really late that morning, though she had not been able to reconcile that with the black truck Mia had seen behind the house near noon that day.

Jaymie now believed that the truck Mia saw that day behind their home had been driven by Franklin. He had borrowed a nondescript black truck from Lew's lot while his son was out of town in case anyone saw him pulling into the property, which is why Mia didn't recognize it as a Vance tow truck.

It wasn't the first time Franklin had manipulated Erin. Jaymie suspected that he, using his insurance fraud connection, had her car stolen and torched in the woods, which necessitated her getting another vehicle, which she obviously would do through her brother-in-law. When Lew suggested the pickup truck, Franklin ridiculed Erin buying it — which, as he hoped, made her determined to have it — then he suggested to Jace that the brakes on it were unsafe, making it necessary to jack it up and take a look at the brake liners.

The rest was open to conjecture. In one scenario Jace had gone along with a plot to pull an insurance scam, intending to have the car lowered on him — Franklin would have assured Jace there would be safety measures in place — so he could claim a difficult to disprove back injury for the rest of his days. In another grimmer scenario Jace was doing Erin a favor, not knowing that the jack had been rigged to fail by his own father. It was a horrendous plot either way.

After Franklin was arrested people came forward with tales of his bullying in high school, and how they had witnessed his constant harassment of Russ Krauss. It was now widely believed that Franklin had, as Russ at first insisted, been the one who fought the guy who died. Russ had pled guilty, true, but he had only done so after threats on his life and, more importantly, the life of his baby daughter, Alicia. He was probably the only one who had never underestimated the full profundity of Franklin's malevolence. Going to jail was the only way he knew to protect his family.

From a schlub Russ Krauss had been elevated to something like a folk hero for all he had suffered. The *Wolverhampton Weekly Howler* was having a field day. There was so much to the story that Brianna Sheridan had been retained as a stringer to look into the massive insurance fraud that the Vance family had perpetrated over the years. Their own insurance scams were comprehensive, but they had also connived with others, even including Alicia, who besides the garage burning had gone along with Franklin, likely out of fear when he suggested she be the victim of a crash and dash. She had paid endlessly for her misjudgment in getting involved with him.

The police never found any note in Alicia's belongings. Wenda Puchala still insisted that Alicia had spoken of a note and maybe she had written one pointing the finger of guilt at her father-in-law/ lover and later destroyed it, but no one would ever know for sure.

Lew was being charged with his involvement in the insurance scam, but was cooperating with the investigation into his father. He claimed he had known nothing about Franklin setting up Jace's death, and the police had no evidence to the contrary. Jaymie had been puzzling over how Mia had known someone helped her father put up the jack the day he died. She thought it would eventually come out that Lew had accused his father of tampering with the jack on the day Jace died. Mia had likely overheard them argue and misunderstood. If that was true it would all come out in court.

Why had Lew not turned his father in if

he suspected him of killing Jace? Maybe that, too, would come out in trial. Jaymie could guess, though: Franklin denied it and Lew chose to believe him. Who would believe that their father was capable of cold-blooded murder, especially of a son?

There was finally a memorial service for Alicia. It rained all day that day. Jocie and Mia had stood hand in hand at the grave-side, and then hugged. Jaymie wept. Jakob held her. Kim, white and frail-looking, had been propped between Erin, who openly sobbed, and Russ, who was recovering from a lifetime of fear. It was a harrowing time and the wounds, deep and real and trauma-tizing, would take time to heal.

Canadian Thanksgiving arrived on the second Monday in October. Jaymie, Jakob and Jocie went north and celebrated with Grandma Leighton and Jaymie's parents. She made a version of her chicken à la king out of turkey . . . Turkey à la GiGi, Jocie called the new dish, referring to her Great-grandma Leighton as she carefully picked out the little red pimento bits to lay on the edge of her plate.

Fall was advancing swiftly, painting the countryside in warm shades of umber and sienna, like the pretty colors in Jocie's favorite new gift from Jaymie's parents, a watercolor art kit. In the woods across from the Müller property Jaymie, Jakob and Jocie gathered with Kim, Mia, Erin, Russ and — standing a little apart from them and not able to meet anyone's gaze — Lew. Lise and Arend Brouwer were there with their son Bram and his son Luuk, as were Detective Vestry and Police Chief Deborah Connolly, both wearing their dress uniforms. Valetta joined Jaymie and her family.

They were not in the spot where Alicia had died. Instead the Brouwers had chosen a clearing nearby, where shafts of sunlight pierced the gloom. Following the tradition of their church, Arend Brouwer asked that they all take a moment to remember and celebrate the lives of Alicia and Jace Vance.

Lise Brouwer, leaning heavily on a walking stick, stepped forward when the prayer and moment of silence was done. "As a woman in this world, I hope for a day when all women, and all children and yes, all men, walk in safety and peace, able to enjoy the silence of the forest, and the joy of solitude. The Brouwer family has always cherished this beautiful sylvan glade," she said, her soft voice inflected with the remnants of her Dutch birth. She looked to her husband and smiled, then to her son and grandson. "And we dedicate this forest to the memory of Alicia Vance, and for her beloved daughter, Mia."

She looked to the child who stood, uncertain and solemn, with her grandmother. "My dear Mia, we will create, in our woods, a path to wander, and the trail will be Alicia's Trail to honor her. I hope we will see families here, as our good friends the Müllers build their holiday market across the road, and maybe someday you will play in these woods with Jocie and Luuk and your other school friends. Would you both say a few words to this gathering?"

Kim, looking nervous, stepped forward, with Mia's hand in hers. "Thank you all. It's been . . . a difficult time." She looked over her shoulder, toward the far edge of the woods. "I think of my daughter starting out from her house, heading to the woods, and I . . ." She broke off. Her eyes filled. She squeezed her granddaughter's hand and held it to her, covering it with her other hand.

She swallowed, took a deep breath, and continued: "I thank the Brouwers for their kindness. Alicia never thought twice about walking in the woods. When she was a child and we would go camping she'd happily go off by herself into the woods to collect pinecones and rocks. Used to drive me crazy! We'd always tote home a box of her finds, and she'd display them in her room until the next time. I want Mia to experience that. The house beyond these woods is hers now. We'll be looking after it until she's old enough to take care of it. And I hope . . ." Her voice broke. She cleared her throat and resumed, "And I hope we will walk in these woods and leave flowers for Alicia."

There was silence after she stepped back, a solemn, kind, respectful interlude. A blue jay squawked and scolded noisily, breaking the stillness, and Kim smiled past her tears.

"My mom told me that the forest is a home for all creatures," Mia said, speaking up in a surprising moment.

"And so it is," Lise Brouwer said with a soft smile. *"All things bright and beautiful, all creatures great and small,"* she sang.

Detective Vestry had been chosen to speak for the police because of her hiking experience. She stepped forward. She looked to Kim and Mia, and said, "Ms. Hansen, Mia, as an avid outdoorswoman I am committed to making our town and countryside a safe haven for all hikers and walkers and nature lovers." She looked around the circle gathered. "To that end a few friends and I are starting a group called Walking Together. The Brouwers have kindly offered to help with creating and grooming a trail through these woods."

There was applause and it was Jaymie's turn to speak. She took a deep breath. "In the year and a half I've lived here with my husband and daughter I have come to love these woods as a place to bring Jocie for a break, for a walk, for a quiet time, for a talk when life gets crazy. For a while tragedy changed that and it was all I could see and feel here, but though I'm not sure I believe in healing energy, maybe it's true — maybe the force of good humans coming together with love and hope can make this a place for quiet reflection and gentle togetherness." She looked to Jakob. "I hope one day it will be said of these woods . . . *love is here*." She scanned the crowd. "We'd like to invite you all back to our place across the road to talk to each other, get to know your neighbors and make new friends and contribute ideas to the plan for Alicia's Trail."

At the cabin they all mingled near Jocie's treehouse as the children played above. Mia was carried there by Lew, who, Kim told Jaymie, had proved to be a steadfast friend and uncle, grieving as he was the loss of his brother and his sister-in-law/girlfriend, and suffering through the knowledge that his father was responsible for both losses. He was out on bail on insurance fraud, but claimed he never suspected his father's worst actions. Jaymie believed him.

"I suspected him for so long," Kim said. "But he bore it with . . . I don't know the word for it."

"Grace?" Jaymie said.

Kim looked startled for a moment, then nodded. "Grace. Yes, maybe that's it. He hasn't held it against me. He's done some wrong, but in time . . ." She sighed. "He loved Alicia. I suppose I'm happy that Mia at least has one Vance left."

Jaymie thought back to how she had suspected Russ, mistaking Mia's words about her grandfather to mean him, when she was really referring to her mom banning Franklin from coming near them. Many mistakes had been made. They were fortunate that they had come through it. As early autumn twilight descended and the gathering dispersed, Jaymie and Jakob gathered paper cups and napkins and plates for recycling. Jocie had gone home with Kim and Mia, invited for a sleepover.

The sun descended behind the trees and Jakob took Jaymie into his arms to watch the light fade in the woods across the road.

Work on Alicia's Trail would begin tomorrow with Bram Brouwer marking a trail and beginning the process of clearing it. They would be holding a fundraiser on the level ground where the Müllers had cleared space for the market that would be built there in the spring.

"I hope someday Mia will live in that house on the next road and maybe Jocie will live in this house. They will be friends, brought together in heartbreak but growing up knowing that they can become strong women in the face of tragedy."

Jakob hugged her and dark descended as the last of the purple twilight faded to indigo. "Let's go in," he whispered. "The dishes and the rest of the cleanup can wait until morning."

Words to make any woman's heart sing.

AFTERWORD

"BASED ON A TRUE CRIME"

How often have you heard that a book or movie was based on true-life events? Often, likely. And I'll say it here: one of the murders in *A Calculated Whisk* is based on a true crime.

In late 2008, Levi Karlsen, a young father of two daughters, was convinced by his father, Karl Karlsen, to work on a truck in a garage on Karl's property. Levi crawled under it, though it was propped up only by a shaky jack, to take a look. He was found dead hours later by his father — who had been gone for several hours, attending a family funeral with his second wife — the truck having collapsed off the jack, crushing him. That was the story Karl told, and it was ruled an accidental death.

However . . . Levi's stepmother was suspicious. It wasn't the first time tragedy had stalked the family as Christina Karlsen,

Levi's mother and Karl's wife, had died seventeen years earlier in a horrific house fire, from which Karl collected a $200,000 insurance payout. In this case, Karl was Levi's newly minted heir, according to a will that had just been signed and notarized. Karl was also the recipient of a $700,000-plus payout from his son's life insurance. The money was supposed to be for the benefit of Levi's daughters, but much of the money instead went into financing Karl's gourmet duck farming business.

Where did some of the money also go? Into paying for a $1.2 million life insurance policy on Cindy, Karl's second wife. She left Karl, told her suspicions to the police, and helped convict him. As much as we recoil from that, a father can and will and did, in this case, kill his son simply for the insurance money. Which brings me to the (sordid?) business of true crime, a booming industry in books, TV shows and podcasts. I've wrestled, as Mrs. Stubbs does, with the morality of true crime as a source of entertainment. True crime stories relate the horror of the worst period of the victims' lives, and the torment of those left behind to live through the sorrow and devastation murder inevitably causes. How can that be excused?

And yet . . . perhaps I'm rationalizing, but

true crime tales have been with humankind as long as we've been telling stories. Many years ago the tales were told in poem and song by traveling balladeers, and now there are podcasts. We're a curious species. Sometimes we revel in the misfortune of others, experiencing schadenfreude, pleasure in another's misfortune, as we watch the great fall from their pedestals. Other times we experience a delicious frisson of fear and live vicariously through thrilling terror, as we read about Jack the Ripper or John Wayne Gacy.

But sometimes we feel particular satisfaction when we read or watch or listen to a true crime tale that ends in justice for the dead. In most cases these stories are written or relayed with the help of those left behind, who, above all, don't want their loved ones forgotten. Along with the tragedy, we hear about their lives, including, in this case, that Levi Karlsen was a good father who loved his children, and a good man his sisters remember with great fondness. I don't think we are awful for being drawn to true crime tales, we're just . . . human.

What do you think, gentle readers?

VINTAGE EATS
BY JAYMIE LEIGHTON MÜLLER

CHICKEN À LA KING

Trying to find the origin of this vintage recipe is tricky. It's named after a Mr. or Mrs. Keene in 1890s New York City, or a Mr. King, a hotel owner in New York in 1898, or one of a number of other Keenes and Kings. But no matter . . . it became a staple of American cuisine and was featured in many cookbooks in the early to mid part of the 1900s.

It's comfort food, pure and simple, basically just creamed chicken over something, but the original version is made with egg yolks and coffee cream and sherry, and that is just too much trouble for the easy weeknight recipe I wanted.

So, on the following pages is my streamlined, modernized version with a few simple substitutions. What makes it a great weeknight recipe is that it can be made no matter what you have on hand: you can poach your own chicken breast, but you can also use leftover roasted chicken or even the meat from a store-bought rotisserie chicken. Likewise, though my version is served over *vol au vent* (pastry) shells (store-bought in the frozen aisle), you can serve it over rice, noodles, or even, as one vintage version suggests, toast.

Serves 4

1/2 pound fresh mushrooms or 1 can of mushrooms

1/2 tablespoon fresh thyme

1/2 green bell pepper, chopped. *Optional! I didn't use green pepper because I don't particularly care for it. If you really want that green and red look and don't like green pepper, sprinkle a little fresh parsley over the finished product, or add frozen peas, which I suggest cooking ahead of time.

1/2 cup butter

1/2 cup flour

1 teaspoon salt

1/4 teaspoon pepper

1 1/2 teaspoons chicken bouillon powder

2 cups milk (or cooking cream, or evaporated milk, whatever suits your fancy, but cream will make the mixture thicker)

1 cup chicken stock (packaged, canned, homemade)

3–4 cups chicken; approximately one pound fresh chicken breasts poached and chopped will work. *Note: if you're poaching your own chicken, do so in chicken stock with more of the fresh thyme, and use the poaching liquid as your chicken stock for the recipe.

4 ounces pimentos (I used jarred . . . is
there any other type?)

For a classic Chicken à la King look, you will need homemade or frozen *vol au vent* pastry shells, one for each person, available in most grocery stores, or whatever else you will serve the dish over, like noodles or toast.

Cook the mushrooms, thyme and green peppers (if you've used them) over low heat in the butter until softened, but do not brown the butter! Blend in flour, salt and pepper and cook until bubbly, but again, not browned!

Stir in bouillon powder, milk and chicken stock; simmer for a few minutes until the mixture is thickened. You want this cream sauce to be thick, but not gloopy (extremely technical chef term; gloopy means congealing into unpleasant blobs), so you may need to thin with additional milk or stock.

Stir in cooked chicken and pimentos and warm thoroughly. A word about the pimentos: I didn't think they'd be much more than color, but they do add a unique flavor to the dish, so, unless you must, don't leave them out!

Serve over prepared *vol au vent* pastry shells, rice, noodles or toast and enjoy!

This versatile recipe is great to use up leftover chicken, or as a Thanksgiving day-after meal, with leftover turkey!

ABOUT THE AUTHOR

Victoria Hamilton is the pseudonym of nationally bestselling romance author Donna Lea Simpson. Victoria is the bestselling author of three mystery series, the Lady Anne Addison Mysteries, the Vintage Kitchen Mysteries, and the Merry Muffin Mysteries. Her latest adventure in writing is a Regency-set historical mystery series, starting with *A Gentlewoman's Guide to Murder*. Victoria loves to read, especially mystery novels, and enjoys good tea and cheap wine, the company of friends, and has a newfound appreciation for opera. She enjoys crocheting and beading, but a good book can tempt her away from almost anything . . . except writing! Visit Victoria at www.victoria hamiltonmysteries.com.